"This might be a little above and beyond your normal duty..."

Uncomfortable under Trey Wentworth's scrutiny, Kelly looked out the tinted windows and noted the ferry had pushed away from the dock. Wow. She was on her way to Collins Island. Imagine that. She'd always been curious about the legendary place.

"I apologize if I insulted you by offering you money," Wentworth said in a low voice. "Please forgive me."

"Don't worry about it," Kelly said. "A hot shower will be more than enough reward."

"Oh, I think we can do better than that," he said, and smiled a lazy smile. Somehow a dangerous smile, Kelly thought.

This man was accustomed to getting his own way and doing exactly what he want...

Dear Reader,

I'm thrilled about the publication of *The Billionaire's Son*, the first book in my new miniseries, The Rookie Files. The Rookie Files will follow the journeys of five rookie cops who meet in police training, become friends, and then learn and grow in their law enforcement careers in Miami-Dade County, Florida. And of course they fall in love!

Kelly Jenkins, the heroine of *The Billionaire's Son*, had a rough childhood but fought against the odds to achieve success. A police officer once helped her, and his assistance inspired her to become a cop and provide similar help to others.

When Kelly rescues Jason, the son of sexy billionaire Trey Wentworth, she has little use for the father since he appears to spend most of his time partying. But traumatized Jason clings to Kelly, and she can't say no to the child. Before she knows what's happening, she's living in Wentworth Villa where she solves the mystery of who kidnapped Jason. But she also needs to solve the mysteries of her own heart. How could she fall in love with a man who is her complete opposite?

I hope you enjoy Trey and Kelly's story as much as I enjoyed writing it! I love to hear from readers. Please visit my website at sharonshartley.com.

Namaste,
Sharon

SHARON HARTLEY

The Billionaire's Son

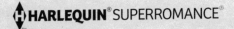

Recycling programs
for this product may
not exist in your area.

ISBN-13: 978-0-373-64056-0

The Billionaire's Son

Copyright © 2017 by Sharon S. Hartley

This edition published by arrangement with Harlequin Books S.A.

For questions and comments about the quality of this book, please contact us at CustomerService@Harlequin.com.

® and TM are trademarks of Harlequin Enterprises Limited or its corporate affiliates. Trademarks indicated with ® are registered in the United States Patent and Trademark Office, the Canadian Intellectual Property Office and in other countries.

Printed in U.S.A.

Sharon Hartley is so fascinated by cops and the dangerous people that complicate their world that she attends every citizens' police academy she can find. Having worked as a court reporter for many years, Sharon plays "what if" on her old cases and comes up with fictional ways to inject them into her stories. After time on the computer creating plots where the bad guys try to hurt the good ones, she calms herself by teaching yoga, plus hiking and birding in the natural world. Sharon lives in St. Petersburg, Florida, with her soul mate, Max, hundreds of orchids and a Jack Russell Terrorist. Please visit her website at sharonshartley.com.

Books by Sharon Hartley

HARLEQUIN SUPERROMANCE

The Florida Files

The South Beach Search
Accidental Bodyguard
Stranded with the Captain

Her Cop Protector

To Trust a Cop

Visit the Author Profile page at Harlequin.com.

For law enforcement officers all over the world.

CHAPTER ONE

HER STRIDES LONG and sure, Kelly Jenkins picked up her speed as she turned into Peacock Park, confident she was on pace to beat her old time. Jazzed because she hadn't scored a personal best on her favorite morning run in months—not since she'd entered the police academy—Kelly pushed harder. That was the key to success.

The shade of the public pavilion with its promise of cool water came into view, but she refused to risk a glance down to her wrist chronometer. She might lose a second or two. Patience was another path to success. She'd know within two minutes.

"Mommy!"

As the terrified wail of a small child registered, Kelly turned her head and spotted a young boy running toward her as fast as his little legs could churn. Two men chased him. She slowed her stride just before the child flung his arms around her thighs.

"Mommy," he sobbed. "Mommy, Mommy."

Knocked off balance, Kelly windmilled her arms to keep herself from falling and stared down at the boy clutching her as if she were a lifeline, guessing he was about four years old.

Before she could say anything, like "Hey, kid, I'm not your mom," the two men arrived.

"Sorry, lady," one of them said, a rough-looking

dude who hadn't shaved in days. Tats covered both forearms, and Kelly recognized the insignia of a local gang, but couldn't remember which one. Greasy brown hair hung to his shoulders. There was a gun-size bulge in his jeans pocket that worried her.

"I'll take the kid," he snarled.

"No," the boy shrieked, clutching her legs tighter, sharp fingernails digging into her bare thigh. "No! Mommy, no."

Her cop instincts slamming into gear, Kelly reached down and picked up the child. "What's your name, sweetie?"

"His name is Jason," the man said, his voice hard, with an underlying edge of threat. "I'm his father. Hand him over."

His entire little body trembling violently, Jason buried his face in Kelly's shoulder, turning away from his "father."

"This child is terrified of you," Kelly said.

"Yeah, well, that's none of your concern, lady. Just give me the kid."

Kelly hesitated, assessing the two men. The second man was thin and shorter than the so-called father, but she noted a resemblance between the two. Same hair and cheekbones. Maybe brothers. The brother looked like he'd spent several years on the streets while this child was well nourished and wore expensive clothing. *Something is wrong here.*

"My name is Kelly Jenkins," she said, "I'm a police officer."

"Damn. She's a cop, Adam," the second man said.

"Jason seems very confused," Kelly continued. "Is there anything that I can do to—"

Adam took a step forward, his arms out to snatch the child. "I don't give a rat's ass who you are. Just give me the damn kid."

Jason looped the straps of Kelly's jog bra through his tiny fingers and squeezed tight. "No, Mommy," he managed, now barely able to get the words out.

When Adam placed his hands on either side of Jason's waist, Jason wailed loudly and shrilly. Kelly stepped back, noting fellow runners had gathered to observe the unfolding scenario.

Wishing she'd been a cop longer than two months, Kelly debated her next move. *Maybe it takes a village, but I have no right to keep a son from his father.*

Yet the gangbanger only referred to Jason as "the kid," never "my son." And he never once spoke to the child directly, tried to soothe him or comfort him. *What kind of a father acts like that?*

"Is this your daddy?" Kelly whispered to Jason.

His face bright red, his screams now diminished to great gulping sobs, the child shook his head emphatically *no*. He locked his feet around her waist.

"Shit," the smaller man said. "Get the kid, Adam. We gotta get out of here pronto."

"Adam, right?" Kelly asked, deliberately using the name. Always good to make it personal. "Where is his mother?"

"Yeah, good question," said a female jogger Kelly didn't know by name but waved at every day.

"None of your fricking business," Adam said. "Give me the kid, or else."

"Or else what?" a male runner asked.

"Or else this." Adam pulled a Glock 19 from his pocket.

"He has a gun," someone yelled.

"Run!"

Her fellow joggers scattered.

Kelly tightened her grip on the kid, transferred her weight to her back leg and executed a front snap kick, knocking the gun out of Adam's hand. She felt more than heard a crack, and knew her contact broke at least one bone.

The man bellowed in pain as the Glock went flying, landing on the grass six feet away.

"Oh, shit," the brother said, looking as if he wanted to run. Or maybe hurl.

"She broke my wrist," Adam howled, protecting his right hand with his left. "You bitch."

Out of the corner of her eye, she noted one of her fellow runners on a cell phone. She wished she could access hers but she didn't dare shift her attention.

"Get the gun, Caleb," Adam ordered, his face contorted with obvious pain.

"Just walk away, Caleb," Kelly said, knowing he wanted to and was the weaker link. "The cops are on their way."

Caleb's eyes grew wide and he looked around.

Yeah, you think about that, you scumbag. Kelly backpedaled, keeping an eye on Adam, wanting to put as much distance between them as possible.

Cursing viciously, Adam advanced. She could incapacitate this jerk in two swift maneuvers, but not while she was holding a forty-pound hysterical kid. If she put him down—and that wouldn't be easy considering his death grip—Caleb could snatch him and haul butt.

So her black belt wasn't much use. She needed to figure out what was going on here before she released Jason—if that was even his name—to two lowlifes she was now convinced bore no relation to him at all. And if they were family, some type of abuse was obviously taking place.

"Calm down, Adam," Kelly soothed, continuing to move backward. "Let's talk about this. More police will be here any second." *Yeah, and where the hell are they?*

"Get the gun, Caleb," Adam shouted.

The harshness of the order apparently decided Caleb, and he moved toward the Glock.

"Think about this, Caleb," Kelly yelled. "I'm a police officer. You'll fry if you shoot me."

"Shut. Up. Bitch," Adam said.

Kelly wanted to run, but knew turning her back on Adam was a mistake. She scrambled for something to say or do before she stopped a bullet. She could give them the kid to save herself, but damned if she would. This was why she'd become a cop.

Just as Caleb reached for the gun, a siren screeched its warning into the air. Kelly didn't look, but heard a police vehicle pull up on the street maybe a hundred feet away.

Caleb froze. "Shit. The cops."

"We need the gun," Adam said.

"Yeah, well, then you get it." Caleb sprinted toward the parking lot of the nearby marina.

"Caleb, what the hell," Adam yelled after him.

Caleb didn't turn and didn't answer.

"You'll regret this, bitch." With a last threatening glare at Kelly, Adam snatched the Glock with his left hand and ran.

Releasing a breath, she heard the cops approach from behind. But Kelly kept her gaze on Adam until he disappeared behind the marina's office building.

"What's going on?"

Still holding Jason, Kelly turned to find two uniformed City of Miami officers, one male and one female. *Thank God.*

"I'm Kelly Jenkins with Miami-Dade Police Department, badge number 33349. My commanding officer is Lieutenant Thomas Marshall." She explained what had happened as concisely as possible, aided by interjections from a few of the other joggers who had wandered back to the scene. The officers summoned backup to search the area, but

Kelly knew Adam and Caleb would be miles away by the time anyone arrived.

"So you don't know this child?" the female officer asked. Her badge read L. Rodriguez.

"I never saw him before ten minutes ago," Kelly told Officer Rodriguez. "I'm not even sure his name is really Jason."

"What's your name, kiddo?" Rodriguez asked in that idiotic tone adults use when speaking to a small child. Kelly had used it herself.

Jason burrowed his head deeper into Kelly's shoulder, tightening his grip on her waist with his legs.

Kelly patted his back. She had no clue how to deal with children. What she really wanted to do was shift his weight to her other arm. The kid was heavy.

"Jason, you need to go with the nice police officer where you'll be safe from the mean men," she said.

"No, Mommy, no," the child begged. "Please, please don't leave me."

Rodriguez narrowed her eyes. "Why is he calling you Mommy?"

"No idea," Kelly replied. "Maybe he was so terrified of Adam and Caleb he got confused."

"We'll take him to the station and let DCF sort this out," Rodriguez said.

"Good plan," Kelly agreed. Department of Children and Families was the obvious call in a case like this. They'd locate his mom or find a foster home. But for the fact that Jason was so well dressed, Kelly would assume the mom was a druggie on a bender, Caleb or Adam a boyfriend left in charge. Something just didn't smell right.

Rodriguez reached out to remove Jason, but the child shrieked and refused to let go of Kelly. "No, no, no!" he wailed.

"Shhh, Jason," Kelly soothed, rubbing his head. "It's okay."

The male officer, standing a few feet away taking statements from bystanders, frowned and joined Kelly and Rodriguez. "What's wrong with the kid?"

"He doesn't want to let go of Ms. Jenkins," Rodriguez said.

"Officer Jenkins," Kelly said, to the male officer, whose name was P. Nordan.

"Don't you want to go find your mommy?" Nordan asked.

Jason raised his head and looked at Kelly. She noted he had bright blue eyes and blond hair, the same coloring as hers. Were the officers beginning to doubt her story? She didn't have anything on her to prove she was a cop.

Jason raised a hand and lightly stroked her cheek. "I found my mommy."

"I'm not anyone's mother," Kelly told Nordan. "Didn't the other joggers confirm my story?"

At Kelly's words, Jason began sobbing again, and turned his face into her shoulder.

Nordan released a long breath. "The kid is traumatized. I think the best thing is for all of us to go to the station and notify DCF."

"I'm on duty in two hours," Kelly said.

"Better call in," Nordan said.

Rodriguez placed a hand on Kelly's shoulder, urging her to move toward the police vehicle. "You can do that on the way to the station."

AT THE MIAMI-DADE headquarters of the Federal Bureau of Investigation, Trey Wentworth paced. The depressing utilitarian room they'd stashed him in contained everything they thought he might want—chairs, a recliner, coffee, tea, soft drinks, bagels—even a plate of frosted fruit pastry. As if he could eat. Three so-called special agents continuously observed him, trying to pretend otherwise, definitely waiting for him to lose it. Expecting him to.

He wouldn't give them the pleasure.

Even though everyone in this room knew something had gone very wrong.

He glanced at his watch for the hundredth time in the last fifteen minutes. The ransom exchange should have been completed two hours ago. He should have heard something by now. He should have been assured his son was alive. But Agent Ballard had returned without Jason, saying the kidnappers didn't show at the drop site. Trey shook his head. He knew the agents had gone to the wrong park in Coconut Grove, but the idiots wouldn't believe him.

His mistake was trusting law enforcement. He shouldn't have involved the FBI. The kidnappers had instructed him not to, but his attorney had counseled the feds were his best option. He trusted Brian, who'd been a friend longer than he'd been his lawyer, but he sure didn't trust the yokels sitting in this room watching him slowly disintegrate.

Soon there'd be nothing solid left of him to hug his son when—*if* he ever saw him again.

The FBI didn't know what the hell they were doing. He should have insisted on accompanying Ballard on the exchange. He shouldn't have given in to their vaunted expertise. He shouldn't have listened to Brian. Of course the kidnappers said not to contact the cops or they'd kill Jason. Wasn't that what they always said?

Trey shot a glance at Walt Ballard, the thirty-ish but already balding agent in charge of Jason's case. Since returning with the bad news, the man worked his phone in a chair by the door, leaning forward, forearms on his knees, wearing a grim expression. Texting? Checking email? Was he receiving information about Jason from the agents still in the field? Was it bad news?

Trey stopped moving and took a deep breath. Not here. He'd fall apart later, away from the public eye. *That was the Wentworth way.* Trey heard his father's clipped voice inside his head and pushed away the sound. The bastard couldn't be bothered to fly in even though his only grandson had been abducted.

Where was his attorney? Shit. Why hadn't they heard something?

Trey glanced at his watch. How much longer? Jason had been through so much in the last year. Would he ever see his son again? Would they even find Jason's body?

Kids disappeared without a trace all the time.

Ballard's phone rang, the sound startling in the quiet of the room. Everyone turned.

"Ballard," the agent barked into the phone. A few beats of silence. "What?"

The shock in Ballard's voice forced Trey into a chair. *Oh, God. No. Jason.*

"Where?" Ballard demanded. Then, "Got it. We're on our way."

Ballard disconnected and looked directly at Trey. "We've got him. We've got your boy."

"Alive?" Trey stood on shaky legs, not trusting his hearing. "Is he hurt?"

"He's fine. He's in the custody of the City of Miami Police."

"No mistake this time?" he demanded.

"No mistake," Ballard said.

Choking back a sob, Trey sagged into the chair again, unable to formulate a response.

"City of Miami arrested the kidnappers?" This

question came from another agent, a female. Trey couldn't remember her name. All he could focus on was the knowledge that Jason was alive and unharmed.

"No," Ballard said. "Apparently the kidnappers remain at large."

"What the hell happened?" asked another agent.

Ballard shook his head. "I don't have all the details yet, and they can wait." He nodded at Trey and grinned. "Let's go get your son."

INSIDE A FRIGID interview room at the Coconut Grove police substation, Kelly couldn't remember when she'd ever been so cold. The AC had to be set at about forty degrees, and she might as well be naked since all she had on was flimsy nylon running shorts and a cotton jog bra. Making things worse, her flesh and her clothing were sweaty.

Officer Rodriguez had wrapped a towel around the shivering Jason, and that helped, but Kelly's legs were freezing. They'd given her a cup of vile lukewarm coffee, but that had cooled and was of no help.

There was a reason for the chill of course. The police didn't want their suspects or interviewees comfortable. She had a bad feeling they considered her a suspect—of what she wasn't sure, but something. She'd heard chatter of a statewide BOLO as they'd snapped photos of the kid, so maybe they knew who he was. For his sake, she hoped so. The misunderstanding would all be straightened out eventually, but she was going to be late for her shift.

She'd called her sergeant on the way in to explain, but he hadn't sounded happy. Shit. She'd been number one in her rookie class and intended to be the highest-performing rookie that had ever entered the Miami-Dade County PD. Missing roll call this soon wouldn't help with that goal.

So where was a social worker? DCF was notoriously inefficient, but this delay was ridiculous.

She needed to contact her lieutenant, but the kid remained glued to her, his legs hooked around her waist. If she shifted his weight to her other side, she could access her phone in her jog pouch. At least she was getting his body heat. He still insisted on calling her Mommy, which was beyond weird, but the kid was confused. Definitely traumatized.

Maybe Caleb and Adam had drugged him. The kid hadn't so much as twitched since she'd sat on this hard chair. His breathing sounded ragged, but he was stuffed up from crying. Maybe he'd fallen asleep.

"Jason," she whispered.

He snuggled deeper into her shoulder and twisted her halter straps tighter. Not asleep.

"Hey. I'm going to move you to the other side, okay? My arm is really tired."

He raised his head to look at her. "You won't let go?"

The fear and longing in his voice made Kelly's breath catch. She had no experience with children.

"No, I won't let go," she told him. *As if I could.* She rubbed his back reassuringly, the way she'd seen mothers do. "I just need to make a phone call. Okay?"

"Okay," he said, and went willingly when she transferred his weight to her left shoulder, which of course now made her right side cold. He placed his hot cheek against her neck and stuck his thumb in his mouth.

Thinking the kid was too old for thumb-sucking, Kelly unzipped the pouch around her waist and withdrew her cell phone. A quick glance told her she didn't have service. Likely the signal had been blocked.

"Damn," she muttered and stuffed the phone back inside.

She was a rookie. How much trouble would she be in for missing a shift? She glanced at her watch. Roll call was in thirty minutes.

Maybe it was time to make some noise, attract some attention. She and the kid had been slowly turning into ice for close to an hour. She knew the drill, and someone watched her through the one-way glass on the far wall. She'd never been good at waiting, but had been extremely patient this morning. She was tempted to give her observers the finger, but knew that wouldn't help anything. And her lieutenant would definitely hear about it.

"How old are you, Jason?" she asked to pass the time.

"Four," he stated, as if she were very stupid. But of course his mother would know his age.

"Who were those guys you were with?" she asked.

He closed his eyes.

"Did they hurt you?"

"They hit Maria," he whispered.

"Why did they do that?" Kelly asked, encouraged by his response. Who was Maria? Maybe the kid had recovered enough to give her some answers.

Jason shivered and turned his warm face into her neck.

"Did you know those men, Jason?"

He released a giant sigh, but didn't say another word.

"Okay, okay," Kelly said, patting his back. "We don't have to talk about them."

The door burst open and four men entered the room. None of them were in uniform. Short hair. Jackets and ties. Feds. DEA? FBI?

"Jason," someone shouted in a relieved tone.

Kelly focused on the speaker as he rushed toward her, and wondered if her mouth fell open. She stared at a man so impossibly good-looking he belonged on a movie screen or in a magazine. Dark hair, intense dark eyes. His jacket, his slacks—everything about him reeked of money and sophistication. The gold watch on his wrist belonged in a museum.

This god-come-to-earth squatted before Kelly and held out his arms to the kid. "Jason," he said in a choked voice.

The kid lifted his head but didn't release his hold on her. If anything, he tightened his grip and glared at the man.

"Jason?" The man shifted his gaze to Kelly, and she felt as if she'd been assaulted by an unseen force. Raw power flowed off him in waves. And arrogance mixed with anger. He didn't like being denied anything. And who would want to refuse him?

"Who the hell are you?" the god demanded.

"Kelly Jenkins. Who the hell are you?"

His eyes widened in surprise as if she was supposed to know who he was. Maybe he *was* some big-deal movie star. Maybe she had seen him before, now that she thought about it, but she never had time for movies or TV. His nails were manicured; his leather shoes buffed. His skin was smooth, unlined, as if he'd never experienced a worry in his life.

"Officer Jenkins, this is Trey Wentworth and you're holding his son, Jason," one of the suits said.

"Thank goodness," Kelly said, thinking, yeah, the name rang some bell, one associated with stacks of cash. She attempted to pass the kid to Wentworth.

"No, Mommy," Jason wailed, and turned his face from his dad.

Wentworth flinched as if the kid had struck him, and rose in a smooth athletic movement.

The feds all exchanged alarmed glances.

Coming to her feet, Kelly asked softly, "Don't you want to go to your daddy, Jason?"

"No. I want to stay with you, Mommy."

"But you know I'm not your mommy," Kelly said.

Jason began to cry again.

Kelly tried to pry his fingers from her clothing and hand Jason over. This kid had a problem far beyond her limited expertise as a rookie cop. He needed serious help, likely a shrink. She felt for the poor little guy. She'd had plenty of experience with shrink stuff.

"Jason, come on," she said. "Let go."

"Stop it," Wentworth ordered.

The force of Wentworth's command caused everyone in the room to look at him.

Kelly met his furious gaze, and again that strange sensation of raw power flowed over her.

"You're upsetting him," Wentworth said. "Leave him alone."

"*I'm* upsetting him?"

"Just give him a minute, okay?" Wentworth ran a hand through his perfectly cut hair. "He's confused. He's been through a lot."

Kelly plopped back down in the chair. "Yeah, well, so have I. What's going on here?"

One of the suits stepped forward. "Officer Jenkins, I'm Special Agent Walt Ballard."

"FBI?"

"Yes."

Kelly nodded. "I knew you were a fed."

"Why don't you fill us in," Ballard said. "How did you meet Jason?"

Beginning with her first sight of Jason, Kelly relayed what had occurred in the park.

"You used martial arts to knock a gun out of the man's hand?" Wentworth interrupted in a shocked voice.

Kelly nodded. "Instinct. These guys were amateurs. I mean, come on, they let a kid get away from them."

"An amateur could still shoot my son." Wentworth glared at her as if she were the criminal.

"You're upset because I kicked the gun from his hand?" Kelly demanded, glaring right back. "So I should have just handed him over to the bad guys?"

"Go on, Officer Jenkins," Ballard said.

Kelly squared her shoulders and continued, ending with concise descriptions of Caleb and Adam.

"The last I saw them they were hauling ass toward the marina. The Miami PD sent officers after them. I assume this is a kidnapping?"

"Yes," Ballard replied. "Apparently there was a miscommunication on the drop site."

Wentworth muttered something about the Keystone Cops.

Ballard turned to Wentworth. "Jason is safe, Mr. Wentworth. Your continued sarcasm isn't necessary or helpful."

"Safe?" Wentworth spit out. "He's clinging to some strange woman I've never seen before who almost got him shot, and he thinks he found his mother."

"Yeah, well, this strange woman likely saved your son's life."

"If you had done your job correctly, the way I—"

"Hey, guys." Kelly shouted over the rising voices. She placed her hand protectively on Jason's head as he burrowed into her shoulder. His entire body shook with the force of his sobs.

Wentworth whirled on her.

Kelly met his penetrating gaze. "This is so *not* what this little boy needs right now," she told him in a quiet voice.

CHAPTER TWO

TREY STRUGGLED TO control his frustration as he watched his precious son—his blessedly *alive* son—weep on the female cop's shoulder. Why was he lashing out at Ballard? The angry voices only confused Jason—upset him worse. But the way his son looked at him had pierced him to his core—like everything bad in the world was his daddy's fault. And maybe it was.

Officer Jenkins murmured soothingly to Jason, and his sobs gradually diminished.

"Gentlemen," the woman said in a level tone, her hand cupping Jason's head. "This *strange* woman is freezing her ass off and really would like someone to call her lieutenant."

After a long quiet moment, she said, "Please?" in a hopeful tone.

Noting gooseflesh on Jenkins's long legs, Trey removed his jacket and wrapped it around her and Jason. He took the opportunity to give his son a quick kiss on his flushed cheek before stepping back. Jason's gaze locked with his briefly before he turned away.

"Thank you," Jenkins said meaningfully. "You have no idea how much I appreciate that."

"Of course," Trey said.

Ballard raised his phone. "Give me a number," he said. "I'll explain the situation to your department."

She gave Ballard the information, and the agent stepped out of the room with his two colleagues, leaving Trey alone with Jenkins and his son. Trey sat in a chair beside them. His son still refused to look at him and sucked on a thumb, something he hadn't done in a while. Trey rubbed Jason's back, grateful the agents had left.

"Thank you for rescuing my son," he told Jenkins.

"You're welcome." She glanced down to Jason then carefully mouthed, "Where is his mom?"

"Dead," Trey mouthed back.

She closed her eyes.

"Hey, buddy," Trey said. "How are you doing?"

Jason buried his face deeper into the officer's shoulder.

"Don't you want to say hello to your daddy?" Officer Jenkins prompted. "I know he's been very worried about you."

After a moment, Jason raised his head. "Hi, Daddy," he said in a small voice.

With a rush of relief, Trey nodded his thanks to Jenkins.

Jason placed his small hand on the woman's cheek. "Don't send Mommy away again, Daddy."

Jenkins's bright blue eyes widened.

Trey shook his head. "Of course not, buddy," he soothed. He knew Jason blamed him for his mother going away. He was too young to understand divorce, the accident or Darlene's death, and right now was crazy mixed-up. He needed time and more therapy to get his memory straight.

Jenkins eyed him suspiciously, probably wondering what he'd done to make the kid act so hostile toward him. God, she likely thought he was some kind of monster. He tried to smile at her reassuringly, but she only narrowed her eyes.

His son had certainly picked the right stranger to help him, and he got why Jason had latched on to her. Definitely pretty, though rough around the edges. Blond hair, blue eyes, tall, slender, all the same as Darlene. When she couldn't get pharmaceuticals, Darlene used running to control her weight and often took Jason with her in a special stroller. Likely the physical resemblance and the jogging had gotten his son all twisted up. What his daddy needed to do was untwist him without causing more damage.

He needed to get Jason home. If his son fell asleep in his own bed, maybe when he woke up in familiar surroundings he'd be grounded in reality again. Dr. Carico could resume regular therapy. Obviously, they'd cut back on treatment too soon.

The immediate problem was getting him to let go of the female cop. Trey knew he should be grateful to Kelly Jenkins, but couldn't help but resent the way Jason clung to her. He wished his son would just once demonstrate the same sort of affection toward him. Not likely. Well, no way was he or anybody else wrenching his son away from her. Whatever the reason, this woman made Jason feel safe, and he had to respect that no matter how much it rankled.

How much would it take to convince her to accompany them back to the villa? Probably not much. Cops were notoriously underpaid.

"Listen, Officer Jenkins, I was wondering if you—"

Ballard swept into the room with his entourage and handed his phone to Jenkins. "Your commanding officer wants to speak to you."

Jenkins held the phone to her ear away from Jason and shifted his son higher on her lap. Trey felt a twinge of sympathy. He knew how heavy a four-year old could get.

"Yes, sir?" she said. "That's correct, sir. Of course, sir." After several nods she said, "Thank you, sir," and handed the phone back to Ballard.

"Are we good?" Ballard said into the phone. "Right. You'll have my report as soon as it's completed. Right. Thanks for the cooperation."

"You're square?" Ballard asked Jenkins.

"Released from duty for the day thanks to you," Jenkins said. "But I'm going in as soon as we're done here. He's pissed, and I don't want to be in his shitcan."

Trey winced at her choice of words.

"Maybe you should take the day," Ballard suggested.

"Can't do that," Jenkins said. "So what now, Mr. Wentworth?"

Jenkins shifted her gaze to Trey, eyebrows raised.

"How would you like a hot shower and some hot food?" Trey asked.

"A hot shower sounds like heaven on earth, but what about your son?"

"Look," Trey said. "Obviously my son is confused because of the abduction. Forcing him away from you right now will only upset him further, agreed?"

She glanced down at Jason and shrugged. "Yeah, that seems to be the situation."

"Come with us back to our home. Jason will likely fall asleep on the ride. I can put him to bed, you can have that hot shower, something to eat, and I'll see that you get home."

Jenkins shook her head. "Sorry, Mr. Wentworth, but I'm a rookie. My lieutenant isn't happy, and missing a shift won't look good on my record."

"Of course I'll compensate you for your time. What about a thousand dollars?"

Her startlingly blue eyes widened again. "A thousand dollars?"

"Two? I'm not sure what's appropriate for your daily wages."

"You've got to be kidding."

"I assure you I'm not. In fact, since we still have the ransom money, I can give you cash right now."

She stared at him for a long moment. So long he was tempted to look away.

"You don't have to pay me," she said finally, a disgusted note in her voice.

He'd insulted her. He hadn't given the offer much thought, but the woman had saved his son's life. Of course he'd have to reward her somehow.

"Please," Trey said. "My son has been through a great deal of turmoil in the last year. All I'm asking is you help me get him home where he'll feel safe without traumatizing him more."

She nodded, her jaw set, as if she was about to be tortured. "Okay. Anything to get out of this meat locker."

"Thank you," Trey said. He turned to Ballard. "I assume we're free to go."

Ballard hesitated, but shrugged. "Yeah, okay. We'll be in touch."

"Oh, I just bet you will," Trey said.

Trey caught a flash of annoyance in Ballard's eyes, but the agent said, "We'll find Jason's kidnappers, Mr. Wentworth. You can count on it."

"I'm not counting on anything," Trey replied. "And I'm hiring my own security team to protect my son."

"That's your right," Ballard said, and turned toward the female cop. "Officer Jenkins, I understand why Mr. Wentworth wants to get Jason settled first, but we need you to work with a sketch artist to get a likeness of the kidnappers. And you'll need to look at a photo lineup to see if either of them has been arrested."

"I'll come back after my shift," she said.

"Not good enough." Ballard shook his head. "The sooner the better. You know that."

"Shit," she muttered.

"Please watch your language around Jason," Trey said. The woman had a sewer mouth.

She rolled her eyes, but glanced at Jason whose arms remained locked around her neck. "Sorry."

"What about if we send the artist to Wentworth Villa?" Ballard asked. "The quicker we get the sketch out to the public, the sooner we'll apprehend Jason's kidnappers. It's possible they could leave the area."

"Sure, whatever," Trey said. "But right now we're leaving." He jerked open the door. "After you, Officer Jenkins."

SHIT, SHIT, SHIT. Pissed—and thanks to the kid, she couldn't even curse out loud—Kelly stomped through the open door, refusing to look at Wentworth. The jerk wasn't the least appreciative of law enforcement's efforts to help his son. He insulted her and the FBI at every opportunity. Typical.

She was glad to escape the arctic room, but the last thing she wanted to do was accompany this kid, who weighed a ton, and his arrogant father anywhere. How had this happened to her? She had an interesting assignment today paired with Sergeant Rudy McFadden, who could teach her a lot. She'd been looking forward to backing him up during patrol.

Instead she was on her way to a rich man's home to do his bidding. She'd managed to remember a few details associated with the Wentworth name. Billionaires, snooty old money. Trey Wentworth, the playboy heir who spent all his time partying, had tried to throw some of that money at her. He thought he could buy her.

Yeah, sure, she agreed this course of action was the best thing for a kid who was beyond screwed up at this point. The abduction had obviously terrified him into fantasyland. And his mom was dead. Kelly patted his back. Poor little thing. How long had his mother been gone? Kelly knew only too well that it didn't matter how long it'd been; the kid would hurt from that loss forever.

As they walked, Kelly listened to Wentworth's authoritative voice behind her instructing someone to meet him in front of the police station. Who? She'd assumed the FBI would give them a ride to wherever Wentworth lived. Probably in the penthouse of a waterfront condo on Brickell Avenue, which fortunately wasn't too far away. She really looked forward to a hot shower and something to eat. And she had to admit it'd be interesting to work with a sketch artist. She'd help however she could to get Adam and Caleb off the streets. That's why she became a cop.

Dirtbags belonged behind bars.

A blast of hot air enveloped her like an old flannel robe as she exited the police station. *Thank goodness.* She narrowed her eyes against the bright light. Realizing how tense she'd held herself because of the cold, Kelly consciously relaxed her shoulders. As soon as she thawed out, she'd give Wentworth back his jacket.

A sleek black limousine pulled to a smooth stop in front of the station. A uniformed chauffeur exited, hurried around to the passenger side and opened the door.

"Thanks you, Hans," Wentworth said.

Kelly stared at the limo. She'd never been inside one before.

"What's wrong?" Wentworth asked.

"Nothing." Kelly wrapped both arms around Jason, ducked her head and climbed into the vehicle. No graceful way to do it in running shorts. Facing the front, she planted her almost bare butt in the seat, and ran her palm across supple, luxurious black leather, breathing in its distinctive scent. She noted a bar to her left with two crystal decanters and matching glasses. Certain the amber liquid inside the decanters was some sort of liquor, she wished she could take a long swallow for quick warmth.

Better not. She needed to stay sharp.

Wentworth sat facing her and Jason. He gazed at his son with such longing that her resentment softened just a bit. When the driver shut the door, it instantly became quiet, making Jason's harsh, erratic breathing very loud.

Wentworth's eyes narrowed. "Is he okay?"

"I think his nose is stuffed up from all the crying."

Wentworth leaned forward and reached his hand inside his coat pocket, his hand brushing against her flesh. She stiffened, but he withdrew a handkerchief and handed it to her.

"See if you can get him to blow his nose."

She dangled it in front of the kid's face. "Blow your nose, Jason," she said.

"Hold it close," Wentworth instructed.

But Jason turned his face away.

Wentworth placed the cloth next to Jason's nose. "Come on, buddy. Blow for Daddy."

The kid made a honking sound.

"Again," Wentworth said.

After several more blows, the kid turned away again, placing his cheek against Kelly's shoulder with a deep sigh, refusing to look at his father. But his breathing sounded better.

Kelly couldn't read the expression on Wentworth's face as he stared out a window. With a start, she realized they were moving. The vehicle was so solid, so quiet, or maybe the driver so expert, she hadn't been aware that they'd entered traffic.

"Where do you live?" she asked after a few minutes.

"We spent the winter at the family villa on Collins Island."

Kelly didn't know what to react to first—the fact that it was currently spring, not winter, or that he had a *villa*, no less, on a private island accessible only by boat. No one could get on or off Collins Island without permission from an owner who resided on the Forbes Best or Most Whatever list.

Wentworth brushed lint off his trousers. "Jason has been receiving therapy from a child psychiatrist associated with Miami Children's Hospital, so we stayed on this year."

She nodded. So the kid had already been screwed up before the kidnapping.

"Have you called his doctor?" Kelly asked. "To let him know what's going on?"

"Her," Wentworth said. "Dr. Carico has rearranged her schedule and will meet with Jason this afternoon."

"Good," Kelly said. "That should help get him straightened out."

"God, I hope so," Wentworth muttered, glancing back to his son, then meeting her gaze. "Are you warm enough?" he asked. "I told Hans not to turn on the AC back here."

"Thanks," Kelly said. "I'm comfortable now. Do you want your jacket?"

Wentworth smiled. "I'm fine. And I don't want to disturb Jason. I think he's fallen asleep."

Kelly gazed down at the kid. His breathing was regular, although still too loud, and his body had relaxed into slumber.

"You're right," she whispered. "That's probably the best thing for him."

"Maybe not," Wentworth said. "He has bad dreams."

"Nightmares can't be worse than the reality of a kidnapping," Kelly said.

"You'd think not."

Wentworth lapsed into silence after that cryptic statement, and Kelly leaned her head against the plush seat back. The adrenaline rush of the encounter with Adam and Caleb, plus the misery of the cold room, had drained her usual energy. She closed her eyes, feeling the easy rush of pavement beneath the limo's eight tires. A far smoother ride than her own compact car. *Like floating on air.*

She woke when the limo came to a stop at the ferry landing for Collins Island. Jason remained sound asleep. And so was her arm beneath him. She wiggled her fingers. Pain shot up to her shoulder.

"Are you okay?" Wentworth asked. "You just made a horrible face."

Well, excuse me, Mr. Billionaire. We certainly can't have that. Apparently high-class people didn't do anything so gauche as have pained facial expressions.

"My arm is numb. I don't want to wake him, but I have to move him."

"Just transfer him to your other shoulder. He might rouse for a second, but he'll fall right back to sleep."

"Ouch," Kelly said as icy needles assaulted her arm.

Wentworth leaned forward and efficiently moved the kid to her right shoulder. Jason fussed for a few breaths, then eased into sleep again.

"Thanks," Kelly said, knowing she made another face as blood rushed into her left arm.

"I should be thanking you, Officer Jenkins. I know this is an imposition for you to remain with my son like this. We're total strangers to you."

"It's my job to protect and serve," she said, trying to make a joke. And remind him that she *was* law enforcement no matter how unprofessional she appeared in her skimpy jogging outfit.

Wentworth didn't crack a smile, only evaluated her with his intense dark stare. "This might be a little above and beyond your normal duty."

"A little." Uncomfortable under his scrutiny, she looked out the tinted windows and noted the ferry had pushed away from the dock. Wow. She was on her way to Collins Island. Imagine that. She'd always been curious about the legendary place. Most everyone in Miami was, but few ever got to see a Shangri-La reserved for that special one percent.

"I apologize if I insulted you by offering you money," Wentworth said in a low voice. "Please forgive me."

"Don't worry about it," Kelly said. "A hot shower will be more than enough reward."

"Oh, I think we can do better than that," he said, and smiled a lazy, somehow dangerous smile. This man was accustomed to getting his own way and doing exactly what he wanted. *How nice for him.*

But she didn't want anything from him.

Wentworth gazed out at the water, apparently lost in thought.

Kelly followed his gaze and noted they already approached the island's dock. Short trip, but they only had to cross the narrow channel known as Government Cut.

Before long they motored off the ferry and reached a pair of towering wrought iron gates with the initials "WWV" inscribed at the top in a handsome flowing script. A decorative iron barrier surrounded the estate.

As the gates swung open, Trey focused his attention on his son again. "We're home. Let's try not to wake him."

Kelly nodded.

The passenger compartment door opened after the driver stopped the limo. Kelly carefully shifted Jason so she could support him with both arms as she climbed out of the vehicle. Trey exited first and held out his hand to assist her, but she was afraid to release the kid who was dead weight in her arms.

Thankfully, she made it out without stumbling, and hoped she didn't gape at the size of the structure before her. *Villa indeed.* Architecture was hardly her thing, but she recognized good design when it slammed her in the face. Wentworth's home reminded her of photos she'd seen of estates in Tuscany. Coral roof tiles, classic columns and graceful arches made her think there might be a vineyard somewhere close by instead of the Atlantic Ocean.

She hefted the still-sleeping kid into a better position, and trudged up white marble steps toward the arched entranceway. Wentworth moved ahead with long easy strides and opened a massive door with the "WWV" monogram carved into the rich, dark wood. Inside, the first thing she noticed was the pleasant sound of a gurgling fountain in the corner.

The second thing she noticed was that the Wentworths' villa was almost as cold as the police station. She could hardly wait for that hot shower.

"Let me take Jason," Wentworth whispered. "I'll put him down and get you settled."

"Thanks," Kelly said. Maybe she needed to increase her reps in weight training.

But Jason roused when she transferred the kid to his father. As he realized what was happening to him, he struggled to escape Wentworth's grasp.

"No, Daddy! No," the kid screeched. He reached his arms back toward Kelly. "I want Mommy."

Kelly sighed and accepted him back. Jason wrapped his arms around her neck and linked his feet around her waist.

"Show me his bedroom," she said, averting her gaze from the tight expression on Wentworth's face.

A uniformed Hispanic woman whose left eye was swollen and bruised appeared in the marbled foyer, apparently alerted by Jason's shrieks.

"*Jasonito*," she exclaimed. Hurrying forward, she made the sign of the cross on her chest. "*Gracias a dios*."

"Hello, Maria," Wentworth said.

Kelly evaluated Maria. Dark hair and eyes, round face, five two, early thirties. Was this Jason's nanny? The kid said the kidnappers struck someone named Maria, and this woman sported a nasty black eye.

"Welcome home, Mr. Wentworth," Maria said. "So the ransom exchange went well?" she said in a hopeful tone.

"No," Wentworth said. "But Jason is home safe, thanks to Officer Jenkins here. Officer Jenkins, this is Maria, my housekeeper and Jason's nanny."

"Please call me Kelly," she said, tired of the formality.

"What happened?" Maria asked.

"I'll explain later," Wentworth said. "Right now we need to get Jason down for a nap."

"Of course," Maria said, reaching for the kid.

"No," Jason whined, tightening his legs. "No!"

"*Jasonito?*" Maria asked in a hurt voice.

"I'm sorry," Kelly said to Maria. "I'm his safety blanket right now."

"Maria, please ready a guest room so Kelly can take a shower."

"Of course, sir." She swiped away a tear, bowed and left the foyer.

"Follow me," Wentworth told Kelly.

The room she hurried through was a blur of white marble, dramatic, subtly lit angles and well-made furnishings, again mostly white. *No place for a kid to play, that's for sure.*

They ascended a grand, sweeping staircase and entered a bedroom that had to be Jason's because an artist, and a pretty good one, had decorated the walls with cartoon characters, colorful balloons and pretty flowers, creating a cheerful space for a child.

Kelly spotted an elaborate bed designed to look like an airplane and moved toward it. Wentworth turned back the bedspread, and she gratefully placed Jason onto crisp, pale blue sheets.

He turned on his side, reached out and grasped her hand. "Don't leave, Mommy," he begged.

"Okay," she said, suspecting the kid would be back asleep within minutes.

Wentworth moved a plush chair close to Jason's bed, and Kelly sat. "Thanks," she murmured. "I'll just wait here until he conks out again."

Staring at his son, Wentworth said, "I'll instruct my chef to prepare something to eat." But he didn't move. After a sigh, shaking his head, he leaned over and kissed Jason's cheek. "Sleep tight, buddy," Wentworth whispered. He stepped to the windows, closed the shades and then left them alone.

Kelly blew out a breath, relieved to finally lose her burden and enjoy a little solitude.

Jason's eyes drifted shut. His grip on her loosened. It wouldn't be long before she could enjoy that promised shower.

She gaped at the number and variety of toys on display in the room. Like photos she'd seen of an avalanche of presents under the tree for some lucky brat on Christmas morning. Not her though. Her Christmases were spent in foster care where she was lucky if she got a hot breakfast.

This poor kid had everything he could possibly want and yet was so totally miserable he'd confused her for his dead mom.

CHAPTER THREE

TREY HURRIED DOWNSTAIRS. Jason was home. His son was safe. That was all he could and should focus on.

When he entered the spacious kitchen, his plump chef, the wife of his chauffeur, sat at the center island reading one of her many cookbooks. She stood immediately, her pleasant face split by a huge grin.

"Jason has safely returned home?" Greta asked.

"Yes," Trey said. "We got lucky."

"Thank God." Then she held herself stiff. "What can I do for you, sir? Is he hungry?"

"I need you to prepare some sandwiches and hot soup. My attorney and Dr. Carico will be arriving, plus we have a visitor."

"Yes, sir," Greta said. "What about dinner?"

"Whatever you had planned," Trey said. He couldn't think that far ahead right now. First he needed to get Kelly Jenkins showered, fed and sent home. Maybe when she was gone, Jason would return to himself.

In his office, Trey moved to his desk and called the island pro shop, instructing them to deliver women's golf shorts and a shirt. The Jenkins woman would need clean and more suitable clothing after her shower. "Size eight or—maybe six. Better bring one of each. I don't care what color. Throw in some socks. Do you have lingerie? No? Okay. But make it quick. There'll be a generous tip."

He leaned back in his swivel chair and closed his eyes. *What else needed to be done?* He couldn't think of a thing. His staff was efficient. Maria would see that Officer Jenkins—Kelly—got her shower and the new clothes.

He'd hoped when Jason got home he would forget this fantasy of his dead mom come back to life. No such luck. Poor Jase. Was there lingering trauma from the crash? Darlene had been so drunk she hadn't bothered to strap him into his car seat, so he'd struck his head. The surgeons said all swelling had resolved, but maybe not. What other explanation was there for his strange behavior? Could Dr. Carico get him straight again?

At a light rap on his office door, Trey opened his eyes. Brian Howell stood there holding a document. Trey leaned his chair forward. He needed to talk to someone he could trust, and Brian was both his personal attorney and a good friend since their undergraduate days at Princeton.

"How are you doing?" Brian asked as he entered, his gaze sweeping Trey over his reading glasses. An avid runner himself, Brian was tall, thin and the most focused man Trey had ever known. *Except for my father, Alexander Asswipe Wentworth the Third.*

"I've been better. But I've also been worse." *Like this morning before I got Jason back.*

"You look terrible."

"No doubt. I haven't slept since the abduction."

"How's Jason?"

Trey sighed. "He thinks the cop who rescued him is Darlene."

Brian halted his steps. "What?"

"He won't let her out of his sight and insists on calling her Mommy."

Brian sat in a chair before the desk. "That's bizarre behavior even given what he's been through. Have you contacted Carico?"

"She'll join us any minute."

"What happened?"

Trey told the story of how Jason somehow escaped his abductors and glued himself to a woman jogging through the park. "I think it's because Kelly Jenkins physically resembles Darlene and was jogging. Remember, Darlene used to take him on runs."

"You're sure that's the whole story?" Brian asked.

"The Miami Police corroborate her version, and they interviewed bystanders," Trey replied. "Why?"

"Like I said, bizarre. Where is this woman now?"

"Upstairs with Jason. She'll join us for lunch when he falls asleep."

"So you've allowed this stranger into your home? Is that wise?"

"I didn't have much choice without sending Jason into full-out hysterics. I couldn't do that to him."

"I'd like to talk to her with you present," Brian

said. "See if she tells the story the same way twice." He removed his glasses and tapped them on his cheek. "I'd also like to run a background check on her."

"She's a police officer. As soon I feed her, she'll be out of our lives."

"Maybe."

Trey shrugged. "Whatever you think. What's that?" Trey nodded to the document in Brian's lap.

"Part of the reason for my caution. This is a demand letter from Darlene's father—or rather Darlene's father's new attorney." Brian handed Trey the paper over the desk.

"My ex-wife didn't have a father."

"Oh, she had one. He just wasn't in her life following conception. One Jeff Lawson just got out of prison, found out who the bundle of joy he never laid eyes on married, and thinks—like his daughter before him—why not dip into the deep Wentworth pot for a little extra spending money."

"You've got to be kidding me." Trey stared at the letter in outrage. Lawson's attorney, a sole practitioner, had a post office box for an address.

"Don't worry about it. I had to tell you, but it's nothing but a nuisance, a bottom-feeder lawyer making some noise. I'll deal with it."

Trey sat back and closed his eyes. "Yeah, please handle it. Right now I've got to focus on Jason."

"Carico is good. She'll get Jase straightened out."

"I hope so," Trey said. The phone rang, and Trey

checked caller ID, surprised to see his father's private number. Was he actually taking time to check on Jason?

"Excuse me," Trey told Brian. "It's my father."

Brian stood. "I'll check on lunch."

"Hi, Dad," Trey said into the phone.

"Trey. I got your message. Excellent news."

"Yes, it is."

"I trust you'll make certain Jason is better protected from now on."

Trey didn't respond. His dad never missed an opportunity to get in a dig. This one was a low blow, but better not to react.

"I hope you haven't forgotten the Alzheimer's benefit," his father continued.

"What did you say?"

"You're scheduled to appear at The Turf Club tonight."

Trey closed his eyes. No way could he attend a formal party now. The idea sickened him. How typical that his father expected him to go.

"Sorry, Dad. Under the circumstances, I won't be able to make it. I'll send regrets and a large check."

After a long silence, his father cleared his throat. "Hundreds of very expensive tickets were sold based on your appearance. The Wentworth name is all over this event."

"Dad—"

"Don't let the family down, Trey. Jason is fine. He'll likely sleep the night through."

"How do you know Jason is fine?"

"He's home, isn't he? Just put in a brief appearance, shake a few hands and down a few glasses of champagne. It's your job, son. I expect you to attend."

And with that his father disconnected.

Trey smothered a curse and replaced the receiver. What made him think this time his father would demonstrate some normal human emotion?

So he was going to The Turf Club tonight. Putting on a cheerful smile and glad-handing strangers was impossible. How would he get through the evening? He didn't want to go, but this was the unholy deal he'd made with his father, the only sure way to protect his mother. A deal that had never chafed worse than right now.

What if Jason were still missing? Would his father still expect him to put on a tux and promote Wentworth Industries?

What the hell. He'd make it quick. He wouldn't sleep tonight anyway without a sedative, and he didn't want to take one. Jason might wake up and need him.

WHEN CERTAIN JASON was asleep, Kelly slipped her hand from under his limp fingers and tiptoed toward the door where she flipped off the overhead light. A small nightlight in the shape of a green frog glowed dimly, and a bit of sun filtered in through the windows, so the room wouldn't be totally black if he awoke.

As she eased the door shut, Kelly wondered if Jason was afraid of the dark.

Carrying a pile of thick towels, Maria waited in the hallway and offered a shy smile. "Is *Jasonito* asleep?" she asked.

"For now," Kelly said, wincing at Maria's discolored face. "You were with him when he was taken, right?"

Maria's smile disappeared. "Yes. We were at the park. I tried to stop them, but they—" She raised her hand to her swollen eye. "I could not protect him. That must be why he is mad at me."

"I don't think he's mad at you," Kelly soothed. "He's just a mixed-up kid right now."

Maria glanced at the door. "He is sweet boy."

"Yeah, he is," Kelly said. *Although damned heavy.*

"Thank God he is home safe. Thank you for rescuing him."

"Just doing my job," Kelly said.

At those words, Maria roused herself. "Let me show you to your room."

Following Maria down the hall, Kelly thought of her own mother, something that didn't happen often lately. Was it the way the housekeeper moved? Kelly's mom had worked as a maid for most of her life. When she was sober enough to hold a job, that is. But never in a grand house like this, Kelly thought bitterly. Usually fleabag motels—where she'd turn the occasional trick if the opportunity arose.

They entered a large bedroom where again the theme was mostly white, although the furnishings, including a desk, provided pleasing splashes of dark brown. A wooden frame without a curtain surrounded a huge bed overflowing with plump, carefully arranged pillows. Arching white orchids perched on bedside tables. Kelly's gaze was drawn beyond the flowers to windows on either side of the bed and a spectacular view of blue-green water in the distance. The Atlantic Ocean.

Maria placed the towels on the bed and stepped to a closet where she slid open doors and withdrew a—of course—white terry cloth robe. Maria handed Kelly the robe, and motioned toward a door that Kelly guessed led to the bathroom. "After you shower, please come downstairs. Lunch will be waiting."

"Thanks," Kelly said.

Maria moved to one of the side tables, opened a door and withdrew a glass bottle.

"In case you are thirsty," Maria said, presenting the bottle to Kelly. "Help yourself to whatever is in the refrigerator."

"Thanks again." Kelly twisted off the cap and took a long drink of chilled water with a refreshing lemon flavor.

"*Por nada,*" Maria said. "It's nothing."

With a slight bow, Maria exited, closing the door behind her, and Kelly released a sigh. Had she fallen down a rabbit hole today, or what? She grabbed the robe, draped it over her shoulders and stepped to a window to check out the view.

Wow. Yeah, the white-capped ocean took her breath away, but the huge pool, surrounded by towering palm trees swaying in the breeze, was equally spectacular. Swimming was her favorite form of exercise, but hard to manage with her schedule.

Yeah, right. Mr. Trey Wentworth would have no problem with her making herself right at home with a dip in his pool.

What a paradise. Wondering just how big this so-called villa was, she shook her head as she imagined the cost to maintain this palace. She couldn't wait to tell Lana and Patrice, two of her fellow rookies, about her adventure into billionaire-land.

But first she needed to shower, warm up and get out of here. Kelly grabbed a towel from the bed and hurried into the bathroom, where the tasteful luxury made it a perfect place to dreamily soak your troubles away.

Under different circumstances. *Get moving, rookie.*

Kelly stepped to the shower and swiveled on the water. She placed the robe on the gleaming marble counter, removed her running shoes and socks, then stripped and stepped through a mist of steam into a strong stream of hot water. Finally. Relishing the warmth, she turned her back to the cascade and on the other wall spotted another set of nozzles. Wondering what would happen, she turned those on, too, and soon jets of delicious heat seeped into her muscles from front and rear.

She washed her hair with shampoo from a pump container conveniently built into the wall, and then rinsed it with a silky conditioner that released the same citrus fragrance. She lathered all over with a shower gel that left her skin soft and smooth.

She emerged from the shower a new woman, relaxed and ready to tackle any problem. After drying off, she enfolded her warm, happy body with the robe, cinched the tie and realized she had to put back on the same damp clothing she'd arrived in.

Maybe Wentworth would loan her some sweats.

Kelly found a comb next to the sink, ran it through her shoulder length hair, and then used the blow dryer to take her hair from soaking to damp. *All the amenities of a hotel.* Except a toothbrush, so she rinsed her mouth with the lemon water and exited the bath to find several sets of shorts and polo shirts laid out on the bed.

Well, how about that. A quick check told her Wentworth had guessed her size correctly. Or, anyway, he'd managed to narrow it down to two choices. The man obviously knew his way around a woman's body. His thoughtfulness elevated her opinion of him.

Was he considerate or just didn't want her walking around looking sloppy? She frowned at her thoughts. She was being judgmental, and she was way too relaxed for that.

Not to mention too hungry.

As she loosened the robe's tie to change into the new clothes, Kelly heard a commotion in the hallway and turned toward the door. Someone was stampeding past the door.

"Mommy!" she heard Jason scream. "Mommy! Where are you?"

What the hell?

Kelly stepped into the hall and spotted the kid running furiously in the direction of the staircase screaming for his mother.

"Jason," she said. "Here I am."

The kid turned, spotted her and reversed direction.

"Mommy," he shrieked.

She tried to brace herself, but Jason launched himself into the air, grabbing her around her hips, and she lost her footing.

Kelly twisted so she took the force of the fall. As her butt landed on the marble floor, she protected Jason's head by holding it against her soft middle with both hands. Kid was screwed up enough already.

"Ooomph," she heard herself say as she hit the floor. Pain shot through her hip, but she tightened her abs to prevent her own skull from slamming down. Out of breath, she lay still for a moment and stared at the ceiling as she assessed her body for damage.

So much for my relaxing shower.

She felt cool air where she shouldn't at the same time she heard noises from Jason, and raised her head to gaze down to where she cradled him against her abdomen. Her bare abdomen. Damn. The robe had come open. Her breasts were exposed. Talk about a wardrobe malfunction.

Jason lifted his cheek and their gazes met. He grinned and began to giggle. *Thanks a lot, kid.*

But it was the first time she'd seem him smile and this *was* ridiculous. A laugh bubbled up from Kelly's chest. She needed to cover herself, but the robe had slid off her shoulders and the terrycloth was all tangled beneath her.

"God, are you two all right?"

Kelly's gaze snapped toward the demanding male voice. Trey Wentworth stood frozen at the end of the hallway wearing a horrified expression. *He saw everything.*

Releasing a breath, she closed her eyes. This day just kept getting worse and worse.

TREY WATCHED AS Kelly leaped to her feet and hurriedly secured the front of the robe. Jason reached his arms up, and she hefted him onto her hip.

"That was fun, Mommy," he said.

Trey hurried down the hall toward them doubting if she agreed. He couldn't help but notice she'd deliberately taken the brunt of the fall, protecting his son.

"Are you okay?" he asked.

"Fine," she said, her face a healthy pink, unable to meet his gaze.

Trey shifted his gaze to his grinning son. "Jason, it's not nice to knock people down."

His smile faded. "Sorry, Daddy. I woke up and got scared 'cause I couldn't find Mommy."

Trey evaluated his son. He hadn't slept long enough to clear his head, and most likely he'd experienced troubling dreams again. Maybe Dr. Carico could give him a sedative and ensure he slept through the night.

"No harm done," Jenkins said. "Except to my dignity."

"I'll bet you end up with a nasty bruise."

"Maybe," she said. "Hey, thanks for the clothes. Much appreciated."

"You're welcome. Lunch is waiting," Trey said. "Come downstairs when you're ready."

Jason grumbled when she returned him to the floor, so Trey stepped forward and took his hand. "Let's go eat, Jase. Mommy needs to get dressed."

Jason frowned, remaining stubbornly in place. "Why can't we stay with Mommy while she gets dressed?"

Trey glanced to Kelly. When their gazes collided, an unexpected arc of awareness shot between them. Yeah, he'd definitely like to watch her get dressed.

Her breasts were magnificent. Perfectly formed and completely natural, a rare thing among the women in his social circle. He wouldn't mind confirming the rest of her body was just as stunning.

"I'll be right there, Jason," she promised, breaking the moment. "Just give me a minute, okay."

"Greta made your favorite sandwich just for you," Trey said, wondering where his inappropriate thoughts had come from.

"Peanut butter and jelly?" Jason asked in a hopeful voice.

"Yes."

"Grape jelly?"

"Of course."

"Okay, Daddy."

Trey breathed a sigh of relief as Jason scampered toward the stairs. "Grape works every time," he told Kelly. "We'll see you downstairs."

"Sure," she said, and disappeared inside the guest room. Trey followed Jase downstairs, his thoughts returning to Kelly's body. He'd also noticed an old burn mark near her collar bone. Its shape suggested someone had ground a lit cigarette into her flesh.

He shook his head, not wanting to think about how much that must have hurt. "Uncle Brian!" Jason spotted Brian and ran across the room toward the attorney, his arms extended wide. "Airplane ride."

Smiling at his son's display of normal childhood enthusiasm, Trey dismissed thoughts of Kelly Jenkins's possibly troubled past. He had enough problems to worry about and didn't need to add hers to his pile.

Making whooshing sounds as if he were a flying airplane, Brian swept a giggling Jason high into the air, and then placed him back on the floor.

"Ready for some lunch?" Brian asked.

Jason nodded and they moved into the dining room where Greta had laid out a buffet of sandwiches, a tureen of soup, cut melon and fresh cookies. Dr. Donna Carico sat at the huge thick glass table speaking on her cell phone with an untouched sandwich before her. She looked up when Jason ran into the room and terminated her call.

Trey nodded at the doctor, knowing she'd had to reschedule appointments. "Thanks for coming, Donna."

She nodded back, and a troubled smile crossed her face as Jason sat down beside her. "Hey, Jason," she said.

"Hi, Dr. Donna."

Trey thought Jason sounded shy. Their eyes met briefly, but then Jason turned back to the doctor.

"Are you here to talk to me?" Jason asked.

"Yes, sir. If you want to talk to me."

Jason shrugged and focused on his sandwich. He took a bite. Then another. "Okay," he mumbled around the bread in his mouth and held out his hand to the doctor.

Trey relaxed. Jason was willing to talk to his therapist, so maybe Donna could make some progress. Trey was beginning to doubt the wisdom of carrying on the charade that Kelly was his son's mother. Perhaps the longer that went on, the harder it would be for Jason to face reality.

Maybe the break should be a clean one. Like ripping off a Band-Aid.

Donna accepted Jason's offered hand, and the two left the room to go to Jason's play room where they usually spoke. Dr. Carico would know the best way to proceed. He'd filled her in on the tumultuous morning during their phone call.

Trey nodded at Greta who hovered by the door in case she was needed. "Please take their lunch to them in the play room."

As Greta gathered the plates, a fully dressed Kelly Jenkins entered the dining room looking as if she were on her way to play nine holes on the Collins Island course. Stunned by the transformation, Trey came to his feet and had to jerk his gaze away from her long, tanned legs. Her blond hair hung loosely around her shoulders, framing a pretty but serious face. *She cleaned up nice,* an old saying of his mother's, filtered through his brain. The only thing that spoiled the image was her filthy running shoes.

He noticed Brian was also on his feet and openly checking her out.

"Brian, please meet my son's savior, Officer Kelly Jenkins. Kelly, this is my attorney, Brian Howell."

She stepped forward and pumped Brian's hand. "Pleased to meet you."

"Charmed," Brian said. "I understand you're quite the heroine."

"Just doing my job," she said.

"Do you feel better?" Trey asked. "At least warmer?"

"Much better," she said, her focus on the buffet. "I heard something about lunch?"

"Please help yourself," Trey said.

"Thanks."

She piled two sandwiches, a huge mound of melon and three oatmeal cookies onto a plate. Next she scooped a ladle of steaming minestrone from the tureen and sniffed it. Apparently deciding the mix was satisfactory, she poured the thick liquid into a small bowl, sat at the table and took a giant bite from a turkey sandwich. She kept her eyes down, chewed quickly and didn't speak.

As Trey watched her, he thought she seemed protective of her food, worried someone might take it away.

He glanced at Brian and found his friend also staring at Kelly's strange behavior. Their gazes met, and Brian shook his head.

As if sensing the scrutiny, Kelly looked up. She swallowed the food in her mouth and asked, "What?"

"Nothing," Trey said.

"Are you from the south Florida area?" Brian asked.

"Born and raised."

"Where did you go to high school?"

"Why?"

Brian shrugged. "Just curious. We're about the same age, and I'm also from Miami."

"We didn't go to the same school," Kelly stated.

"How long have you been a police officer?" Brian asked.

Kelly narrowed her eyes at Brian. "Is this an interrogation or something, Mr. Lawyer?"

Brian sighed. "I was hoping you could tell me what happened in the park with Jason and the kidnappers."

"You can read the police report," Kelly said. "I've told the story at least ten times, and I'm not going over it again with you now."

Brian held up his hands in surrender.

"Where's Jason?" Kelly asked.

"Talking to his therapist," Trey said.

"Excellent," Kelly said, and resumed eating. To his surprise, she finished both sandwiches, all the fruit and started on the soup, loudly slurping the still-hot liquid from her spoon.

Trey nibbled at his own sandwich, wondering where she learned her table manners and why she was so prickly about her background. He understood why she didn't want to go over her confrontation with the kidnappers again, and had to laugh at the expression on Brian's face when she shut him down. Not many people had the nerve to speak to Brian Howell that way.

"Well, I'm definitely full," Kelly said after a few minutes, gazing regretfully at her untouched cookies. "Thanks for lunch, but I really need to get going."

"You can take the cookies with you," Trey said, relieved the complication of Kelly Jenkins was soon to be over and she'd be out of his life. And his son's life.

She bit her lip, and he could tell she considered grabbing the cookies, but shook her head and rose. "That's okay. You'll make sure I get home, right?"

"Of course," Trey said. He nodded at Greta who had returned to her post. "Please summon Hans."

Trey turned to Kelly again. "Officer Jenkins, thank you. I can't express how grateful I am for your assistance with my son."

"No problem."

Trey smiled. Why did people politely say "No problem," when there actually was a problem? Rescuing his son had created chaos for this woman. He could tell she was uncomfortable even now.

"How will I get these clothes back to you?" she asked.

"There's no need for that. Please accept them as a very small token of appreciation."

She hesitated, but said, "Okay."

Maria appeared at the door holding a small bag. "Officer Jenkins, this is your clothing. I laundered it for you, but it might still be a little damp."

"Thanks, Maria," Trey said, relieved there'd be no excuse for Kelly Jenkins to reappear in his world. Although, frankly, she seemed to be in as big a hurry to escape as he was to see her go.

"Should I say goodbye to Jason?" Kelly asked, looking from Trey to Brian.

"Don't you think it would be better if you left without him knowing?" Trey said. "He might get upset."

"But what will he do when he learns I'm gone?"

"He's with his therapist. Dr. Carico will handle any problems."

"Better to make a clean break," she said with a nod, echoing his earlier thoughts.

"I'm glad you agree."

Trey accompanied her to the foyer, and they stepped outside where Hans waited beside the limo.

"Thanks again," Trey said.

"Sure." Kelly hurried down the steps with a backward wave. She bent over to enter the limo when a blur dashed past him.

"Mommy," Jason shrieked.

Trey reached for his son but missed.

Out of breath, Dr. Carico appeared beside Trey. "He wanted me to meet her. He really believes this woman is his mother."

Trey watched in horror as Jason threw his arms

around Kelly's legs, surprising her, knocking her off balance again.

But she recovered without falling, and knelt to speak with him.

Trey and Dr. Carico hurried down the steps.

"I'm so sorry," Dr. Carico told Kelly.

"Come on, buddy," Trey said. "Mommy has got to go."

Sobbing, Jason buried his face in Kelly's shoulder and clasped his hands around her neck. "Take me with you, Mommy," he pleaded. "Please."

CHAPTER FOUR

MURMURING SOOTHING SOUNDS, Kelly placed the still-sobbing Jason back in his airplane bed. She knelt, not letting go of his warm sticky fingers. Dr. Carico moved beside them and quickly administered an injection into his upper arm. The child didn't react to the prick of the needle.

"He'll be out soon," the doctor said softly.

Kelly nodded, her attention focused on the child, stroking damp hair away from his flushed face. Unbearably sad blue eyes stared into hers. Poor little dude.

"Don't go," he whispered.

"I'm right here," Kelly said.

He heaved a sigh, closed his eyes and within a minute or two his breathing grew steady. He didn't rouse when she released his hand.

Feeling older than her sergeant, she came to her feet and faced Carico who stared at her now sleeping patient with a worried frown.

"Maybe I should have sedated him earlier, but he seemed fine."

"He's fine until I leave his sight," Kelly said. "Now what?"

"He'll sleep the rest of the night."

"Will his head be straight when he wakes up in the morning?"

Carico met Kelly's gaze. "I don't know."

"At least you admit it." Kelly looked away from the question in Carico's probing gaze. What did these people expect her to do? Sure, she felt bad for the little dude—the kid was in a very bad place—but she wasn't anybody's mother. And she had a career to get back to.

"Let's go downstairs and talk to Trey," Carico suggested.

Kelly followed the doctor down the elegant stairs, across the marbled living room into the dining room where Wentworth and his lawyer pal sat at the massive glass banquet table deep in conversation. Lunch had been cleared, but they each held a graceful crystal glass full of red wine. An array of cheese and crackers worthy of being on a magazine cover sat between them, along with the open wine bottle.

Well, it's five o'clock somewhere.

With a start, she realized it was after 6:00 p.m. Where had the time gone? The sun would soon set on the most surreal day of her life. Not the most frightening, but definitely the strangest.

Wentworth glared at her with an expression so full of resentment she squared her shoulders. Did the jerk blame *her* for this fiasco? Geez. Like it was her fault Jason preferred a stranger's comfort to his father's.

"How is Jason?" Wentworth asked.

"Asleep," Carico said. "And he'll stay that way the rest of the night."

"Good." Wentworth nodded. "Would you like some wine?"

"No," Carico replied as she seated herself. "Thanks, but I have a meeting later that I can't miss." Glancing at her watch, she added, "In fact, I'll have to go soon. The ferry is crowded this time of day."

"Kelly?" Wentworth asked.

"Wine sounds great," Kelly said, taking a seat across from Wentworth at the table.

A plump blonde woman who'd been lurking at the door rushed in and placed a clean wineglass on the table.

"Thank you, Greta," Wentworth said. He dribbled wine into the new glass, then pushed it across the table toward Kelly.

"Thanks." She took a swallow, surprised to find the taste wasn't sweet like the crap she usually drank. She swirled the liquid in the glass like she'd seen on television and took another sip. Not bad actually. This must be what the wino experts called dry, and no doubt more expensive than anything she'd ever swilled in her life.

She lowered the glass and found Wentworth staring at her, along with his lawyer and his son's shrink.

The lawyer cleared his throat. "We seem to have a situation here."

"No shit," Kelly blurted, and immediately regretted her choice of words. At least the kid was upstairs snoozing.

During an awkward silence, Carico helped herself to several slices of cheese and crackers and placed the food on an elegant white plate. When she resumed her seat, Kelly met her gaze. The shrink narrowed her eyes and nodded, as if she'd arrived at some sort of conclusion.

"What do you think, Donna?" Wentworth asked.

"The kidnapping made Jason regress," Carico said. "That was to be expected."

Wentworth nodded. "Is there a possibility he'll continue to think Officer Jenkins is his mother when he wakes up?"

"I can't answer that question. We'll have to wait and see."

"Is there any chance he's making this up, that he knows this woman isn't his mother?" Wentworth asked.

Kelly took a sip of her wine to cover a snort. Wentworth was clueless. He'd seen Jason's reactions. How could anyone possibly think the little dude was playacting?

"Not from what I've observed," the doctor said, shaking her head.

"Have you ever seen anything like this before?" the lawyer asked.

"I've never treated a patient with this kind of transference, but I've read about it. It's rare."

"Transference?" Kelly asked.

"In therapy, transference usually happens when a patient projects their feelings or thoughts about one person onto their analyst. The analyst comes to represent some person from the patient's past, and it can provide a useful window of information about what a patient desires or wishes to avoid."

"Jason desires his mother to be back," Wentworth said.

Carico nodded. "The abduction traumatized him, made him long desperately for his mom to protect him. When he spotted Officer Jenkins, who physically resembles his absent mother, he latched on to the idea she'd returned to save him. A mental defense mechanism created by a terrified child."

"Jason knows his mother is dead," Wentworth said.

"But can a four-year-old truly understand the finality of death?" Carico asked gently.

Kelly stared into her wineglass. She'd seen her mother everywhere for years after her murder. And she'd been thirteen, a teenager who definitely understood the meaning of death.

"Plus, in our sessions, Jason mentioned his mom used to take him with her jogging."

"The healthiest thing she ever did," Wentworth said, in a tone full of sarcasm.

Kelly glanced at Wentworth. Definitely not too fond of his late wife.

"Jason's symptoms also vaguely remind me of

conversion hysteria," Carico continued, frowning. "But usually in such cases there is a physical ailment, such as blindness or paralysis, that develops. I intend to do a lot of research."

Wentworth leaned forward. "Whatever it takes."

Carico flashed Wentworth such a brilliant smile that Kelly almost choked. What was up with that? Did the good doctor have the hots for her patient's father?

"But the gorilla in the room is what do we do about Officer Jenkins," Carico said.

Kelly met the shrink's direct gaze and didn't like what she saw. Uh-oh. No question she was going to hate what came next.

"After careful consideration," Carico said, "it is my opinion that Kelly should be available when Jason wakes up. Just in case."

TREY CLOSED HIS eyes to block out the outraged expression on Kelly's face. She obviously didn't like the idea of hanging around. Hell, he didn't want her here, either. He'd hoped to be rid of her, but what choice did he have when Donna recommended she remain?

Jason needed her.

"Just in case what?" Brian asked. "I think we need to be clear here."

"In case Jason becomes agitated that his mother is gone again," Donna said. "You've seen how he reacts when Kelly attempts to leave. His personality is extremely fragile because of everything he's been through. We don't want to push him into a full-blown episode of hysteria. From what I saw earlier, he was very close, and that could be quite damaging, perhaps take years to recover from."

"I have to agree," Brian said. "I've never seen any child react the way he did when we tried to separate him from Officer Jenkins."

"What concerns me most is how he stiffened his limbs," Donna said. "That's a symptom of catatonia. We want to avoid pushing him into such a dangerous state."

Remembering the sight of Jason's rigid body when he tried to separate him from Officer Jenkins, Trey stared into his wine. What was happening to his son? Even with all his resources, he was helpless to prevent Jason's downward spiral.

"Come on, guys. You can't expect me to stay here," Kelly said, her gaze shifting around the table.

"I know it would be a tremendous imposition, but couldn't you remain just one night?" Donna said. "I've done it several times, and this villa is quite comfortable."

"You can stay in the guest room you used earlier," Trey said. "I'll place my staff at your disposal."

"No way," Kelly said. "I have to work tomorrow."

"I'll have Hans drive you to your station in the morning."

"Roll call is at ten a.m. What if Jason isn't awake by then?"

Donna smiled. "You obviously aren't familiar with little boys. I'm certain he will be up long before that."

Kelly shook her head. "But what if we're just putting off the inevitable? What if he gets hysterical when I leave in the morning?"

"We'll deal with that possibility then," Donna said.

"Will you be here to do that?" Kelly demanded.

"Yes. Trey has asked me to return to evaluate his condition."

Trey nodded when Donna shot him a smile. Thank God for Donna. Anything to convince the cop to stay. He understood she had a life, but how could she refuse to help a frightened child? Was she heartless?

"If Jason doesn't settle down, my recommendation will be to treat him in-patient," Dr. Carico said. "I've consulted several colleagues, and they all recommend institutionalization. Trey wants to avoid that at all costs."

Kelly released a sigh. "Yeah, I get that."

"When she was alive, Jason's mother left him with nannies all the time," Trey said, relieved Kelly appeared to be softening. He couldn't force her to stay, and he'd already insulted her once by offering payment. "I think he'll understand your need to go to work."

"Did his mom work?" Kelly asked.

"Not after we married, but she attended a lot of luncheons."

Kelly's mouth tightened. "This is nuts."

"He's a scared, confused little boy," Trey said. "And I'm only asking for one night."

She shook her head and stared at the cheese tray. "I'd have to swing by my apartment in the morning to get my uniform."

"That's not a problem," Trey said. "Like I said, whatever it takes."

"All right," Kelly said, throwing up her arms in surrender. "I'm not convinced it's the right thing to do, but I'll stay."

"Thank you," Trey said, putting as much meaning into the words as he could muster. "Please feel free to make yourself at home while you're here."

The cop looked interested in that idea, but before she could ask a question, Maria appeared at the door to the dining room, uncharacteristically twisting her apron in both hands. Jason's condition was hard on everyone in the house.

"The police are here with a sketch artist," she said. "They want to work with Officer Jenkins."

"Of course," Trey said. "Show them to the solarium."

"Damn," Kelly murmured, coming to her feet. "I forgot about that."

"So I guess it's good you didn't leave," Trey said.

TWO HOURS LATER, Kelly nodded her approval at the completed sketches of Adam and Caleb. Rafael, the artist, had captured their likenesses quite well. Not exact, of course, but close enough to give patrol officers a good tool to work with.

"I wish everyone had a memory as good as yours," Rafael said as he packed his drawing materials into a huge canvas satchel. "You made my job easy."

"It would be hard to forget those scumbags," Kelly said.

"Did you hear someone on scene filmed your encounter with the kidnappers on their phone and gave the video to Channel Eight?"

"Seriously?" While she'd been banished to fantasyland, the case—*her* case—had developed leads and moved forward in the real world without her. She was totally out of the loop because she'd been busy babysitting a screwed-up kid.

"Yeah, but the video is of you holding the Wentworth kid," Rafael said. "They didn't manage to get a good head shot of either perp."

"Sounds about right."

"Good thing, or I'd be out of a job. Channel Eight showed the recording on the six o'clock news. Congratulations on your thirty seconds of fame."

"Gee, thanks." But she was curious about what had been captured. Maybe she could catch the footage at eleven o'clock. She hadn't seen a TV anywhere in this mansion, but there had to be one somewhere.

Laughing, Rafael turned to look out on the pool deck through the huge plate glass windows of the solarium, a room full of casual wicker furniture, colorful prints and green plants, including more blooming orchids. Kelly followed his gaze and found the two officers who had driven him over sitting at a table with a glass pitcher of what looked like iced tea and another cheese-and-fruit tray. Both men had their feet up. A glorious sunset was in full view behind them, creating a scene fit for a slick travel magazine—if it weren't for the two cops in black uniforms with loaded guns on their hips.

"Now, there's a duty I could get used to," Rafael said.

"You think so? I'd be bored sick sitting around and doing nothing."

"That's a sickness I could take," Rafael said. "I guess a stay on Collins Island is your reward for saving Wentworth's kid." He nodded at the remains of a buffet the blonde cook had laid out for them. "Damn, but that food was amazing."

"I'm leaving in the morning."

Rafael turned back. "Good job, by the way." He gave her a high five, the slap of their palms sharp in the quiet room. "I've already heard talk of a commendation for you."

"Thanks." A feeling of pleasure tickled her belly. A commendation? Really? Still gazing at the resort-like view, she added, "But I did what anyone would."

"Yeah, right. Anybody would karate-kick a gun out of a perp's hand. How's the kid by the way?"

Kelly shrugged, ashamed of her resentful thoughts

about babysitting Jason. Poor little dude's head was in a super bad place. What was one day out of her life? "Asleep. Hopefully he'll be himself again when he wakes up."

"And if he's not?" Rafael asked.

Kelly shook her head. "I don't know." But she did know, and she didn't like the idea of Carico stashing the little guy in a loony bin. Even if they found one for kids. Even if the hospital was as luxurious as this villa. Jason needed to be with his father and in familiar surroundings. She wasn't any shrink, but she knew the only way he'd get better was to be around people who loved him.

And his father might be a jerk, but he loved his son. That was Wentworth's only saving grace. Well, besides his looks.

Rafael hefted his satchel over his shoulder. "Let me roust my ride and get going. Having to use that ferry takes forever." At the last minute, he stepped to the buffet, wrapped two sandwiches in a napkin and stuffed them in his bag. He winked at her. "For my wife."

"You may have a hard time getting those guys out of their chairs," Kelly yelled after him.

With a backward wave, the artist disappeared. She heard a voice in the hall—probably Maria—directing the way out.

Kelly turned back to the view. Man, but she longed for a swim in that pool, had wanted to dive in since she'd first laid eyes on it. And hadn't Wentworth told her to make herself at home? Unfortunately, she didn't have a bathing suit. Or goggles.

A few minutes later, Rafael appeared on the pool deck next to the officers. She smiled as she watched the exchange. She couldn't hear the conversation but could imagine the jokes about not wanting to leave the good life. When the three men walked off the deck, she felt suddenly alone, as if her posse had abandoned her with the enemy.

Which was ridiculous, of course. Wentworth wasn't her enemy. But he wasn't her friend.

She glanced at her watch. Eight fifteen. Now what? She wasn't used to having nothing to do. She rotated her neck as frustration and pent-up energy ate at her. If she were home, she'd be studying or exercising. Yeah, definitely exercising after all the extra calories she'd consumed today.

What she needed was a workout. If she couldn't swim, why not go for a run? Or at least a walk around billionaire island. Maria had laundered her running gear. Even better, maybe the mansion had a gym. Would it be rude to search?

Yes, it would. Her mother had managed to teach her that much at least. But she could ask.

With a sigh, Kelly left the solarium, hoping she didn't get lost in this monstrosity of a house. When she entered the hall, she found Maria waiting for her.

"Would you like something more to eat, Miss Kelly?" the housekeeper asked.

"After that buffet? No, thank you, Maria. I'm stuffed."

Maria nodded, her blackened eye appearing even more swollen now. "Is there anything I can get for you, Miss Kelly?"

"To tell you the truth, I really need to burn off some energy. I'm wondering if there's a gym or any sort of exercise equipment around that I could use."

"Of course."

Kelly followed Maria to a one-story building off the pool deck. Inside was a large gym with free weights, pneumatic equipment, treadmills and spin machines.

"Sweet," Kelly murmured. This state-of-the-art gym was equipped better than what the department had available at the West Dade training facility. Being a gazillionaire did have its perks.

"Any chance your boss will want to work out tonight?" she asked.

"No. Mr. Wentworth comes here in the morning."

"So he won't mind if I use his gym?"

"He said to let you do whatever you want."

Kelly glanced down at the clothing provided by Wentworth earlier in the day. Comfortable enough, but designed for a golf game, not a serious workout. "I'm going up to my room to change first."

"Can you find your way, Ms. Kelly?"

"Second right at the top of the stairs. Thanks, Maria."

Energized because she had a plan, Kelly hurried to the room she'd used earlier, picking out landmarks so she could find the gym again. More clothing, two pastel golf sets similar to the one she had on, were laid out on the bed. This time even clean lingerie had been provided. She fingered a white lacy bra and matching panties created by a French company she would never dream of splurging on. Wentworth had nailed her cup size.

But of course he had. Her face warmed as she remembered he'd gotten a good look at her bare breasts.

She ought to be grateful he'd provided clean underwear for her to put on in the morning. So why did she feel resentful of Wentworth's courtesies? Maybe because with his bottomless pockets the man could do whatever he wanted, and that kind of power bred a dangerous kind of arrogance. And contempt.

She didn't belong here. All this luxury wasn't her thing and never would or could be. Really, who laid out such a lavish buffet for two people? What waste. She could remember days when her belly had ached from hunger.

She picked up one of the outfits to check the size, and found a bright red bikini bathing suit underneath. Hardly appropriate for swimming laps, but no doubt the type of swimwear Wentworth's bimbos wore to parade around his pool. Should she be grateful or insulted?

Shaking her head, Kelly moved to the window and gazed down at the pool deck, now illuminated by hidden lights. Barely visible, in the distance the dark Atlantic Ocean stretched into an unseen horizon.

She leaned against the window frame. God, what a gorgeous piece of real estate. A laugh bubbled up as she considered the ludicrous proposition of her squad making a domestic call to this island paradise. Anyone in trouble would bleed out before the cops could manage to get on and off that slow ferry.

At the sound of voices, she refocused on the deck and stood up straight. Trey Wentworth, dressed in a black tux that fit him as if custom made—and likely was—spoke to a giant, muscled dude that looked as if he were straight out of special forces. She figured the big guy had to be a bodyguard or security of some sort, but she couldn't take her eyes off Wentworth.

Smooth and sophisticated in black tie, he made her think of James Bond. South Beach style. God, but he looked good enough to eat.

Why was he so dressed up? But she knew why. Obviously the man had a date. That couldn't be right. His son had been kidnapped, rescued—by *her*, thank you very much—flipped out and then drugged into oblivion, but Wentworth, obviously not a candidate for dad of the year, was going out on the town to some swanky shindig?

What kind of a father did that?

When he looked up at her window, Kelly jumped out of the way, hoping he hadn't seen her. This family's dirty laundry was none of her business.

She quickly changed into her clean running shorts and jog bra. Feeling better in her own clothes, she hurried back down the stairs only to encounter Wentworth striding across the loggia toward the front door—looking even more delicious in the brighter light. As his arm moved, she caught the flash of gold at his cuffs, and again stepped out of sight. Things were awkward enough between them without the man thinking she was a stalker.

Hans opened the door to the limo, and Wentworth climbed in. Kelly moved forward to watch the black vehicle drive away.

Well, do have such a good time, Mr. Billionaire. Oh, and don't worry about your traumatized son. I'll be here in case Jason wakes up and needs a parent to comfort him.

She whirled away from the disappearing tail lights and marched toward the gym. Man, did she ever need that workout.

CHAPTER FIVE

HURRYING UP THE marble steps into his home, Trey focused on one thing: Jason. How was he? Had his son woken? Cried out for his mother or his father?

Probably not. Donna said Jase would sleep through the night and it was only 11:00 p.m.

He'd remained at the benefit the minimum amount of time, escaping at the first opportunity after less than two hours, ninety minutes of a frozen smile and feigning interest in a cause that was no doubt worthy but one he couldn't care about right now.

All he cared about was his son.

At the top of the stairs, Trey slipped off his shoes so he wouldn't make any noise as he approached Jason's room. The last thing he wanted to do was wake him if he remained asleep.

Trey edged open the door to Jason's room and exhaled a relieved breath. Jase lay on his side with his favorite stuffed animal, a pink, ragged chimpanzee named Chimpie, clutched against his body. His son's chest rose and fell steadily. He looked like any normal four-year-old, happy, at peace with his world.

Trey prayed that tonight his son's slumber wasn't inhabited by violent nightmares.

Shutting the door, Trey headed toward the bar.

He needed a drink. He'd held himself in check at the party, refusing anything but club soda, afraid alcohol might loosen his tongue and allow him to say things in public he shouldn't. Things about his father.

The most heartless son of a bitch on the planet.

Trey removed his jacket, tossed it over a chair and poured himself an inch of his favorite whiskey. He downed the liquid in one swallow, welcoming the fiery burn that trailed down his throat into his belly and then poured another.

He was sick of people, of being polite and sociable. All night, every hand he'd pumped, every perfumed cheek he'd kissed, every lame joke he pretended to find amusing, all he could think about was whether Jason had woken up frightened and missing his daddy.

But he hadn't. Jase was safe in bed and sound asleep. Trey drank his whiskey and added more to his glass. He could stop obsessing about his son and indulge in a little blessed solitude.

He longed to forget the present and return to a time when Jason had been a happy, well-adjusted little boy who adored his parents. Holding the crystal tumbler, Trey moved to the window and stared outside onto the illuminated pool deck. He wanted to forget a reality where his son despised him for taking away his mother. Where the world had warped to the point where Jason had latched on to a stranger and anointed her his absent mom.

When Jason woke up in the morning, would he still insist Kelly Jenkins was his mother? It couldn't be good for Jase to allow him to carry on with that delusion. At what point did he bring it to an end?

What a terrifying mess. Trey removed his tie and slammed it to the bar.

Donna insisted time would heal his son's wounds, but Trey wasn't so sure anymore. And he was helpless to do anything for Jase. A father should be able to help his son.

Nursing his drink, Trey stepped outside. Maybe a little fresh air would make him feel better. He breathed in the scent of something blooming mingled with a salty ocean breeze. What he ought to do is turn on the court lights and whack a few thousand balls over the net. The idea appealed, but the growing effects of the whiskey made him doubt the wisdom of that plan. Maybe tomorrow.

At the sound of a splash, he turned toward the lit pool in time to witness two legs kick into the air and push off the wall, propelling a blur of crimson toward the other end.

Just who was swimming in his pool at this hour? He moved closer to the edge of the water and watched the swimmer's efficient strokes.

It was Officer Jenkins, executing flip turns as if she were a professional. He took a deep breath. He'd told her to make herself at home and was pleased she'd been able to do so.

He moved back when she approached his end

of the deck again, not wanting to get water on his pants when she flipped.

But she stopped. Breathing hard, she placed her hands on the side of the pool.

"Good evening, Officer Jenkins," Trey said, his words coming out more slurred than they should.

She jumped back and raised her arms in a defensive posture, eyes wide, ready to fight. He'd startled her.

She lowered her fists. "Mr. Wentworth."

"Trey," he said. He took a sip of whiskey and gazed down at her. She had a classically oval and quite lovely face. His gaze lowered, but the rippling water obscured the rest of her body.

She nodded and glanced around as if looking for an escape route, no doubt embarrassed. "I'll get out of your way," she said. "I'm sure you wanted privacy."

"You're fine." Surprised by her obvious discomfort, Trey sat on a lounge chair with a towel draped over the back. He didn't care if she enjoyed his pool. Few guests ever did.

"You're an excellent swimmer," he said.

"Thanks." Her answer sounded more like a question.

"But listen," she blurted. "I'm grateful for the bathing suit. I figured if you provided one it was okay to use the pool."

"Of course." Had he provided a bathing suit? He couldn't remember.

"Okay," she said. "I'm getting out now."

"Good. You could get chilled now that you've stopped moving. Hypothermia can be dangerous."

And her lack of movement had calmed the water, making it obvious she wore a rather skimpy red bikini, likely the source of her reluctance to exit the pool. His staff certainly had excellent taste.

With a quick glance his way, she placed her hands on the edge of the pool and easily boosted herself out of the water, turning to place a firm derriere on the concrete. Then she brought both feet up underneath her and stood defiantly before him, water sluicing over her smooth flesh.

He couldn't breathe as his gaze feasted on her stunning body.

Their gazes locked. He couldn't speak. He couldn't look away.

His brain, befuddled by whiskey and the glorious warrior woman, created an image of both of them wet, naked, writhing together in his pool.

KELLY TOOK A deep breath and fought the urge to shield herself like a modest virgin, which she most assuredly was not. But she wasn't a slab of meat, either.

Wentworth's pool had looked so refreshing, and the night had been so lovely—God, she loved a night swim—she just couldn't help herself.

And apparently Wentworth couldn't stop himself from staring.

"Could you please hand me the robe?" she asked.

"Robe?" Wentworth appeared dazed. How much booze had he enjoyed at his little shindig?

"Behind you on the lounge chair," she said. "If I come close to grab it, I'll drip all over you."

He hesitated, the hint of a smile playing on his lips. What was he thinking?

Finally, Wentworth reached behind him, grabbed the white terrycloth, then rose and carried it to her.

"Thanks."

"You're quite welcome."

She took the robe from his hands, covered herself and tied the waist with a quick jerk. Wentworth returned to his seat and this time lifted his legs and leaned against the back. He continued to gaze at her as he took a sip of whatever was in his glass.

Still wary, but more at ease now that her boobs weren't staring him in the face, she used the hood of the robe to squeeze water from her hair. She ought to go to her room, but curiosity about wherever he'd gone held her in place.

"You must have gone to some fancy soiree tonight."

His dark eyes stared at her. "A benefit for—what was it?" He shrugged. "Alzheimer's I believe was the disease of the night."

"You're home early," she said. "Boring party?"

"You have no idea."

His tone irritated her. Like she had no clue what a black-tie party for the super-rich would be like.

He was right, of course, but the jerk didn't need to rub it in.

"You don't think I should have gone out," he stated.

"None of my business," she said.

"Believe me, I didn't want to go. I hated to leave Jason."

"So why did you?"

"I'd committed months ago. Tickets were sold based on my appearance."

"Your son getting kidnapped seems a good enough excuse."

"Yeah, you'd think so," Wentworth murmured. "The old man disagreed."

He looked away, gazing over the pool. Who the hell was the old man? Probably his father.

Wentworth's expression was so mournful she almost felt sorry for him. Almost. At least he had a father to be mad at. She never even knew who hers was.

"Jase was asleep when I checked. Did he wake up while I was gone?" Wentworth asked.

"No," Kelly said. "I checked on him a couple of times and he was snoozing away."

Wentworth returned his focus to her. "Thank you."

"Of course."

This was her opportunity to leave. But she had questions, lots of them. And Wentworth seemed to be talkative for the first time, probably because of the booze. So she sat on the lounge chair next to his.

"How long ago did Jason's mother die?"

"Six months. Car crash. She died instantly."

Kelly sucked in a breath at his blunt reply. "I'm sorry. I know it's rough when death comes unexpectedly."

Wentworth gazed over the pool again. "Jason was in the car with her. He survived even though she didn't bother to strap him into his car seat."

Kelly's sympathy for the dead mother dwindled at that bit of news. How the hell do you respond to such negligence?

"She was drunk," he said. "Never felt a thing."

Kelly smothered the curse that rose to her lips. This was Wentworth's beloved dead wife, after all, mother of his child. Better tread carefully. "Was Jason badly hurt?"

"Head trauma." Wentworth gazed at her again. "Which could partly explain his confusion about you. We'd been divorced for over a year and shared custody."

"I'm sorry." Uncomfortable with his frank revelations, Kelly wanted to get out of here. This was definitely none of her business. "I don't mean to be intrusive. It's just—"

"The whole messy story was all over the tabloids," Wentworth said. "I'm surprised you don't know the sordid details."

"I'm not much of a tabloid fan," she said.

He nodded and took another sip of booze. She could smell the strong fumes. Time to get out of here. History had taught her being around men that were too drunk could lead to big trouble.

She rose. "Well, roll call comes early. I'd better get some sleep. Thanks for letting me use your pool."

"Anytime," he said, gazing off into space again.

Kelly sensed his thoughts were far away from her now. No doubt on the dead wife. She shouldn't have asked. For the hundredth time she reminded herself the problems of the rich and famous had nothing to do with her.

She was out of here first thing in the morning. She'd arranged for Hans to drive her home at 7:00 a.m. Plenty of time to dress and make her 10:00 a.m. roll call. Maria promised breakfast would be laid out at six.

One thing for sure, people definitely ate well in Wentworth Villa.

She shivered when she entered the air-conditioned house and hurried up the stairs. The door to Jason's room stood ajar, which halted her steps. She'd closed it when she peeked in on her way down to the pool,

But maybe Wentworth left it open when he'd checked on his son. Or maybe not. She glanced around uneasily.

No question about the fact that someone had helped the kidnappers get to Jason. Could that someone be a member of Wentworth's staff?

Kelly edged open the door. Jason snored softly in the glow of his night light. Shaking her head, she eased the door shut and continued to her room. She'd mention her worries to Ballard, but right now a warm shower awaited and a hopefully soft bed after that.

And then she was so out of fantasyville.

What if Jason woke up still insisting she was his mom? She didn't want to go through another hysterical scene with the kid. He'd been through enough already.

But no matter what happened with the little dude, she *would* be at roll call. Nothing Wentworth said could make her miss another shift.

CHAPTER SIX

KELLY DIDN'T HAVE any trouble finding the dining room when she descended the stairs at 6:00 a.m. All she had to do was follow the scent of bacon and freshly baked bread.

She took a deep breath. Yes, and there it was. Strong hot coffee.

Hurrying toward the lure of caffeine, she resisted the urge to rearrange the underwear Wentworth had provided. Damn, but these fancy thong panties were uncomfortable. Why did women wear them? There were some places that lace just shouldn't go.

For sure she couldn't work wearing this nonsense. She'd change as soon as she got home.

Kelly spotted Maria in the living room, but the housekeeper didn't notice her. She was too busy struggling to open a container of what looked like prescription meds. But who didn't have trouble with that childproof packaging?

Greta waited inside the dining room where, as promised, a buffet of hot and cold breakfast goodies awaited. This place was like a hotel.

"Good morning, Officer Jenkins."

Kelly nodded. "Good morning, Greta."

"Sit anywhere you like. Would you like some coffee?"

"Yes, please. Black."

Kelly took a seat, and Greta immediately poured steaming hot liquid into the china cup at her place.

"Please help yourself to the buffet when you are ready," Greta said. "Hans will be waiting for you out front when you are ready to go."

"Is Jason up?" Kelly asked.

"Mr. Wentworth is in his room now with the doctor," Greta said. "They should be down for breakfast soon."

"Dr. Carico is here?"

"Yes, ma'am."

"Good." Thinking the good doctor must be on some sort of retainer, Kelly glanced at the spread of food. Maybe she ought to make her escape while she could, but everything smelled too good.

She went to the buffet, grabbed a plate and heaped it with creamy eggs, crisp bacon, hash brown potatoes, grits, cantaloupe, a chocolate croissant— Lordy, way too much food. She couldn't help herself.

Her typical breakfast, when she had time, was a bowl of cold cereal. Man, she really needed to get out of here. Another day in fantasyland and she wouldn't be able to squeeze into her uniform.

She opened the newspaper Greta placed next to her coffee, and a headline screamed some nonsense about corruption inside the Miami-Dade Police Department, her employer. Kelly ate and read until the sound of little feet thundering in her direction interrupted her concentration.

She lowered the paper just before Jason launched himself into her lap.

"Mommy!" he shouted, throwing his arms around her neck.

Kelly gave Jason a hug, meeting Wentworth's cold dark stare over his son's head.

"JUST A FEW more days, Officer Jenkins."

"And I said no."

Trey paced the dining room as he glared at Kelly. Carico had taken Jason to his playroom so he could talk privately with the officer. He needed to find a way to convince her to stay. What could he offer? He was usually good at persuading people, but this woman was adamant.

"All I'm asking is a little more time to give Dr. Carico a chance to treat Jason, to get his head on straight again."

"What you're asking will jeopardize my career." Kelly shook her head. "I've worked too long and hard for that."

"You can commute from here. I'll put my staff at your disposal to make sure you don't miss any work."

"Great. So I show up at my station every day in your limo?"

"We can bring your car here. Or you can use one of mine."

"Which will take twice as long because of that stupid ferry."

"So we'll use the Wentworth Industries helicopter."

Her eyes widened. "Oh, that's an awesome plan. I can hear my sergeant now."

"I'll talk to your sergeant, explain the situation."

She looked away. "How can it be healthy for your son to continue to believe I'm his dead mother? He'll have to face the truth eventually. Why put it off?"

"Dr. Carico believes we should ease him into the truth gradually or risk damaging him further."

"That sounds like quack talk to me."

"Because you're such an expert in child psychology?"

Her jaw tightened. Great. Trey stopped moving and placed his hands on the back of a chair to get control of his own temper. He needed her on his side. No, on Jason's side. What could he say to convince her?

Hard to believe this was the same woman he'd spoken to at the pool last night. She'd seemed softer somehow, but maybe it had been her lack of clothing and the killer body. He'd been sorry when she covered up. Kelly Jenkins was a beautiful woman, one who never played up that beauty. She even tried to hide it.

But how could she be so unfeeling? She'd spent time with Jason. She knew how desperate he became whenever she left him.

Not meeting his gaze, she lifted her coffee and took a quick swallow.

"Look, I don't want to insult you by offering you cash again, but—"

"Then don't." Her cup clattered to the saucer.

"So I'll donate money to your favorite cause or charity, help out your mom or your great aunt. Give to the Police Benevolent Association. Pay off your student loans."

Kelly stared into her empty cup. "Contrary to your obvious belief, Wentworth, money cannot solve all problems."

Trey sucked in a breath. This woman had no idea how well he understood that painful truth.

"I'll do whatever it takes to persuade you to stay."

She raised her startling blue gaze to his wordlessly.

"He's just a mixed-up little boy who misses his mother," Trey said. "Can't you find it in your heart to help him a little longer?" Maybe she didn't have a heart.

She closed those eyes.

"I'll make certain you don't miss any more work," he added.

"All right," she said. "You win."

Trey exhaled forcefully, relief making him want to hug her. He could just imagine the reaction *that* would get. "Thank you."

"I'll give you another day, maybe two. But nothing you do or say can make me blow off another shift. In fact, I need to leave right now or risk being late."

"Greta," Trey called out.

Greta materialized at the door, having obviously listened to every word of his exchange with Kelly.

"Hans is waiting in the limo out front," she reported.

"Go," Trey said to Kelly. "I'll explain to Jason that you had to work."

Kelly rose and moved toward the front door.

"But I can tell him you're coming back tonight, right?" Trey asked.

She whirled on him. "I said I would, didn't I?"

"Yes."

"It'll be late, though, probably around seven or eight. After my shift, I'll need to go home to pack some clothing. Do whatever it takes so I can drive my car onto the ferry."

"Are you sure you don't want me to send the limo?"

"I don't want to be trapped on this island without wheels."

"You can use one of my vehicles whenever you want."

She shook her head, and Trey raised both hands to indicate he'd back off. Kelly obviously had a stubborn streak as deep as his father's.

"We'll hold dinner for you," he said.

A smile threatened her mouth, a rare occurrence.

"One thing's certain," she muttered. "I sure as hell won't starve."

CURSING BECAUSE THE scene with Jason and then the tug-of-war with his father had taken so much time, Kelly unlocked her third-floor apartment and hurried toward her bedroom. No way could she be late today. She'd only given in to Wentworth because she kept seeing Jason's puffy, tear-streaked face in her mind's eye, hearing his sad voice begging her to stay. How could anyone say no?

The poor little guy had enough troubles without her adding to them.

A quick look around told her nothing had been disturbed. She had no pets or plants to suffer during her absence yesterday. She paused after tossing her clothing into the hamper. What did that lack say about her life?

That she was a dedicated cop. That's what. She had no time for anything else.

Except now, apparently, Jason Wentworth and his father.

She'd already showered at Wentworth's castle, so she pulled a clean uniform out of her closet. After dressing—and thankfully disposing of the lacy thong—she strapped on her duty belt, which weighed close to twenty pounds, rearranged it on her hips and grabbed her car keys. She relocked her front door, pleased with how quickly she'd gotten ready. Even with all the delays, she'd still arrive at the station early for roll call. She'd come home after her shift to pack.

How much trouble would she be in for missing

yesterday? Agent Ballard's phone call should go a long way to smooth her absence with the brass—still, you never knew. The sketch artist said he'd heard talk of a commendation, so maybe she wasn't in that much trouble.

And what could she have done differently? She'd been over yesterday's events a hundred times, and she wouldn't change a thing about what she'd done.

She moved across the deserted parking lot toward her car when a sudden movement caught her attention. Kelly tensed, unsure why her cop instincts roared into life.

She scanned the area. A figure stood under the trees to her right maybe fifty yards away. A man. Dark hair and clothing, six feet, thirty years old. Watching her through binoculars, his right wrist in a cast. She slowed her steps. Something about him rang a bell. She knew this man. Who was he?

Shit. It was Adam, one of Jason's kidnappers. Surveilling *her*. He had binoculars. Did he have his gun? How did he know where she lived?

Kelly drew her weapon and aimed it at Adam in a two-handed grip. "Police. Stay right where you are."

But of course he ran. Kelly lowered her weapon and hauled butt after him, but he had too much of a lead. He leaped into a waiting silver Corolla and disappeared in a roar.

Someone else was driving. Caleb?

She managed to get a partial tag. Breathing hard,

she took out her notepad and jotted down three letters and one number.

She glanced back to her dirty white Ford, dread knotting her gut. Jason's abductor knew where she lived. Did he know her vehicle? Had he been in her car?

No way was she getting inside until it'd been processed. Maybe they'd find fingerprints on the door handles that would lead them to Adam.

She had to call it in. Damn. She'd miss roll call again after all.

Before she could unclip her phone from her belt, an explosion boomed into the quiet morning, rocketing the hood of her car into the air.

CHAPTER SEVEN

TWO HOURS LATER, standing next to Lieutenant Marshall and Special Agent Ballard, Kelly watched the remains of her car being towed away by the FBI. Trucks from several local television stations had set up for remote transmission on the other side of police barricades.

A life she had carefully planned and arranged for so long was now spiraling out of her control. She'd once sworn she'd never be a victim again, and now this.

"As bombs go," Ballard said, "that one wasn't much."

Kelly silently disagreed. Yeah, no one had been harmed, but she was out a three-year-old Ford that she still owed a ton of money on. Would her insurance even cover an incendiary device?

"You're certain the man you saw was Jason Wentworth's kidnapper?" her lieutenant asked, his tone indicating he had his doubts. But at least he'd come to the scene. His presence signaled the department took her situation seriously.

"I'm certain," Kelly said. "But I didn't get a look at the driver."

"Excellent police work, Officer Jenkins," Ballard said. "The fact that you remained alert to your surroundings likely saved your life."

Kelly nodded, fully aware of how close she'd come to getting killed or seriously injured. According to the techs, the bomb had been triggered remotely. Adam had blown up the car to destroy any evidence he might have left behind, hoping she'd already gotten in the vehicle.

"So your theory is he wanted me out of the picture so I couldn't ID him as the kidnapper?" Kelly asked. She planned to look at mug shots today to see if either Caleb or Adam had been arrested. If it weren't for Jason's mixed-up head—and Wentworth's money and influence—she'd have already done that.

"Bingo. And this is the first good lead we've had since yesterday," Ballard said.

"But how did he know where I live?" A cop's home address was always kept private. Law enforcement didn't even have to reveal it when they testified.

"Yeah, I'd like to know that, too," Marshall said.

"Probably something to do with the media coverage," Ballard suggested, with a nod to the trucks. "They've been all over this story."

"Great," Kelly said. She still hadn't seen the video of her encounter with the kidnappers. She'd forgotten about her fifteen minutes of fame, and now she'd likely get fifteen more. This couldn't be good for her career.

"What happens next?" she asked.

"Your partial tag came off a stolen truck," Ballard said, "but so far that's a dead end. We're in the process of obtaining your apartment's video feed from this parking lot. We'll need you to review it. Maybe we'll get lucky and find an image of our guy around your vehicle."

Kelly shot Ballard a look. The man actually seemed happy, but she'd hardly call it lucky that a dangerous criminal she could identify had somehow learned what car she drove to work every day. And where she lived.

And Adam was still out there somewhere. Was he planning another attempt on her life?

"I need to contact my insurance company," she said. "How long will you keep my vehicle?"

"No way to know." Ballard's phone rang, and he removed it from his belt. "We'll be in in touch," he said, moving way.

This just kept getting better and better. She was beginning to agree with Wentworth about the FBI.

Kelly waited for her lieutenant to speak. She barely knew the man and couldn't get a read on his mood, whether she was in trouble or if Marshall agreed with Ballard that she'd done good police work by spotting Adam before getting into her car and getting blown to smithereens.

"Are you fit for duty, Officer Jenkins?" Marshall asked.

She came to attention. "Yes, sir."

"You're not too shook up, need the day?"

"No, sir. Absolutely not."

Was that a gleam of approval in his steely gaze? She couldn't be certain. The man was like granite.

He nodded. "Come on then. I'll give you a ride to the station. Your squad went on patrol a unit short again today."

KELLY PULLED HER squad car into the lot of the Coral Bagel deli and parked next to Patrice Skinner's unit. Patrice was her closest friend in the department. They'd formed an instant connection during training and, if circumstances allowed, they often met for lunch. Other members of their four-unit squad occasionally showed up as well, especially if they wanted to break down an eventful call. Sometimes even their sergeant, Rudy McFadden, who patrolled the same area with his squad, joined them.

But today she didn't want to talk to anyone but Patrice, who was addicted to popular culture and celebrity gossip, a habit Kelly often teased her about. Kelly intended to pump her friend for info about Trey Wentworth. If anyone knew the scoop, Trice would.

After alerting dispatch she was on break, Kelly entered the quiet diner. To get in and out within thirty minutes, they deliberately took lunch around two, long after the noon rush.

She spotted Patrice in their favorite corner booth, sitting across from Lana Lettino, another rookie from their class. Kelly heaved a sigh of relief at the sight of her friends, both of whom already knew about her encounter with Jason.

Finally a return to reality. People who understood her life.

Trice waved her over, and the waitress arrived immediately with three glasses of water.

"Roast beef and Swiss on rye," Lana ordered.

"The usual," Patrice said.

"One veggie burger," the waitress confirmed. "And you, Officer Jenkins?"

"Just a small house salad and coffee."

"What's up with that?" Lana asked when the server had moved away.

Kelly shrugged. "I'm not hungry."

"You look awful," Patrice said. "And the fact that you're not hungry has got me seriously worried."

"Funny," Kelly said. "But you wouldn't believe the amount of food I've eaten in the last twenty-four hours at Wentworth Villa. I've probably gained five pounds."

Lana laughed. "Come on. You don't like the good life on Collins Island?"

"You have no idea."

"We need details," Trice said.

Kelly filled her friends in on the morning's events. "So now I don't even have a vehicle."

Dark eyes wide, Lana sat back in the booth. "A bomb? No way."

Kelly shrugged. "No good deed goes unpunished."

"So this kidnapper knows where you live and remains at large gunning for you?" Lana asked.

"Until the Bureau can apprehend him. I spent an hour on the computer looking at mug shots before I went on patrol."

Patrice cursed. "Then it's a good thing you're moving to Collins Island. No way the scumbag can get to you there."

Kelly sipped her water. Trice had a point. She would be far safer at Wentworth's mansion than in her own apartment. And maybe a limo back and forth to the station wouldn't be such a rotten idea after all. Although she should let Wentworth know about the threat.

Was it fair to put Wentworth's driver in the middle of the danger? She wouldn't even be having this conversation if she hadn't noticed Adam watching her. She couldn't be on her guard 24/7. Sooner or later she'd make a mistake.

"I guess you didn't spot either of the perps in the mug shots," Trice said.

"No such luck," Kelly muttered.

"Are you worried?" Lana asked.

"A little," Kelly admitted. "But I figure that goes with the job. It's what we signed on for."

"I don't know about you," Patrice said, "but I sure didn't sign up for any bombs in my car. Is the department going to do anything for you? Like give you a rental?"

"I doubt it."

When the food arrived, since they only had fifteen minutes left, Patrice and Lana dug in.

"Any chatter around the station about me being in trouble?" Kelly asked, pushing the lettuce around on her plate.

Patrice narrowed her hazel eyes on Kelly. "Trouble about what?"

"For missing yesterday."

Patrice shook her head. "Seriously? Come on, girl. You're a heroine. You saved a little boy's life."

"There's even talk about a commendation." Lana grinned. "I'd be jealous if it weren't for the bomb and all."

"You're sure Rudy isn't pissed?" Kelly asked. The squad had already gone out on patrol by the time Lieutenant Marshall delivered her to the station, so she hadn't been able to talk to her sergeant.

"He did mention he wants to chat with you before you check out this afternoon," Trice said.

So she *was* in trouble. "You don't know what about?"

"Nope." Patrice shook her head.

"You still got that crush on our sergeant?" Lana asked.

Patrice's cheeks flushed. "Don't be silly. I respect the guy, that's all."

"Yeah, right," Lana said. "I've seen the way you look at him."

"At least I'm not still hung up on my high school sweetie," Patrice said.

"I am not hung up," Lana said. "I just need to find his murderer. Your thing for Rudy will bring you nothing but trouble, girl. He's already taken."

"I know that."

Remaining silent, Kelly shook her head. Trice all but swooned over their married sergeant while Lana couldn't get over some dead boyfriend from high school. Kelly had no use for romance. In her opinion—only reinforced since she'd been on the job—men did nothing but create chaos in a woman's life. Her two best friends were proof of that.

"So what's Trey Wentworth like?" Patrice said in an obvious attempt to change the subject. "Now, there's a man who is serious eye candy."

"Agreed, but I've hardly spoken to him." Kelly leaned forward. "What can you tell me about him?"

Patrice took a swallow of water. "The Wentworths are old money."

"Legal old money?"

"That's the word. Their base of operations is Manhattan, and they're very private. His father rules the family with an iron fist, and it's rumored he pays a publicist to keep their dirty laundry out of the tabloids. But the antics of Trey's rock star wife were too outrageous to keep quiet."

"She was a rock star?" Kelly asked.

Patrice sighed. "I keep forgetting how literal you are. No, a model, a gorgeous girl, but one with a serious drug habit. After she married Wentworth, she quit working, had a kid, began to party and quickly self-destructed. An all-too-familiar story."

"He told me she was killed DUI."

"Oh, really?" Patrice sat back. "That's sounds like a rather intimate discussion for a man you've barely spoken to."

"We've had a few conversations about the kid."

"So come on. Give," Lana said. "What's he like?"

"The kid? He's totally screwed up."

"You know I mean Trey Wentworth."

Kelly took a swallow of lukewarm coffee. How should she describe Trey Wentworth? "Arrogant. He thinks his money can solve any problem."

"Maybe because, hey, it usually can," Lana said.

"Money can't get his son's head unscrambled. So there's never anything in the tabloids about Trey, just his ex?"

"He is known as a party animal," Patrice said. "That's how he met his ex."

"That much I've heard. Anything else?"

Patrice raised her eyebrows. "All these questions from the woman who made fun of my subscription to *Celebrity* magazine?"

"If I'm going to be living in his house, I need all the intel I can get."

"Oh, I'm sure that's all it is. Let's see. Like I say, the family manages to keep most things out of the public eye, but Trey is or was an excellent tennis player. He won some big-time tournament as a junior player—maybe the US Open—and was considered good enough to go on the professional tour. No one was surprised when he went to work for Wentworth Industries instead."

"Why? Professional tennis players earn a ton of money."

"That sort of common entertainment was deemed beneath the Wentworths." Patrice made quote marks in the air around "common."

"Seriously?" Kelly rolled her eyes.

"How does he act toward you?" Lana asked.

Kelly shrugged. "Most of the time he's polite enough, but he hates cops. He thinks we're all incompetent."

Lana leaned forward and lowered her voice. "Is it true the FBI screwed up the drop?"

"Apparently. Wentworth is grateful that I saved his kid, but he thinks I'm some kind of hick from the wrong side of the tracks."

"I wouldn't be so sure about that," Patrice said.

"What do you mean?" Kelly asked.

Trice smiled. "You're exactly his type. Blond hair, blue eyes, great body. You actually resemble the dead ex."

"Yeah, apparently the little dude thinks so, too. And, man, if you ask me, that's just creepy."

CHAPTER EIGHT

"WHEN WILL MOMMY be home, Daddy?"

Sitting on the pool deck after a long romp in the water, Trey paused towel-drying Jason's hair. This was the fourth time his son had asked about his mother in the last hour. Each time the question pierced him like a knife straight to the gut.

Jason showed no signs of regaining any memory of Darlene's death. His son preferred to live in a world where his mother still breathed, and who could blame the kid.

"She'll be home later, son," Trey said. "After your nap."

Jason yawned huge. "I don't want to take a nap."

"But you know you have to, right?"

Jase nodded, and Trey began briskly rubbing his head again. His son was exhausted but as usual would never admit it.

"Will Mommy be here when I wake up?" Jason asked from underneath the terrycloth.

Trey lowered the towel. "I can't promise. She might have to work late."

A confused look passed over Jason's sweet young face. "I wish she didn't have to work."

"Me, too, buddy. But she wants to. She likes to work."

"Why?"

"Why do you like to play in the pool?"

"'Cause it's fun."

"Well, maybe her work is fun, too." But how could that possibly be true of police work?

"Come on. Let's find Maria and get you into bed."

When Jason was settled into his airplane bed, he looked up and asked, "Is Dr. Donna coming back today?"

"No," Trey replied. "She'll be here in the morning. Do you like talking to Dr. Donna?"

Jason yawned again. "She's okay."

Trey drew the drapes and moved to the door where he dimmed the overhead light. The frog night light illuminated his son's bedroom with a soft green glow.

"Sweet dreams, buddy," Trey said. He closed the door quietly and moved downstairs into his office.

With a vague intention of getting some work done, he sat at his desk. He was days behind on correspondence and reports, but couldn't yet concentrate on the questionable decisions his father had been making lately. And he needed to pay attention. Allies on the board were worried the old man was seriously damaging Wentworth Industries.

Trey came to his feet and moved to the window. Was it the right thing to let his son continue to believe Kelly Jenkins was his mother? Dr. Carico insisted they should let Jason come to the realization his real mother was gone forever gradually, on his own.

That sounded great, but what if he never did?

Maybe it was time for a second opinion. He respected Donna, but this was his son's life. He didn't want to take any chances.

His phone rang. He'd been ignoring texts and calls all day to devote his time exclusively to Jason, but this was the ring tone he he'd programmed for Kelly Jenkins so he'd know when she called.

"Hello, Officer Jenkins," he said.

"Hi. Listen, I've got a problem," she said. "Is it possible you could send your limo to pick me up at my station at six after all?"

"Of course. I'll tell Hans. What's the problem?"

She hesitated before answering. "You haven't talked to Agent Ballard?"

"I've been with Jason all day."

"Ballard said he'd notify you."

"Notify me of what?"

When she hesitated again, Trey closed his eyes, certain he was about to receive more bad news.

"What's going on, Kelly?"

"The kidnappers somehow tracked down where I live and planted a bomb in my car."

"What?" The word exploded out of his mouth. "Are you all right?"

"I'm fine. I'll explain everything when I get there, but the FBI took what's left of my car for processing, so I need you to send a ride. Okay?"

What's left of her car? "But you weren't injured?"

"I wasn't inside when it blew. How is Jason?"

Trey shook his head. "He keeps asking where his mother is, when she'll be home."

"I'll also need Hans to swing by my apartment and wait while I pack, but I'll get there as quickly as I can."

"Is that wise? You said the kidnappers know where you live."

"The FBI has my apartment under surveillance."

Trey snorted. "For all the good that will do."

"I doubt the bad guys will go anywhere near the place now. And I need uniforms, clothing."

"Right." Sick of feeling helpless, Trey ran a hand through his hair. What could he do? He should be able to protect Officer Jenkins.

"Please be careful," he said.

"I'm a cop. I'm always careful. But warn Hans just in case, okay?"

"Don't worry about Hans. The man is ex-military. Nothing rattles him."

"Still, he should know there's a bull's-eye on my back."

And that target that had been planted there because she'd rescued his son. No question he owed her. "I'll tell him."

"Good. Listen, I've got to get back. Make sure Hans is here at six. I'll be waiting at the back entrance."

Trey immediately placed a call to the Protection

Alliance, the security company he'd contracted to guard his son. Hans was a good man—trained in martial arts and more bodyguard than chauffeur—but Trey wanted one of PA's people to accompany Hans when he picked up Kelly. He didn't want to take any chances with Kelly's life. His son needed her right now, and that meant he did, too.

After he explained the situation, Lola, PA's office manager, promised to have another operative available within the hour to take the place of the one who accompanied Hans to get Kelly.

"Sounds like the bad guys want to eliminate a witness who can identify them," Lola said.

"Is there any way you can have one of your people protect her while she's on the job?" Trey asked.

"Isn't she a cop?"

"Yeah, a rookie."

"That would be tricky. Even a rookie would pick up a tail, and my operative would have the whole department on his ass."

"What if I clear it with Officer Jenkins's boss?"

Lola laughed, a throaty sound. "Yeah, you do that."

Trey disconnected, his thoughts darting a thousand directions. The kidnappers had found Kelly and had tried to eliminate her. Did that mean they planned to make another attempt to snatch Jason? What else could he do?

His father wanted them to relocate back to Manhattan. Much as he hated that plan, maybe it was time to give a move serious consideration. Surely the kidnappers wouldn't follow them, and he could get that second opinion on Jason's condition without hurting Donna's feelings.

But moving would mean tearing Jason away from Kelly Jenkins. Unless—was there any way he could convince her to go with them? Strangely, the thought of having her along didn't seem quite as abhorrent as it had twenty-four hours ago.

But no. There was no way Kelly would ever consider accompanying him to New York, so Jason would lose his mother again.

Trey went to find Hans. His security team needed to know the stakes had just been upped.

KELLY WANTED TO wait for her sergeant. She really did. If Rudy McFadden needed to speak to her, she wanted to speak to him. He likely wanted to counsel her about her attendance, although she'd seen him around 5:00 p.m. when all units had converged on a call, and he hadn't said a word about needing a conversation.

He was now hung up on a different incident, a domestic with about ten priors, and he might not return to the station for hours. She sent him a text and pushed out the back door. She'd talk to him tomorrow.

Wentworth's limousine slid beside Kelly the second she entered the parking lot. Hans nodded at her through the windshield just as the limo's back door swung open.

She blinked. How had he managed that? Some special billionaire remote control function? Kelly climbed inside and almost into the lap of another man.

"Who the hell are you?" she demanded. She'd seen him before, talking to Wentworth on the pool deck last night.

"Scott," he replied. "Your new bodyguard."

"My what?"

"Mr. Wentworth is concerned about your safety."

"I'm a cop," she said. "I don't need a protector."

"Yes, ma'am," Scott said, folding his beefy arms. "I'm sure that's correct. Although there was some mention of an incendiary device in your vehicle."

"He's here to back me up," Hans said from the front seat. "Give me your address."

Back him up? Shaking her head, Kelly gave the address and remained silent for the rest of the trip. She figured Wentworth would hire extra security for Jason after the kidnapping, but *she* didn't need a guardian.

When Hans pulled to a stop in front of her building, she said, "I'll be quick," and jumped from the car.

Scott came with her.

She whirled on him. "What are you doing?"

"Going with you."

"That's not necessary," Kelly said, with a quick glance around. Was the FBI watching?

"You can't talk me out of it, Officer," Scott said. "I'm being paid to make sure nothing happens to you."

"Fine," she ground out. This was ridiculous.

They didn't speak as the elevator ascended to her floor. Before she could jam her key into the lock on her door, Scott stuck out his muscled arm, bent over and peered at the mechanism.

"Does anything appear different, Officer?" he asked when he straightened up.

"I'm a trained officer, not an idiot."

Scott nodded. "Unlock the door, but let me clear the room."

After turning the key, Kelly stepped back and waved her arm with a dramatic flourish, indicating he could enter first. Scott drew a Sig Sauer from under his jacket, pointed it at the ground and entered.

Kelly folded her arms as she waited, hoping none of her neighbors came into the hallway. The thing she hated most in the world was feeling like a victim.

At the age of thirteen she'd made a solemn vow to never be anybody's prey ever again.

Scott reappeared in the doorway. "You're good."

Refusing to give in to the snarky remark lurking on her tongue, Kelly entered and packed quickly, tossing underwear, socks and casual clothing into her ragged suitcase. She didn't bother with toiletries since Wentworth had all anyone would need—oh, except her toothbrush. After adding that to the pile, she grabbed workout gear, her competition-style bathing suit and goggles, the book she was studying for the sergeant's exam, which she intended to sit for as soon as she was eligible.

She grabbed clean uniforms from the closet, threw them over her arm and glanced around her bedroom. What was she forgetting?

"Are you ready, Officer?" Scott asked.

Her gaze fell on the gun locker she used for her service weapon. She stowed it inside her luggage and clicked the latches closed. "I am now."

Scott grabbed the bag and hefted it easily. "Let's move."

Kelly wanted to snatch her suitcase out of the man's hand, but followed him into the hallway.

This guy was just following orders, and she was a cop who understood chain of command. Her problem wasn't with a guy doing the job he was being paid for.

Her problem was with Trey Wentworth.

CHAPTER NINE

WHEN KELLY ENTERED the foyer, Trey stood back while his son launched himself into her arms. They'd been waiting for her return ever since Jase had woken up from his nap demanding to see her.

"Mommy," he shouted in a voice so full of joy that Trey's stomach clenched.

So in his son's mind, Kelly was still his mother. He'd hoped that after so many hours apart Jason would realize the truth when he saw her.

To her credit, Kelly knelt and hugged him close. "Hi, Jason."

"I missed you, Mommy."

"Well, I missed you, too," she replied in a way that made Trey doubt if she'd given him a single thought all day.

She stood and their gazes locked. Trey blinked at the difference in her. He'd never seen Kelly in her police uniform before. Was this even the same woman? She'd somehow acquired edges he'd never noticed.

If Kelly wanted to disguise the fact that she was beautiful, a dark blue police uniform made of sturdy synthetic fabric certainly did the job. But the trappings also gave her an aura of authority, the sense that this was a woman not to be trifled with. And right now she looked seriously angry about something.

Although, didn't she always?

His gaze zeroed in on her weapon. Now there'd be a loaded gun in the same house as a curious four-year-old.

He cleared his throat. "Are you hungry? Dinner is ready."

"I need to talk to you," Kelly said. "It's important."

Lugging a suitcase, Scott entered the foyer. "Where should I put this?"

Kelly narrowed her eyes at the PA operative, making Trey wonder if there was a problem between the two of them. Was that what she wanted to talk to him about?

Maria appeared and said, "I'll show you."

"Go on into the dining room, buddy," Trey told Jason.

Jason took Kelly's hand and tugged. "Come on, Mommy. I'm hungry."

"Daddy needs to talk to Mommy for a minute," Trey said. "You go on, son."

"But Mommy just got home."

"Can our discussion wait?" Trey asked Kelly. "Jason's been anxious to see you."

He thought she'd refuse, but after a pause she nodded. "Sure. Let's eat."

"Thank you," Trey told her.

"No problem. But I'd like to drop my gun belt first."

"Where are you going, Mommy," Jason demanded when she untangled her hand from his.

She knelt so they were eye level. "Mommy needs to go to the bathroom to wash her hands. I'll be right back."

"Promise?" he asked.

Trey bit his lip. How could anyone be immune to the longing in that little boy's voice?

"I promise."

She stood and hurried away, unbuckling her belt as she took the stairs.

Where would she hide her gun? Was there any chance Jason could get at it? Unlikely, but he needed to speak to her about that possibility. He needed to procure some sort of a safe.

"Why is Mommy dressed like that?" Jason asked. "She looks funny."

"For her job," Trey said quickly. "You ready to eat, Jase?" Trey asked, in an attempt to change the subject. "I know you're hungry."

Jason heaved a big sigh, his gaze glued to the staircase where Kelly had disappeared. "I'll wait for Mommy."

So Trey waited beside his son for Kelly to return.

When she descended the stairs a few minutes later, Jason rushed forward to grab her hand. She still wore that ghastly uniform, but her hair looked different. Before it'd been tied back somehow, but now it framed her face, softening her serious expression. Her step appeared lighter without all that weight around her waist.

As he followed ersatz mother and son into the dining room, she spoke easily to Jason, making him giggle. He skipped along beside her, appearing truly happy and at ease for the first time all day.

Inside the dining room, Greta had set three places at the table. Trey helped Jason into his booster seat and indicated Kelly should sit across from his son. He sat at the head of the table.

"No buffet tonight?" Kelly asked, unfolding a napkin into her lap.

"Greta will be serving us," Trey said.

Greta pushed in her cart containing the first course and placed a steaming bowl of minestrone soup before Kelly.

"Thanks," she said, and gazed at it as if she'd never seen food before.

He should be grateful to this woman. His request had disrupted her career, but for the most part she was being a really good sport. Especially considering her life was now in danger.

Then why was he still so uncomfortable with her presence in his home? Maybe because he had his doubts that all this playacting was the right thing for Jason's mental health.

WHAT SEEMED LIKE hours later, Kelly followed Jason and his father upstairs. It was finally time to put Jason down for the night. She'd planned to speak to Wentworth immediately after dinner about the bodyguard situation, swim forty laps and then retire to her room to study. No such luck.

Wentworth gave Jason permission to watch his favorite Disney movie before bed, and of course she had to watch it with him.

Finally, at nine, Wentworth had told Jason it was bedtime, and apparently it was some sort of bizarre family ritual that Mommy and Daddy both had to put the kid down. Why did it take two people? She'd managed to go to sleep as a child without anyone ever tucking her in.

When the three of them entered his room, Jason climbed into bed. Wentworth arranged the covers for his son and kissed his forehead. "Good night, buddy."

"Good night, Daddy."

Kelly waited for Wentworth to turn out the light, but father and son both turned to her.

"Mommy?" Jason said.

Kelly stepped forward "What, Jason?"

"Aren't you going to kiss me?"

Kelly shot Wentworth a look, and he nodded. She shrugged. Nothing wrong with giving the kid a quick peck.

She leaned over, planted a kiss on his check and breathed in a sweet elusive fragrance from her childhood, a lotion her mother had once smoothed onto her skin after a bath when she was very young.

She straightened, startled by the unexpected rush of memories.

Jason smiled angelically. How could anyone think of harming this adorable little dude?

"Now Mommy and Daddy have to kiss," Jason announced.

What? Kelly shot Wentworth another look.

He shrugged, leaned over and quickly kissed her cheek.

She raised her hand to the spot. Had Wentworth really just kissed her?

"Daddy," Jason said with infinite patience. "You know that wasn't a real kiss."

TREY WANTED TO laugh at the wide-eyed expression on Kelly's face. If only there was something humorous about his son's situation.

Hand to her cheek, she glared at him warily. Good-night kisses had always been part of his family's bedtime ritual. Even when their marriage was beyond repair, he and Darlene had always managed a perfunctory meeting of the lips when they put Jason down for the night together.

Kelly would get over it.

Before she could mount a protest, he gathered her close and pressed his lips to her soft, very kissable mouth. The kiss was quick, but a sudden, unexpected flash of desire shot through him, and he fought it.

He wanted her. He hadn't felt such yearning for any woman in a long time.

She stepped away from him, fingers to her lips, and the moment passed.

"Time for sleep now, buddy," Trey said.

He turned off the overhead light. Kelly followed him to the door. Neither of them spoke, but the memory of how she'd felt in his arms burned in his thoughts.

He'd enjoyed touching her, but this pretend-mother game suddenly felt wrong. And dangerous.

Dangerous for all three of them.

When they got to the bottom of the stairs, he said, "You wanted to speak with me?"

"Yes." She released a breath. "Is there any more of that wine from dinner? It's been a long day."

A glass of wine sounded like exactly what they needed. "Good idea," he said. "Let's move into the bar. Red or white?"

"Red," she said.

Trey selected a pleasant Napa Valley merlot and busied himself with a corkscrew while Kelly perched on a barstool, her long legs dangling.

"So I assume you and your wife had some—I don't know—ceremony every night with the good-night kisses?" she asked.

"Yes." The cork exited the bottle with a soft pop. "We each had to kiss Jason and then each other before he'd go down for the night."

"A heads-up would have been nice," she said.

"Sorry." He dribbled wine into two glasses, and slid one across the bar toward her. "Frankly, I'd forgotten about it myself. It's been a while."

"Thanks." She took a sip of wine. "Does your kid always get what he wants?"

"Obviously not," Trey said. "He didn't want to be kidnapped."

"I understand that. It's just—I don't know." She looked away. "Maybe I shouldn't say this, but don't you think he might be a little, you know, spoiled?"

"Come on. Didn't your mother and father tuck you in at night?"

"Actually," she said, setting her wineglass back on the bar, "I never even met my father. So no."

"Well, then your mother at least."

Kelly started to say something, but pressed her lips together and shook her head. "Never mind that. I need to talk to you about the fact that you've hired a babysitter for me."

"A bodyguard. What's the problem?"

"Surely you understand I can't have this Scott person following me around."

"He's for your protection."

"I don't need protection. I'm a cop. I do the protecting."

"And cops die in the line of duty all the time."

"Not all the time."

"And they don't find explosive devices in their vehicles very often, either. That's my point."

"Come on, Wentworth." She slid off the barstool

and paced the room like a caged animal. "Do you expect this guy to get into my squad unit and tag along while I'm on duty? That's so not going to happen."

She paused her restless movements and faced him. "Well?"

"My name is Trey," he said.

She narrowed her eyes at him. "I know."

"You called me Wentworth."

"Why are we arguing about your name?" She placed her hands on her hips and glared at him.

"We're not." He stepped from around the bar and moved toward her.

"Yeah?" She took a step backward. "You could have fooled me."

"We're arguing about the fact that I kissed you, and we both liked it."

CHAPTER TEN

KELLY SUCKED IN a deep breath and looked away. Had her response to his kiss been that obvious?

The second Trey's lips had touched hers, she'd lit up like a torch. A flash fire of desire had swept through her, a novel experience for her. A man's touch had never done that to her before.

She'd been mortified by her reaction, knowing the kiss had only been to placate the little dude. No big deal. So why couldn't her usually reliable brain formulate any words?

Because Trey was too close—close enough to lean down and kiss her again. And she wanted him to.

She raised her gaze and found his dark eyes burning into hers. She blinked. He was angry. But why? Because she'd called him by his last name? Because she didn't want his damn bodyguard?

She stepped away and managed to squeak out, "It was just one quick kiss."

He moved back toward the bar, and she relaxed. With distance between them, she could breathe more easily, keep her guard up.

"Do you enjoy insulting me?" he asked.

"What?" So much for keeping up her guard. "I didn't mean to insult you."

He retrieved her wineglass and presented it to

her. Her pulse skittered into high gear again when their fingers brushed.

"Then please at least call me Trey."

"Sure. Trey it is." She returned to her stool at the bar and took a gulp of wine. Why was she so nervous? Men never made her nervous. That's why she'd worked so hard to become a black belt, so she'd never feel powerless again.

He sat in a stool next to hers and picked up his wine, his gaze sweeping her body intently.

"What?" she demanded, hating that she smoothed her hair like some goofy teenager. But what was he staring at? She fought an impulse to run to her room and hide like she had as a little girl.

What did she want to hide from? Wentworth? She in no way felt physically threatened by him.

What she wanted to run away from was the way she felt when he touched her. She stared at the smooth wooden bar and tried to sort out her thoughts. Okay. She'd obviously lost her mind and for some absurd reason was attracted to Trey Wentworth. How had that happened? He definitely was not her type. Rich playboy? Please. She needed to get over herself pronto.

And she needed to avoid any more good-night kisses.

"Thank you," he said.

She raised her gaze to his. Were they back to the kiss? "For what?"

He laughed. "Don't sound so suspicious. I don't

think I've properly expressed how grateful I am for you helping my son."

Kelly released a sigh. This subject was far easier to deal with.

"And please don't tell me you were just doing your job," Trey said. "We both know it's not in your job description to move into my home."

She nodded. Now, this was more like it. Actual appreciation from the billionaire. "You're welcome."

When he took a sip of wine, she did the same. Wearing a mysterious smile, Trey reached behind the bar and retrieved a gold foil wrapped box, the perfect size to hold a bracelet, and presented it to her.

She glared at the lovely package without touching it. "What's this?"

"It won't bite you."

"Funny. What is it?"

"Something to demonstrate my gratitude in a more concrete fashion."

She shook her head. "That's not necessary. I've told you that."

He removed the wine from her hand, placed the golden box in her palm and closed her fingers around it. The gift felt warm against her skin.

"Please at least open it," he said softly.

She bit her bottom lip. Whatever was inside this box—and it had to be expensive jewelry—she couldn't accept. Not only because of department rules, but her own ethics wouldn't allow it. She tried to tell herself she didn't want to see what was inside, but frankly, yeah, she did. What was the harm in peeking?

Before she could do anything, Trey took the package from her hand and unwrapped it, revealing a black leather case. He removed a gold watch with glittering diamonds circling the face. The thin, supple band gleamed in his hands as he showed it to her, and she sucked in a breath at the sight. She'd never seen such an exquisite piece of jewelry.

She remained silent while he fastened the stunning timepiece around her left wrist, his fingers warm and steady. She stared at the jewels, transfixed. But where would she ever wear this, even if she could keep it? She raised her arm to read the name of the watchmaker, something Swiss and famous, and knew this gift had cost more than her car.

"This token is nothing compared to the life of my son," Trey said. "I hope you'll accept it."

"It's beautiful," she breathed.

"So you like it?"

"Of course." She shook her head. "But I can't keep this, Trey."

"Why not?"

Kelly removed the watch and placed it back in the box. She closed the lid with a snap, removing temptation from her greedy eyes.

"Even if I thought it was right, that I deserved

a reward for doing my job, cops can't accept gifts. Even the clothing you gave me was a stretch."

"No one has to know," he said, placing his hand on the box, moving it toward her.

"*I* would know," she told him, raising her gaze from the box to meet his. "And you would know."

He stared at her for a long moment, then nodded. "Okay. I understand."

"Thank you for the thought, though."

"So I didn't insult you again?" he asked.

"No. This time I believe you meant well."

"I want to find a way to thank you. I know how much staying here has disrupted your life."

"It has, yes." No point in lying. "I'm used to a routine, but you made it hard to say no. And Jason is such a sweet little dude."

"But a spoiled one?"

She shrugged, sorry she'd made that observation, glad they'd moved on from the watch. "Hey, what do I know about raising a kid?"

Trey shifted his gaze to his wineglass. "Probably as much as I do."

"I've learned that kids need boundaries," she said. "Maybe he thinks he can just pick a new mother out of thin air."

Trey met her gaze again. "You believe he's making this up? Seriously?"

Kelly sighed. No, the kid didn't appear to be faking, and she was a good judge of liars. "I believe Jason is seriously confused."

Trey nodded. "When he got out of the hospital after the wreck, I admit I let him do or have whatever he wanted."

And that would be one hell of a lot of everything, considering how deep the Wentworth pockets were. "I'm surprised he doesn't have his own pony." Kelly shook her head.

Trey added wine to their glasses. "He has two in upstate New York."

Yeah, so little Jason was a little prince.

"You need to learn the word 'no.'"

"He'd lost his mother," Trey said. "He missed her, was hurt by the belief that she'd abandoned him, that his father was somehow responsible. I would have done anything in my power to make him feel better."

"There's nothing you can do to make up for that loss," Kelly said softly. "That I can tell you from personal experience."

Trey met her gaze. "How old were you when you lost your mother?"

"Thirteen." Her voice cracked on the number, and she swallowed. "Thirteen going on thirty."

"What happened to you? You said you never knew your father."

She shrugged. How had she allowed the subject to veer from Jason to her own troubled childhood? "Foster homes."

Trey grimaced. "I'm sorry."

"Yeah, but I was luckier than most. I got out okay."

"Why lucky?"

"You don't want to hear this."

"Yes, I do."

"A police officer—" She hesitated and took a sip of wine. Why was she telling Wentworth this messy story? She'd never told anyone. "He took me under his wing and looked out for me in the system. He was a good guy, the reason I became a cop."

"What happened to him?"

"He retired last year, moved to Daytona Beach."

"It's nice to have a mentor."

"I guess your father was your mentor," she said, pleased she'd found a way to switch the subject back to Wentworth.

Trey laughed harshly. "Oh, yeah. My old man has guided me through life like a kindly and wise sage."

Kelly stared at Trey. Interesting that he had issues, serious issues apparently, with dear old Dad. No one's life was perfect. So maybe Trey did understand that stacks of cash didn't solve every problem. And maybe his relationship with his father was another reason he treated Jason like royalty. He wanted to do a better job at parenting, make sure his son knew he was loved. Maybe she should give the guy a break.

Or maybe she'd had too much wine.

At least Wentworth knew his father.

She set her glass on the bar. She needed to get

away from this man. She was actually starting to feel sorry for a billionaire.

"Listen, Trey, about that bodyguard…"

"You want me to call him off."

She nodded.

"Then it's done," Trey said.

"Thanks." She came to her feet. "I need to get some sleep. It's been a crazy couple of days."

"I understand."

She hesitated. "If you really want to thank me, I do have a suggestion."

"Just name it."

"Ask Greta to prepare food that's a little less, you know, fattening."

Trey laughed softly. "You got it."

"Thanks. Would you mind if I swam a few laps before I turn in?"

"Please, Kelly. You don't have to ask. Everything in my home is at your disposal," he said, giving her such a slow sexy smile that her heart began to gallop again. "Everything."

THE NEXT MORNING Trey moved into his office with his second cup of coffee determined to tackle the mail he'd ignored since the kidnapping. The coffee was gone but he'd made little progress when the phone rang. Caller ID revealed Brian Howell, his attorney.

"Good morning, Trey. How is Jason?"

Trey sat back and rubbed his eyes. "The same. He's in session with Dr. Carico right now."

"Does he still think Officer Jenkins is his mother?"

"He says he does."

"What do you mean by that? Do you think he's faking?"

"I honestly don't know, but you have to admit the whole idea is nuts."

"What does Carico say?"

"Donna's opinion is Jason truly believes Kelly is his mother."

"Surely Jason couldn't fool a professional," Brian said.

"You'd think not."

"And why would he pretend?"

"Kelly would say it's because he's spoiled and used to getting his own way."

"Is she there now?"

"She's on duty. She left before nine."

"I see. Well, you'll be glad to know the background check on Officer Jenkins came in this morning. It's attached to an email I just sent you. That's one reason for my call."

"Hold on." Trey swiveled to his computer, found Brian's message and sent its attachment to his printer.

"That was quick," Trey said. "Thanks. Does the report reveal any problems?"

"I'll let you decide that for yourself."

"What's the other reason for the call?"

"Possible good news. Have you heard from Agent Ballard today?"

"No. What's going on?"

"The FBI brought in Darlene's father for questioning."

"What? Is he a suspect in Jason's kidnapping?"

"Definitely."

"How did that happen?"

"Ballard asked me for a list of people who might have a grudge against you or your family. When I told him about the lawsuit, he jumped on it."

"Yeah, but that doesn't seem likely to me. The man doesn't even live in Miami, does he?"

"Well, that's the thing. They located him in a fleabag motel near the Miami airport."

"Oh, my God." Trey stared out the window. Was it possible that any man could kidnap his own grandson and demand ransom money? Even if the grandfather had never met his daughter or her son, the idea sounded too sick.

"What was Darlene's father's name again?"

"Jeff Lawson."

"Does Lawson resemble Kelly's sketch?"

"Vaguely. But if you try hard enough, a sketch can look like anyone. I suspect they'll bring her in for a lineup soon."

"I hope it's him," Trey said. "If it is, then this nightmare will be over. At least for her."

"Ballard told me about the bomb in Officer Jenkins's vehicle. Lawson spent ten years in the Atlanta federal penitentiary, an ideal place to get an advanced education on pyrotechnics."

"She could have been killed."

"But she wasn't. Read the report. You'll learn Kelly Jenkins is nothing if not a survivor."

CHAPTER ELEVEN

KELLY ENTERED A SMALL, dark room while Agent Ballard held the door. Trying to suppress her resentment, she stared through the one-way glass, but no one had entered the space on the other side yet.

She'd been yanked off patrol before lunch and instructed via radio by Sergeant McFadden to drive her unit immediately to the FBI headquarters in Broward County, an hour away. The feds had a suspect in Jason's abduction in custody. They needed her to come in and make the ID.

"This won't take long," Ballard said.

She took a deep breath and bit back the words, "I hope not." She was missing another tour of duty, and she'd had no lunch. An empty belly always made her cranky.

Yeah, of course she was thrilled at least one of the bad guys had been caught. But why did the kidnapping case have to constantly interfere with her job? She could tell Sarge was angry when he gave her the order, although he didn't go into what was bugging him. He did, however, remind her they still needed to have a conversation, to check with him before she clocked out tonight.

Awesome. Just what she needed today.

Her morning had started off with Jason clinging to her legs and begging her not to leave. Trey had helped calm him down, but the little dude's sad, tear-streaked face had touched something deep inside her, his misery reaching into a place she thought had shriveled up a long time ago. She'd felt like a low-life dirtbag for making a little kid cry.

Was it normal for kids to get that upset when their mothers went to work? How did real moms manage that kind of drama every day?

And ever since that good-night kiss, she didn't know how to act around Wentworth. Trey, she reminded herself. *Think of him as Trey.* Why was using his first name so hard for her? Because she understood the need to keep distance between them.

Being around Trey Wentworth was bad for her mental health.

Ballard pressed a hand to an ear piece, and Kelly heard garbled words.

He nodded at her. "They're on their way."

When the door opened, a tingle of excitement shot through her. She really did hope the Bureau had apprehended Adam. She didn't like looking over her shoulder every second, wondering if she was in someone's sights.

"Just take your time, Officer Jenkins," Ballard said.

Remaining silent, she pressed her lips together. Damn right she'd take her time. She wasn't some unreliable witness off the street. Why couldn't the FBI remember she was a trained law enforcement officer?

Five men, all graying, all approximately the same height, weight and age entered the lineup room. She perceived immediately that neither Caleb nor Adam was among this group, that all these men were at least twenty years older than Jason's abductors. She carefully scrutinized the face of each subject anyway just to be certain.

Ballard accessed an intercom and told the men, "Have them turn sideways, please."

Kelly repeated her examination and finally sighed. "Neither of the kidnappers I spoke to is in this group," she told Ballard.

His face tightened. "You're sure."

"Yes," Kelly said. "They were much younger than this. You don't have the right guy."

Ballard uttered a mild curse, but activated the intercom again. "Release everyone but Lawson," he said.

"Sorry," Kelly said.

"Yeah," Ballard said, staring at the floor. "Me, too."

"No other suspects?" she asked.

Ballard shrugged, and Kelly understood he didn't want to discuss the case with her. But why shouldn't he? Who better than her? She was an integral part of his case and she'd thought a lot about the circumstances of the kidnapping.

"Have you considered Jason's kidnapping could be an inside job?" she asked.

Ballard smiled. "You sound like a television police drama, Officer Jenkins."

"Don't be an ass," she said. "You know I mean someone from Wentworth's staff could be involved."

His smile faded. "We've checked everyone out. Most have been with the family for years."

"So how did the kidnappers get on the island? You know no one gets on a ferry without permission from an owner."

"We've gone through the security logs and no one boarded the ferry without clearance."

"That's my point. Did you check with the marina? Maybe they came and went with their own boat."

"Of course. No unauthorized dockings appear in the records."

"How good is the security at the marina?"

Ballard hesitated. "Good, but not as tight as the ferry."

"What about leaving the island? Does security check for clearance to board the ferry on the return trip?"

"I don't know about that." Ballard frowned. "Why would they?"

"Good question. Did you check out Wentworth's driver, Hans somebody?"

"He's clean, retired special forces."

Kelly nodded. "Well, I've been living in this fantasyland, and I believe Adam had to have help from someone in-house. If assistance didn't come from Wentworth's inner circle, then employees of the management company. Or the security company. You need to check that out."

Ballard eyed her thoughtfully. "We'll go through it again."

"Good. Can I return to duty?"

He nodded. "Thanks for coming in. We'll be in touch. Are you still staying at Wentworth's place?"

"For now."

"Tell Wentworth we need to have a conversation."

Kelly raised her brows. Great. Just what the world needed, more conversations.

KELLY'S SHIFT WAS over by the time she parked her unit at the station and entered the back door. She'd checked in on the drive south, and Rudy told her he'd be waiting for her in the roll-call room.

She pushed open the door and spotted Patrice by Rudy's desk having an animated conversation of her own with their sergeant. As Kelly moved toward where they stood, they broke off and glanced her way.

"Hey, Kel," Patrice said with a nod. "See you tomorrow, Rudy."

Kelly stood at attention before her sergeant.

"Thanks for joining us, Officer Jenkins," Rudy said. "Any luck with the FBI?"

"No, sir," Kelly said. "They had the wrong guy."

Rudy snorted. "Sounds like the feds. So what's going on with you, Jenkins? You've missed a lot of time the last three days."

"I'm sorry, sir. It's because of the Wentworth kidnapping."

"So you're some kind of big-deal heroine, now, huh?"

She stood straighter and lifted her chin. "No, sir. Not at all, sir."

"The kid is back with the father, right?"

"Yes, sir. However, Jason Wentworth has developed the deluded notion that I'm his mother."

"Geez. Because you rescued him?"

"I guess, sir."

"I see."

Kelly could tell her sergeant didn't see at all. He sat behind his desk and slid a yellow sheet of paper toward him. A trickle of unease traveled her spine. Was that a disciplinary memo? What happened to the commendation?

"Also," she said, in an effort to help her case, "the kidnappers placed a bomb in my vehicle."

"I heard something about that," Rudy said. "I also heard a rumor you've moved into Wentworth's mansion. Is that true?"

Kelly nodded, suspecting his source was Patrice. But her situation was no secret. "Yes, sir. Until they can get the kid straightened out."

"How long is that going to take?"

"No way to know, sir."

"Living on Collins Island with nothing but billionaires could be a big distraction for a rookie."

"I won't let it distract me, sir."

"You're off duty tomorrow and Friday, right?"

"Yes, sir. Unless you want me to come in and make up time."

"No. I want you to take the days to get your head together."

"Yes, sir."

Rudy tore the paper once, twice and dropped the ragged pieces into his wastebasket.

"Okay, Jenkins. I'll let your attendance issues slide for now, but consider yourself as having received a verbal warning. From now on, you need to be on time and complete your shifts."

"I understand, sir," Kelly said.

"You'd better, because I'll be watching you."

WHEN TREY'S LIMO rolled off the ferry, Kelly leaned forward and tapped on the window separating her from Hans.

"Yes?" A disembodied voice sounded over the intercom.

"Pull over," she said. "I want to talk to the guards."

Kelly exited the vehicle and walked toward the guard shack. A uniformed male, in his late twenties and Hispanic, watched her approach warily, no doubt surprised to see a uniformed policewoman emerge from a resident's luxury limousine.

She'd first thought to jog over to speak to a guard on her morning run, but realized she'd get more co-operation if she were in uniform.

"Can I help you, Officer?" the guard asked. His badge read Carlos.

Kelly shook his hand. Carlos sounded friendly enough.

"Officer Kelly Jenkins. I'd like to ask you some questions."

"You're the policewoman who saved the Went-worth kid, aren't you?" he asked. "We heard you were staying at the villa."

"It's only temporary," she said. "Believe me."

"You've become a legend around here," Carlos said with a grin. "What do you need?"

Kelly motioned toward the ferry landing. "I'm assisting the FBI with their investigation and want to understand how your security works."

"Sure."

"A visitor can only board the ferry with prior clearance from a resident, right?"

"Absolutely, either on foot or with a vehicle, and they have to present valid ID."

"So you always know what a visitor's destination is?"

"Right."

"Do you follow a visitor to make sure they actually go to that resident's home?"

"Well, we always ask if they know where they're going. If they don't, we offer to lead them on one of our golf carts."

"So you wouldn't know if a visitor didn't actually go where they say they're going?"

Carlos frowned. "I guess that's true."

Kelly nodded. "What about on the return trip? Do you ID then?"

"Why would we? Any visitor has already been cleared."

"Makes sense," Kelly said, gazing at the ferry.

"However," Carlos added, "we do check any bags carried by domestic workers who walk on the ferry to make sure they haven't stolen anything."

Kelly resisted the urge to roll her eyes. How insulting that must be for the workers.

"Are the guards employees of the island or a homeowners' association?"

"We all work for the Protection Alliance."

Carlos announced the name of his employer with a sense of pride.

"That's a private security firm, right?" Kelly asked.

"Right," Carlos said. "You're trying to figure out how the kidnappers got on the island. Aren't you?"

Kelly nodded. "Who from Wentworth Villa can give permission for a guest to board?"

"Let me check," Carlos said. He moved to the guard shack and returned with a clipboard. He flipped a few pages and said, "Of course Mr. Trey

Wentworth, Alexander Wentworth—I believe that's his father—Maria Navarre, plus Hans and Greta Karies."

"Clearance is usually done by phone, right?"

"Usually," Carlos agreed.

"How do you know the person on the phone is the person they say they are?"

Carlos looked blank for a second, and then grimaced. "Well, we check the number on caller ID, but I guess we don't know for sure who is speaking. Do you want to talk to my supervisor about this?"

"Not necessary," Kelly said. "You've answered all of my questions. Thanks very much."

"Anytime," Carlos said as they shook again.

Kelly moved back toward the limo where Hans leaned against the driver's side door, watching her intently.

She shook her head. The security on this island was supposed to be the best in Miami, but as many as three of Trey's staff could have given clearance for the kidnappers to board the ferry.

WHEN KELLY APPEARED in the doorway of the media room, the dread that had knotted Trey's gut loosened its grip. Tonight, he'd been as anxious as Jason for her to return home.

Their gazes locked across the room. She smiled uncertainly, and then focused on Jason who lay on the floor transfixed by the television.

She'd already been up to her room and had

changed out of her uniform into a Miami-Dade County Police T-shirt and blue jeans that hugged her long legs.

Trey held his breath, waiting for his son to notice her arrival. Trey prayed today was the day Jason returned to reality.

Kelly moved into the room. Jason looked behind him and then leaped to his feet.

"Mommy," he cried, throwing his arms around her legs.

Trey sighed.

She bent over and hugged him. "Hi, Jason. Whatcha watching?"

Jason grabbed her hand and related the convoluted plot of his favorite cartoon, one he'd seen hundreds of times. Kelly appeared dazed by the end of the explanation.

"It's almost over," he said. "Then we'll have dinner." A doubtful expression clouded his precious face. "Unless you're real hungry."

"Go ahead and finish your movie," Kelly said, and joined Trey on the sofa.

"Hi," Trey said.

"So I guess I'm still Mom," she said softly.

"It appears so." Keeping his voice low so Jason couldn't overhear, Trey asked, "What happened with the lineup at FBI headquarters?"

"They had the wrong guy," Kelly said. "A giant waste of time."

Trey released a breath. So Darlene's father hadn't

kidnapped Jason. He should be relieved, but that meant the bad guys were still out there gunning for Kelly and maybe Jason again. Far better if Jeff Lawson had been their guy.

"Any problems today?" Trey asked. "More bombs or other incendiary devices?"

"No bombs," she said. "But definitely some problems."

"I hope just normal police work."

Kelly glanced at Jason, but he was caught up in the cartoon. "I'm in trouble with my sergeant for missing duty."

"What? You're kidding?"

"I wish I were."

"Can I do anything to help?"

"No."

"Let me make a phone call."

"Absolutely not," Kelly insisted. "You'd only make it worse. I just have to keep my head down and do my job."

Trey nodded. But he knew Kelly's history now. She'd been through hell and back and had managed to come out on the other side a good person, someone who still wanted to help others. She'd worked two, sometimes three jobs at a time while attending a local university to study criminal justice, graduating with a damned good grade point average. It'd taken him longer to get through Princeton on his father's dime, and he'd never worked a day while in school.

He couldn't let the fact that Kelly had helped his son impact her career. He had to find some way to help her.

"Although," she muttered, "it'll be tough to fly under the radar when I'm delivered to work by a limo every day."

"What about—"

Her eyes widened. "Please don't suggest your chopper."

"I was about to suggest Hans could drive a different car."

Before she could respond, Jason crawled onto the sofa between them and leaned against Kelly. "I'm hungry, Mommy. Let's go eat."

"It's pizza night," Trey told Kelly when all three of them had found their seats.

"I'm surprised anyone would be allowed to deliver to this island," Kelly said.

"Not quite," Trey said with a laugh. "Greta makes her own whole-wheat crust and a fresh tomato sauce. Jason loves it."

"Fresh mozzarella is the secret," Greta said, placing a huge, steaming pizza in the center of the table.

"And fresh basil, which smells heavenly," Kelly said.

Greta placed a slice on the plate in front of each of them.

"Except for an apple, I missed lunch, so I'm starving," Kelly said.

"Why did you miss lunch?" Trey asked.

"My command performance for the FBI."

"You should have said something," he said. "We didn't have to wait to eat."

She shrugged and took a huge bite of her slice. Trey did the same. Delicious, as usual. His cook was a gem. He hoped Kelly appreciated that this was a much simpler meal than usual.

Kelly asked Jason about his day. His son grinned, obviously pleased to have her attention, and began rattling off his activities, including his daily romp in the pool.

Trey listened, surprised at how easily Kelly interacted with Jason. She knew exactly how to draw him out and even appeared to be interested in his responses.

"Daddy," Jason said when they were finished eating, "can I watch TV a little more before bed?"

Trey hesitated. Normally, he allowed Jason to do whatever he wanted. But dinner was being served later than usual because of Kelly's schedule. Maybe it was time for some boundaries. Maybe Jason should go on to sleep.

Or maybe he didn't want to delay a repeat of that good-night kiss with Kelly.

Stunned at the realization he'd been looking forward to kissing her all day, Trey said, "Maria has to give you a bath first and then only thirty minutes of TV. Okay?"

"Okay, Daddy." Jason jumped from his chair and raced into the hallway where Maria waited.

"Come on, *Jasonito*," she said.

"I know what you're thinking," Trey told Kelly when they'd gone upstairs.

"No, you don't."

"You think I'm spoiling him."

"No. I think he should be learning his ABCs, not zoning out while watching television."

"Seriously?"

"Education would be better for his brain than pretend heroes," she said. "Maybe a dose of reality would help ground Jason."

"Reality?"

Kelly shrugged. "Life doesn't always have a happy ending like in cartoons. Education is what helps a kid get ahead."

"He's four."

"So? Some kids are in preschool at that age. I didn't see any educational toys in his room, either."

"Isn't Jason a little young to face the harsh realities of life?"

"He was kidnapped. I'd say he's already faced some pretty serious realities."

"And as a result, he retreated to some safe place inside himself. Look, I know your childhood wasn't all roses, but—"

She narrowed her eyes. "What do you know about my childhood?"

"I hope everything. My attorney ran a background check on you."

"What did you say?"

Startled by the vehemence of her question, the anger behind her words, Trey mentally kicked himself. He'd meant to compliment her on how she related to Jason. Instead he'd insulted her again. He should have known she'd think a vetting was intrusive. And perhaps it was.

"I already knew you were in foster homes," he said. "You told me that yesterday."

"That didn't give you the right to snoop around in my life."

CHAPTER TWELVE

UNSURE WHY SHE was so furious, Kelly pushed back from the table and stood. She didn't have anything to hide. In fact, she was proud of how far she'd come.

But she should have the power to decide who knew the details of her life.

"I routinely get security clearance on anyone who comes near Jason," Trey said in a tight voice.

"I'm a cop," she said. "Why can't people remember that?"

"I know you're a cop, but there are always rotten apples."

"So I'm a crooked cop?"

"You know I didn't say that."

"But you suspected I was involved with Jason's kidnappers?"

"Not anymore." Trey stood and threw his napkin to the table. "But Brian ordered the clearance the first day, and I only received the report this morning."

"I want to see it," she said.

"Fair enough."

"What's wrong, Mommy?"

Kelly whirled at the sound of Jason's voice. With tousled damp hair and clean pajamas, he stood in the doorway of the dining room looking worriedly from his father and then back to her.

"Why are you yelling?" Jason asked.

Kelly took a deep breath. Poor little dude had been through enough without listening to his parents fighting. God, she remembered what it was like when her mother and Roy started hurling furious words at each other. She'd always hid under the bed, waiting for the inevitable sound of the first blow and her mother's piercing wails afterward.

She'd sworn that she would never put a child through that kind of pain. It was one reason she became a cop.

"I'm sorry," she said, her voice shaky. "Just a silly argument. I didn't mean to yell."

"Are you ready for some TV, buddy?" Trey asked.

Jason nodded solemnly.

With a sharp pang to her gut, Kelly intuitively knew he was terrified the angry words meant his mother was leaving him again. Just how many arguments had he suffered through between his real mother and father? Did he think that was why his mom had gone away?

She hurried over, lifted Jason into her arms and hugged him close. Smelling of baby shampoo, he hooked his arms around her neck.

"I'm sorry if I scared you," she said, meeting Trey's gaze over Jason's shoulder. Trey's mouth was pinched. He looked as guilt ridden as she felt. "Everything is okay."

Jason's warm body relaxed in her arms. He trusted her. He believed her. But in her opinion everything was most certainly not okay. So now she was a liar.

"Instead of TV, why don't I read you a story before you go to sleep?" Kelly suggested.

Jason pulled back so he could see her face, his blue eyes wide. "A story?"

"Sure," she said. Surely his real mother read him stories at bedtime. Even her mom had managed that on occasion.

"Do you have a favorite?" she asked. She recalled a shelf full of books in his bedroom.

"I'm sure we can find one," Trey said, taking Jason from her arms. Kelly sighed in relief when the heavy child went willingly to his father.

Inside Jason's bedroom, Kelly selected a book from the shelf whose cover featured an adorable brown-and-white puppy while Trey pulled two chairs next to the bed. When she sat with the book, Jason stared at her with such wide eyes Kelly decided this must be a novel experience. His mom must not have been much of a reader.

She glanced at Trey, and he nodded. By unspoken agreement, their conflict over her security clearance had been postponed.

She began to read. "Rocket was a happy puppy who liked to explore."

By the end of a few pages, she realized she'd selected a story featuring a curious little puppy who wandered away from his mother, got lost and met friends and enemies while trying to find her. She assumed it was a cautionary tale for children about staying close to home.

But this might not be such a great choice for a little boy who'd lost his own mother.

She shot Jason a look to judge his reaction. His eyes were closed. Was he already asleep?

"Why did you stop?" he mumbled. And then yawned.

She continued with the story. When she read, "The end," a short time later, Jason's eyes were still closed, his breathing regular.

"I think he's out," Trey whispered.

Making as little noise as possible, Kelly stood and switched off the bedside light. Jason's face appeared sweet and totally at peace. If only.

She leaned over and kissed his forehead, catching another distinctive whiff of baby shampoo. She quietly backed away from the bed, and Trey did the same, his gaze on her.

"Now Mommy and Daddy have to kiss," Jason said sleepily.

Kelly froze.

Jason's eyes were wide open now, staring at them, waiting.

And then Trey's mouth was on hers, his hands cupping her cheeks. While last night he'd seemed surprised by the kiss, tonight he took possession of her mouth with such intent and control she knew he'd planned this, intended to elicit a reaction from her.

When he drew back, her lips felt ripe and deliciously bruised. Was he the world's greatest kisser or had she never met a man who knew how to do it properly?

He smiled down at her, cupping her cheek with his warm hand. "I'm sorry," he whispered.

She understood his apology had nothing to do with his mouth on hers. But exactly what was he sorry for?

"Good night, son," Trey said.

Kelly allowed him to take her hand and lead her out of Jason's room. She came back to herself halfway down the staircase and yanked her hand from his.

He looked back at her with an unreadable expression. "We need to talk."

"You bet we do," she said.

Her life was spiraling out of control. She'd worked too long and too hard to allow that to happen. She needed to get herself back on track. She needed to get off billionaire island and back to reality.

As KELLY STOMPED ahead of him into the bar, Trey wondered if she was prickly because of the kiss, the bodyguard or maybe it was the security clearance issue. Everything he did made her angry.

Dealing with Kelly Jenkins was like walking on shredded glass.

His feelings about her changed constantly, but his admiration for her ambition and resolve increased steadily. As did his appreciation of her body. Under different circumstances, he would have seen where their kisses led. She could pretend otherwise, but in his arms Kelly turned into a firecracker—one ready to ignite.

She removed a wineglass from the overhead display and sat at a bar stool. When he moved behind the bar, she pushed the glass toward him.

Trey selected a bottle, opened it and poured ruby liquid into her glass. He'd intended to ask Kelly about her history this evening, open up a dialogue to get some more intimate clues about her life, but had reconsidered that idea. He'd talk to Dr. Carico first about how he should approach the subject. Donna might have some professional insight.

"I'm sorry if the security clearance upset you," he said. "It was ordered before I got to know you. Please forgive me."

"You think you know me now?"

"A poor choice of words," he said, pouring wine into a second glass. "Of course I don't know you. I met you two days ago."

"Damn right," she muttered, and took a healthy swallow.

When she lowered the glass, he met her clear blue gaze. She had amazing eyes, but she looked away.

"What are you so angry about, Kelly?" he asked softly.

Her gaze flew back to his.

"And what can I do to make it right?"

She released a sigh, her shoulders relaxing.

He tasted the wine. "If you like, I can arrange for a taxi to take you to work. Just tell me what you need."

"Truthfully, I don't know what's wrong with me. I'm just—I don't know. Unsettled by everything that's going on."

"You don't like our kisses?"

"Oh, I like them, all right," she said, as color crept into her cheeks. "And you know it. That's part of the problem."

"I agree."

Her eyes widened. "You do?"

"I also like our kisses too much."

She smiled faintly and averted her gaze. "How long can this go on, Trey? I can't stay here for the rest of my life. I mean, I like Jason and all. Despite his delusions about me being mother material, he's a sweet kid. But this crazy situation is screwing up my career. My whole life."

"You don't think you're mother material?"

"Absolutely not. I'd be lousy at it."

"Now I do have to disagree. You're wonderful with Jason."

"Are you kidding? Did you see his face when

he caught us arguing?" She closed her eyes as if to shut out that image.

Trey nodded, remembering his son's anxious face. Of course she was right that Jason shouldn't see conflict between them.

"I felt like crying," she said, and took a sip of wine.

"We need to be more careful. Still, Kelly, you'd be a great mom."

"You're as delusional as your son," she said. "I hate kids."

"What? You certainly could have fooled me."

"Well, considering the woman you married, maybe you're easily fooled."

Trey blinked, surprised by how much her comment stung. Maybe the fact that he *had* been a fool to marry Darlene was what made the words so difficult to hear. The truth often was.

"Gee, Kelly," he said. "Why don't you say what you *really* mean?"

At least she had the grace to blush. "Sorry. Like I said, I'm unsettled."

"Right. Unsettled." Trey took a long swallow of wine, disappointment searing his gut. But why? No more kisses? Because this woman didn't want children? Why should he care?

Because Kelly's true opinion of him was all too clear, now.

She'd seen right through him, knew the truth about him. He *was* a fool, a man who had done nothing useful with a life blessed by a fortunate birth. Kelly Jenkins had come from nothing yet had done far more with hers.

"So how do you want to get to work in the morning?" he asked.

"Actually, I'm off tomorrow. I hope to sleep in."

He laughed, the sound harsh to his own ears. "Don't count on it with a four-year-old searching for you."

She nibbled at her bottom lip, looking uncertain. He focused on her lush mouth, remembering how soft and willing she'd been, and fought the urge to pull her into his arms again.

He took a step back from the bar. He needed to get away from her before he made an even bigger fool of himself.

"I trust you can find your room?" he asked as politely as he could manage.

"I think I know the way by now," she muttered.

He bowed. "Then I'll see you in the morning."

Leaving his wine behind, he left Kelly at the bar, feeling the heat of her gaze on his back as he retreated.

He needed to vent a raging frustration that had been building since the kidnapping. Was this what Kelly meant about being unsettled? He felt like he had no foundation anymore, that his life was built on quicksand.

By the time Darlene had died, once every stint in rehab had failed, he'd felt nothing for her but pity.

And then a fierce rage when he learned Jason had been in the vehicle with her.

And, yeah, maybe Kelly resembled Darlene a little, but Officer Jenkins was nothing like his ex-wife at all. Nothing.

He headed toward the tennis court. Smacking a few thousand tennis balls lobbed across the net from the automatic Ballmaster sounded about right.

He switched on the huge overheads. Light flooded the court, clearly illuminating the stark white lines, and he immediately felt better. Tennis was the only thing he'd ever done on his own that he'd been good at. Maybe because boundaries were obvious to him on the familiar and never-changing court.

CHAPTER THIRTEEN

KELLY STRETCHED LONG under the warm, fluffy comforter. She couldn't remember another time in her entire life when she'd slept so deeply or so well. She sighed, not wanting to leave her snug little cocoon.

It was her day off. She could sleep until noon.

And, hey, since she *was* living in Wentworth Manor, maybe she could order up breakfast in bed? She smiled at the thought. What time was it anyway?

She rolled to her right side expecting to read the digital clock on the nightstand. Instead she gazed into the big blue eyes of Jason Wentworth, his feet on the floor, elbows propped on the bed, staring at her.

"Hi, Mommy."

Kelly swallowed, a burst of unexpected pleasure breaking through her sleepiness. "Hi, Jason."

He climbed into bed beside her. She sat against the headboard and quickly pulled the covers over her chest. Was it okay to share this kind of intimacy with the kid? She always slept in a thin cotton tank top and panties. The little dude might think she was his mother, but she wasn't. What should she do?

And where was Trey?

Jason settled himself against her belly, his knees bent. "You slept late this morning."

"Yeah, I guess I did."

"Why?"

"I don't have to go to work today."

A giant smile wreathed his face, and she noticed he'd developed a few freckles on his nose and cheeks. His hair was lighter, too. Probably from all the time in the pool.

"Really?" he asked.

"Really. What do you want to do today?"

"Go swimming."

"Okay," she said. But should she have given permission without checking with his father? Why not? The kid wanted to swim, and so did she.

"Are you ready for breakfast?" Jason asked.

She sighed. So much for sleeping in.

"I'm ready for coffee. That's for sure."

"Jason?" Trey's voice boomed in the hallway. "Where are you?"

"With Mommy," Jason yelled back.

Eyes wide, looking as if a hungry lion were chasing him, Trey appeared in the doorway. What was wrong with him?

"What did I tell you, young man?" he demanded in a voice unlike she'd ever heard him use with his son.

Jason's lower lip stuck out. "Not to wake up Mommy. I didn't."

"No," Trey yelled. "I told you *never* to go into Mommy's room under any circumstances."

Jason's eyes welled with tears at his father's harsh voice. "But I waited for her to wake up."

"It's okay, Trey," Kelly told him. "I don't mind."

"No, it is not okay," Trey said.

"I'm sorry, Daddy."

"I know you are, but this is important, son." Trey exhaled and ran a hand through his hair. "Come on out now, Jase. I need you to go downstairs so I can talk to Mommy."

Deciding something awful must have happened to put Trey in such a foul temper, Kelly gave Jason a hug. "Go on, sweetie."

"Are you coming?"

"I need to get dressed. I'll see you at breakfast."

Moving much slower than he had getting into the bed, Jason climbed down and shuffled past his father into the hallway. When Jason had disappeared, Trey turned back to Kelly with furious eyes.

"Where's your gun?" he demanded, striding into the room.

She blinked. "My gun?"

"Yes. You know, the thing with bullets that can kill curious little boys. Where the hell is it?"

"Is that why you're upset Jase came into my room? You're worried about my service weapon?"

"Yes."

"It's in a locked gun safe."

Trey's expression softened. "You brought a safe with you?"

"Of course."

"Where?" he asked.

"The closet, top shelf."

Trey jerked open the closet door and reached for the gun locker.

"There's no way anyone could get inside," she said. "Certainly not a kid. And I doubt Jason could even lift it."

Trey moved to the bed carrying the safe. "Yeah, it's heavy," he said.

He worked at the box, trying for several minutes to pry it open. Finally, he released a huge breath and met her gaze.

"Sorry," he said. "I feel like an idiot."

"You don't need to apologize for being worried about gun safety. That means you're a responsible parent."

"The hell I am."

He collapsed on the foot of the bed, pulling the comforter off her shoulders. She yanked the sheet back over her chest knowing her nipples stood out like beacons through the thin fabric.

"I meant to ask you where you kept your gun sooner."

"There's been a lot going on," she said.

"And when I realized Jason had gone into your room…" Trey broke off and shook his head. "I guess I panicked. I should have trusted you. You're a professional law enforcement officer."

"Please don't worry about it, Trey. No cop will ever be mad at a parent for worrying about keeping their kids away from guns."

"Thanks." He smiled, and she became hyper-aware that she was in bed, practically naked, and a gorgeous man, one with whom she'd shared several delicious kisses, technically was in that bed with her. And he was reputedly the most eligible bachelor in the world.

"I heard you swimming last night," he said.

"And I heard you whacking a bunch of tennis balls."

"Yeah," he said. "Good thing balls can't hit back."

"I get that." His comment and bitter tone surprised her, although maybe they shouldn't have. Trey Wentworth might have all the cash anyone ever needed or wanted, but everyone always insisted money didn't solve every problem.

She'd just never bought into that before.

"Did torturing tennis balls make you feel better?" she asked.

"Somewhat." He raked a hand through his hair again. "Until I realized Jase had come into your room."

"I heard a rumor you won some big-deal tennis tournament."

"That was a long time ago. Do you play?"

"Unfortunately, none of my foster parents had tennis courts."

"There *are* public facilities, you know."

"Yeah, well, I'm told you need a racket, which costs money."

"I've got rackets you could use. Would you like to learn?"

Would she? Kelly hesitated. She loved sports. Why not learn a new one?

"You could teach me how to play?"

"It would be my pleasure. I'll have the pro shop deliver some clothing," he said, glancing at the clock.

She followed his gaze. Nine thirty. Damn, she'd slept later than she thought. No wonder Jason had showed up at her bedside.

"But first," Trey said, "we have a meeting with the FBI."

SATISFIED THAT JASON could never get at Kelly's weapon, Trey rose and returned the gun locker to the top closet shelf.

"The FBI?" she demanded behind him.

Trey returned to her bedside. "Agent Ballard is on the ferry."

Looking interested, she sat up, and the sheet fell away, revealing her perfect breasts straining against her tank top. He knew he should avert his gaze but couldn't.

"Have they made an arrest?" she asked eagerly.

"I doubt it."

He forced himself to look at her face. A current of something explosive and sensual arced between them. Her eyes widened in awareness. He clenched his fists, wanting to shed his clothing and climb into bed with her.

As worried as he'd been about Jason getting at her gun, he'd actually had a flash of envy when he saw his son snuggled next to her.

He'd just met this woman. She came from a world foreign to him. Was it because of their differences that he wanted her?

And she didn't even respect him. So he once again wanted what he couldn't have? Story of his life.

And all they'd shared were kisses. Good-night kisses for his confused son. Nothing more than that.

Yeah, and he wanted to kiss her again. This time without Jason watching. He took a step toward the bed.

Still holding his gaze, she raised the sheet over her chest. A knowing smile appeared, and he lowered his gaze to her mouth where her tongue darted out and swept her lips.

He took a step away from her. He needed to get out of here before he initiated something he'd regret. Jason needed Kelly. He couldn't screw that up.

"Breakfast is waiting," he said, moving toward the door. "I'll see you downstairs."

"So you're nowhere on Jason's abduction?" Trey demanded.

Agent Ballard turned from the buffet where he'd been scooping melon onto his plate. When Ballard had arrived, Trey had invited him to join them for breakfast, hoping against his better sense for good news.

"You have absolutely no leads at this point?"

"We have leads," Ballard said, "but none of them are credible."

"So why are you here?"

After dropping several of Greta's fresh pastries beside the fruit, Ballard nodded toward Kelly, who was seated at the table gobbling down scrambled eggs, sausage and a huge helping of hash brown potatoes.

"Actually I'm here because of Officer Jenkins," Ballard said.

Kelly looked up, her mouth full.

"What about Officer Jenkins?" Trey asked.

Ballard grinned. "She believes the kidnapping was—in her words—an inside job."

Kelly swallowed and shot Ballard her best glare. Trey hid a smile. No love lost between those two.

"Kelly?" Trey asked.

She wiped her mouth with a napkin and said,

"Jason was taken from the playground. I keep asking myself how the bad guys got on the island."

Trey nodded. "Good question."

"Either a resident put their names on the ferry list or they came by private boat to the marina," Kelly said.

"We've combed through the ferry rosters from that day looking for discrepancies," Ballard said. "There are none."

"And I didn't recognize any names on the list," Trey offered. "What about the marina?"

"We've double-checked there, too," Ballard said. "Impossible for someone to motor in or out without the staff noticing. Everyone had clearance."

"What about a sailboat?" Kelly asked. "A landing on the beach or against the seawall?"

"The island's security team has excellent coverage with surveillance cameras," Ballard said. "We've been through everything the day of the abduction. No unauthorized boats landed or docked anywhere around the island."

"So they had to get Jason off via the ferry," Kelly said. "I checked with security. Guests aren't followed to make sure they end up where they say they're going."

"I understand the playground is seldom used," Ballard said.

"There aren't many kids on this island," Trey agreed.

"Yeah, mostly rich old guys," Kelly muttered.

"As a result, there's no surveillance video of the playground," Ballard said.

"What are you getting at?" Trey asked.

"Because your housekeeper and son were in a rather isolated area, no one heard any screams for help," Ballard said.

"But Maria was knocked unconscious," Trey protested, looking from Ballard to Kelly. "You've seen her black eye. She fought for Jason."

"We're trying to reconstruct a possible chain of events so you'll understand our thinking. You know that Jason's tox screen showed he was drugged," Ballard said.

Trey nodded. He'd allowed Carico to draw blood, even though he'd hated that his son had to go through a needle stick so soon after returning home.

"After drugging him, it's likely they placed him in a large container, maybe a duffel bag, and then possibly in the trunk of a car to smuggle him on and off the ferry," Ballard said.

Trey closed his eyes.

"Someone had to give Adam, and most likely Caleb, clearance for the ferry that day," Kelly said.

"Without clearance, the car wouldn't be allowed on the island," Ballard agreed.

"I checked," Kelly said. "Three members of your staff can put a name on the list."

His appetite gone, Trey shoved away his own

food. "I thought you'd already cleared everyone on my payroll."

"They all passed an initial background check," Ballard said. "Now I'd like them to take a polygraph."

"A lie detector test," Trey said. "I thought that wasn't admissible as evidence."

"It's a tool," Ballard said.

"I can't force anyone to take a polygraph," Trey said.

"But if a staff member refuses, it'll give us someone to focus on," Kelly said.

"We're also looking at the personnel from the private firm that runs security on the island," Ballard said. "Protection Alliance."

"Great," Trey said. "I just hired them to provide another layer of protection for Jason."

"How well do you know your attorney?" Kelly asked.

Trey stared at her. "Brian Howell has been my friend since prep school."

"Check him out, too," Kelly suggested to Ballard. "Maybe he's got money problems no one knows about."

Her words were like a punch to his gut. If Kelly and Ballard were correct, then someone he trusted was willing to hurt his son. But it couldn't be Brian. Not Hans, Greta. Not Maria. They'd been with him for years. But he had other maids, groundskeepers, temporary staff of maybe a dozen people to run the house while he was on Collins Island.

He might not know all of their names, but they were always well treated and paid an excellent wage. And they'd all passed his security check, the one that had so pissed off Kelly.

"You're way out of line here," Trey ground out. This was too much.

"The kidnappers had help getting on and off the island," Kelly said. "Someone who knew Jason would be out of the house."

Kelly had to be wrong. He refused to believe that someone he trusted—he employed—could have stabbed him in the back.

Damn her. He'd asked her to stay to help Jason, but her presence was causing nothing but more turmoil in his life.

CHAPTER FOURTEEN

KELLY SWUNG FOR the ball, trying to smack it with what Trey called the sweet spot of her racket. She connected, and the ball sailed back over the net. She even managed to keep it inside the lines this time.

Trey hit the ball back to her, but she judged the trajectory wrong and her return slammed into the net.

"Better," Trey called.

Sitting on the sidelines, Jason clapped madly. "Good job, Mommy."

Kelly grabbed the fabric of her new white tennis skirt and curtsied to the little dude. A burly bodyguard, wearing sunglasses that hid most of his face, hovered close to him. How did Jason feel about that new and disturbing facet of his life?

They'd been rallying for almost an hour, and she was enjoying this new game, one that forced her to chase down the ball and break a sweat.

How strange that a girl from the wrong side of the tracks would like a country club game.

"Heads up," Trey shouted, and lobbed another ball her way, this time forcing her to use her backhand, which for some odd reason was satisfying.

Tossing a ball in the air, Trey grinned.

"You're a competitive thing, aren't you?" he yelled at her.

"Who, me? No way."

Trey looked like some kind of tennis god on the other side of the net, all gorgeous in his white shorts, muscled legs and arms on full view. Patrice had sent her an email with an attached cover of *Celebrity* magazine featuring his smoothly handsome face. Apparently Trey had been their Hottest Man of the Year a few years ago.

Looking at him right now, yeah, she got that.

His mood had definitely improved since they'd started playing. Man, but he'd been offended by her suspicions. Did the guy want her to keep her ideas to herself? No way. Someone close to him had aided the kidnappers, someone he might deal with every day.

She knew what betrayal felt like. And now so did Trey.

Welcome to real life, Mr. Billionaire.

She slammed a ball back, and realized she wasn't being fair. Maybe she'd misjudged Trey Wentworth.

For one thing, he'd turned out to be a patient coach. He knew intuitively how to help her learn, and never lost his temper or made her feel like an idiot when she screwed up. He encouraged her, complimenting her small successes and improvements. As a result, their rallies were definitely getting longer.

Too bad her boss, Sergeant McFadden, wasn't more like Trey.

"Argggh," she wailed when a ball went long. She was losing her focus.

"That's enough for today," Trey said.

"Okay," Kelly agreed, breathing hard. Tennis was more work than she thought, but had energized her.

Trey grabbed two towels from the sidelines and handed her one when she met him at the net. "You did great today."

Taking the towel, she said, "Thanks."

"We'll have your second lesson tomorrow morning."

She wiped sweat from her face. She wanted to learn more—people paid a fortune for private coaching like this—but didn't Trey have anything else to do with his time but teach her how to play tennis? She knew he was beyond wealthy, but surely he had *some* work to do. Wentworth Industries couldn't run itself.

She shot a glance to Jason. Besides, there was no guarantee she'd still be here tomorrow.

"Tennis is a great game," she said. "Aerobic, but you also have to use your brain. Too bad it's not more accessible to kids that don't belong to a country club."

"But it is," Trey said.

Kelly shrugged. *You just think it is.*

Jason leaped to his feet. "Is it time to go swimming?"

"Sure, buddy," Trey said. "Find Maria and put on your bathing suit."

"He's like a fish," Kelly said, watching Jason scamper ahead, the bodyguard hurrying to keep up with him.

Trey draped the towel around his neck. "He's always loved the water."

"Is Dr. Carico coming today?"

Trey's smile faded. "After lunch."

They walked a few steps and Kelly said, "Jason is showing no signs of getting his memory back."

"No, he's not," Trey agreed, his tone flat.

Sorry she'd mentioned what had to be foremost on his mind, Kelly looked away, and the beauty of Trey's home slammed her in the face. Colorful tropical flowers, swaying palms and graceful structures surrounded her. She took a deep breath of clean, salty ocean air. If she listened hard, she could hear the crash of waves on the beach.

This place was like an artificially perfect amusement park. How long could the three of them continue to live in this fake bubble?

She wasn't a mixed-up little boy's mother, a woman who spent her days playing tennis or golf or whatever hoity-toity game.

Still, under the illusion—the delusion—his mother was alive, Jason was happy. Content. Kelly shook her head. She had grown very fond of the little prince. Too fond of him. And his father.

"It's such a beautiful day," Trey said. "I think I'll ask Greta to serve lunch on the pool deck."

"That'll be nice," Kelly said.

As long as she remained stuck in fantasyland, though, she intended to keep a close eye on Trey's staff. She might not be a detective yet, but life with her junkie mother had taught her to know when people were up to something.

Her bet was on Hans or the lawyer.

TWO DAYS LATER, Trey followed Dr. Carico into his office and shut the door behind them. Her session with Jason was complete, and his son was now in the pool being watched by his new bodyguard and Maria.

"Can I get you anything, Donna?" Trey asked. "Coffee?"

"No, thank you, Trey. If you're looking for an update on Jason's condition, I'm afraid I don't have any progress to report."

"Please have a seat," Trey said, indicating the chair across his desk. "Actually, this isn't about Jason."

Donna perched on the edge of the chair and crossed her legs. "No?"

"Well, I guess it is in a way, but this is more of a…personal matter."

She smiled broadly, and the excitement dancing in her eyes clanged a warning bell for Trey. Donna was hoping to hear something from him. What? Had he given her the wrong impression?

"What's going on?" she asked.

"I need your advice," he said cautiously.

"On a personal matter?" she asked, her voice light, teasing.

"Yes, and I'd like you to keep this confidential." He leveled his gaze at her to judge her response.

"Of course."

"I've received the background report from my investigator on Kelly."

Her smile faltered. "So this is about Officer Jenkins?"

Trey nodded. "She was abused as a child. The abuser was her mother's boyfriend. Her mom was a real piece of work and never did anything to protect her."

Donna sat up straighter in the chair. "That's very sad, although I'm not surprised."

"You're not?"

"I think it's obvious Kelly is from a different class than you're used to dealing with, Trey."

He remained silent. Donna's snobbery annoyed him, but he remembered similar thoughts filtering through his head when he'd first met Kelly. Before he knew her.

"Abuse doesn't recognize class lines," Trey said.

Donna's lips thinned. "Why are you telling me this?" she asked, her tone no longer light.

"You're a therapist." He shrugged. "I wanted your input on how to talk to Kelly about her past."

"Why in God's name would you want to discuss her past abuse with Officer Jenkins?"

Trey didn't answer. Why indeed? When Donna

phrased it in those blunt words, he wondered why he'd even considered bringing up the subject with Kelly. Because he'd seen the burn mark on her chest?

Because he wanted to know everything about her.

Donna nodded and looked away. "I haven't wanted to say anything, Trey, but this conversation has convinced me that we have a problem."

"A problem? Has something changed with Jason?"

"No, and frankly that concerns me, too."

"You expected him to regain his memory by now?"

"It's true I didn't expect him to become quite so attached to Officer Jenkins, but it's her behavior that has me concerned."

He leaned forward. "Kelly? What's she done?"

Donna crossed her legs. "And she's Kelly now."

"That's her name."

"It appears that *Kelly* has wormed her way into your life in a most disturbing fashion."

Trey stared at Donna. Wormed her way? Kelly hadn't wormed anywhere. She'd fought him at every step.

"It was on your advice that I allowed her to remain," he said. "You told me it was the best thing for Jason."

Donna nodded. "I am aware of that."

"So what's changed?"

"Is she here now?" Donna asked, lowering her voice.

"She's back on duty." Which was too bad. He and Jason had enjoyed a pleasant two days with Kelly while she'd been off. Swimming, tennis, watching television. They'd even played a board game together, and Kelly had worked with Jason on his ABCs.

"I wish you could hear your tone of voice," Donna said.

"What's wrong with my tone?"

"It's full of regret because she's gone back to work."

"I like Kelly," Trey said with a shrug. "So does Jason, obviously."

"I've also noticed that she's watching people very carefully, as if she's plotting something."

Trey tapped a pen on his desk. Although convinced Donna couldn't have been involved in the kidnapping, he thought better of telling her Kelly was assisting the FBI.

"She's a cop and naturally suspicious."

"And just listen to how you defend her. I'm truly sorry to have to say this, Trey, but it's become clear to me you're getting as attached to Officer Jenkins as Jason. I did not expect that from you."

Trey sat back. "I know Kelly is not his mother."

"Do you know she's not your wife?"

Trey knew jealousy when he heard it. He'd dealt with it often enough. And right now Dr. Carico didn't sound at all professional. What was this conversation really about?

He steepled his fingers. "Are you saying you think it's best for Jason that I send Officer Jenkins away?"

"I'm sorry, but, yes, I do. I think it would be better for both of you."

"That's your *professional* opinion?"

She nodded. "It is."

"Thank you, Dr. Carico," Trey said. Time to end this discussion. He needed to think carefully about how to proceed. Carico's warning wasn't anything he hadn't already considered. His relationship with Kelly—whatever it was—could never interfere with Jason's recovery. But the two of them were behaving exactly as the good doctor had recommended, and Jason was doing fine, except for the fact that he still believed Kelly was his mother.

Well, he'd asked for advice from Carico, and he'd gotten it.

It had never occurred to him that the doctor had feelings for him, but she quite obviously wanted to get rid of Kelly for her own reasons. What would Carico think if she knew those mandatory goodnight kisses had become the highlight of his day? That he was so pathetic he thought about Officer Jenkins constantly?

He stood. "I'll certainly take your recommendation under advisement."

Carico remained seated and blinked up at him. "Under advisement?"

"I've thought I should get a second opinion for some time now. This crossroads is the ideal time to consult a new child psychiatrist."

She came to her feet. "But I've been treating Jason since the accident."

"I know that."

Hands fisted at her sides, she said, "I've rearranged my schedule, canceled appointments to make myself available to treat your son."

"And I'm grateful for that," Trey said. "You've been of tremendous help to Jason." *And were damn well compensated for your time.*

"Yet this is how you repay my devotion to you?"

Trey stared at the doctor, stunned. "Let's try to keep this professional, shall we, Doctor?"

She took a deep breath and closed her eyes. After a moment, she lifted her chin and said, "Of course it's every patient's right to obtain a second opinion. I'll send you several recommendations when I get back to my office."

"Thank you," Trey said. "I have a tennis game, so I think you can find your way out."

CHAPTER FIFTEEN

AT THE CONCLUSION of his session with Mac Laughlin, the island pro, Trey shoved his racket into its case. He felt better. He always did after playing three sets of tennis. Much more effective therapy than any session with a shrink.

But his conversation with Dr. Carico still rankled. Festered. What was he going to do about Jason's treatment? About Kelly Jenkins?

What was he going to do with his life?

"That was one hell of a workout," Mac said, slinging a towel around his neck.

"Yeah, good session."

Mac took a long pull on a water bottle and said, "What's gotten into you lately, Trey? You're playing like you've finally decided to join the tour."

"I think I waited a little too late for that," Trey said.

Mac laughed. "Same time tomorrow?"

"Yeah. Listen, Mac, you're from Miami. How did you learn to play tennis?"

"Summer camp in North Carolina." Mac shrugged. "I loved the game and was pretty good at it, so my parents paid for lessons. I eventually joined the tennis team at my high school, where I had a great coach, and ended up going to college on an athletic scholarship."

"So high schools have tennis teams in south Florida?"

"The ones in the affluent areas do. The equipment is expensive, as you know." Mac thought a minute and grinned. "Well, maybe you don't know about that little problem."

"So it would be hard for a kid from an underprivileged background to learn to play? There aren't any free clinics at the inner city parks?"

"Free? In Miami? What planet are you from?"

Trey scrubbed his face with a towel. "I'm beginning to wonder that myself. See you tomorrow."

After a shower, Trey dressed and entered his office. Tennis had been a part of his life as long as he could remember. Maybe because the game was the one thing he'd been good at that his father couldn't control.

Until he'd wanted to join the professional tour. Of course professional sports weren't the Wentworth "way." But that was old news. He had bigger problems now. Like the fact that he missed Kelly as much as his son did. What a tangled mess. But she'd given him an idea, one that excited him. He hadn't been excited about anything in a long time.

He checked his phone. As promised, Carico had texted him three recommendations for a second opinion on Jason's treatment. Trey called his attorney.

"Brian, I have three child therapists I'd like checked out. Can your people handle that?"

"You're finally getting a second opinion?"

"Carico became...too close to the situation."

"Anything I need to know about?"

"Just send her an appropriate severance check with one of your best letters."

"Is she angry?"

"I'm not sure."

"How does Jason feel about a new doctor?"

"As long as he has Kelly, he doesn't care." Trey looked up at a knock on his door. Normally stoic-faced Hans waited at the threshold with an expression that Trey didn't like. What now?

"I've got to go, Brian."

"I'll have results for you as soon as possible."

"Thanks," Trey said and disconnected. "What?" he asked Hans.

"Your father is on the two o'clock ferry."

WHEN THE FERRY pushed away from the dock at six thirty, Kelly opened the limo door and swung out a leg.

"Where are you going?" Hans demanded over the intercom.

The window was up, so she couldn't see him. Hard to surveil him when she couldn't see him.

"I need some fresh air," she replied.

He made a disapproving sound, but didn't say more. She and Trey had compromised on the transportation issue. No bodyguard, but she'd agreed to the limo, mainly so she could keep an eye on Hans. But she'd been wrong about him. Her surveillance revealed the guy was a straight arrow and loyal to Trey.

Kelly walked over to lean on the boat's railing. The rush of salty wind blew her hair everywhere, so she controlled it with a ponytail. Her shift had gone well today. She'd been on time and experienced no problems she couldn't handle. No more hateful remarks from her sergeant, thank goodness.

So, hopefully, her career was back on track.

Looking down, she watched the frothy water stream past. She smiled, reminded of Jason splashing in the pool. What had the little dude done today while she was gone? Most likely he spent as much time as he could in the water, and Trey would have been right there with him. She had to admit Wentworth was a pretty devoted dad. She hadn't known such a thing truly existed outside of sitcoms.

Picturing Trey in his bathing suit, she felt a tug of arousal. Man, did she ever need to get over herself. The minute Jason realized she wasn't his mother, Trey would forget she even existed.

How could she put a stop to the good-night kiss ritual? Did she even want to?

Her stomach rumbled, and she decided it was far safer to wonder what Greta had prepared for dinner. Whatever was on the menu was sure to be yummy—at least everything had been so far. It was great not to have to worry about dinner. She loved her job, but was always too exhausted to make anything healthy when she got home.

Home? What the hell? She pushed away from the railing and gazed toward the rapidly approaching dock on Collins Island. She wasn't on her way home. She was ferrying to Wentworth Villa where she was nothing but a temporary guest.

She'd grown to appreciate having Hans to negotiate Miami's nightmare traffic after a long shift. She loved the fifteen-minute ferry trip twice a day. Boat rides were something a kid living under protective services never even dared to dream about.

Worst of all, she looked forward to seeing Jason and Trey.

But they weren't her family. She didn't have a family.

None of these trappings were her life.

Kelly turned from the water, glared at the sleek black limo and mentally kicked her own ass. She was as big a fool as her mother.

WHEN KELLY ENTERED the front door of Wentworth Villa, Maria stood in a corner of the foyer. She spoke into a cell phone, using her palm to shield her mouth so she couldn't be overheard. Looking up, the housekeeper immediately terminated the call and hurried toward Kelly. Maria's shiner had now faded to purples and browns.

"We have a visitor," she said in a hushed voice.

"Ballard again?" Kelly asked. Had there been a break in the case?

Maria shook her head. "Mr. Wentworth's father. They are waiting for you in the bar."

Alexander Asswipe the Third was here? No wonder Maria appeared rattled. Trey didn't talk much about his father, but what few comments he'd made, including that delightful pet name, told her they didn't get along.

"Are you sure they want to see *me*?"

"Yes." Maria ran her palms down her uniform. Normally the definition of calm, Maria seemed jittery, nervous. No doubt she didn't like Wentworth Senior any more than Trey did. Should be an interesting evening.

"Okay," Kelly said. "Let me lock up my gun first."

"Put on something nice, *chica*," Maria suggested, darting a look in the direction of the bar. "No one is in a good mood."

Kelly hurried up the stairs wondering about the need to change clothes. In the strictest sense, her uniform definitely wasn't "nice," but neither was much else she owned. She'd change, but her best jeans would have to do for Trey's charmer of a dad. Too bad they weren't exactly clean.

Another reason to go home. If she stayed much longer, she'd have to do laundry.

She came to a halt when she entered her room. On top of the bed were all of the clothes she'd brought with her, including her underwear, stacked into tidy piles. A stab of guilt made her flinch. Obviously Maria had already washed her clothing.

Kelly sat on the bed. This was too much.

"Mommy! Mommy!"

Hearing Jason's voice in the hallway, Kelly felt a rush of warmth and stood. He came to her door, peeked inside, but didn't enter. Good boy.

"You're home," he said.

"Yeah, I am." Kneeling before him, she hugged him tight, inhaling the scent of his baby shampoo.

"Grandpa Mean Bull is here," he whispered in her ear.

"Grandpa Mean Bull?" She pulled back to look at the little dude. What was that about?

Looking worried, Jason bit his bottom lip and nodded.

So both of the Wentworth men had pet names for the head of the clan. Despite his bad press, Kelly looked forward to meeting the old shit.

"Yeah, I heard we had a visitor." She stood. "You go on now. I'll be right down."

But Jason hesitated, obviously wanting to say something. Finally he blurted, "Grandpa Mean Bull is hungry."

She laughed and said, "So am I. Now scoot so I can change clothes."

When Jason had disappeared, Kelly reached inside the closet for the gun locker, but quickly withdrew her arm and stared at the top shelf.

Her small safe had been moved at least a foot to the left and turned sideways. She was super careful with her gun and knew exactly how she'd left its locker. Fortunately, she always made sure to never leave the numbers on the combination that would open the lock.

She withdrew the box and decided that someone had spun the digits that set the locking mechanism. What was going on here? Did some bozo think she'd left a weapon inside?

Or had Maria moved the locker when she'd cleaned and accidentally changed the digits?

Kelly secured her weapon and placed the safe inside the bottom drawer in the bureau.

She changed into her clean jeans, frowning at how difficult they were to zip up. She put on a bright blue blouse that she believed enhanced the color of her eyes. In the bathroom, she washed her face, released the ponytail she wore at work and brushed out her hair. She found some lip gloss and applied it to her lips.

She stared into the mirror. This was as good as it was going to get.

But she hardly recognized the woman glaring back. It wasn't just the lip gloss. Good Lord. Her cheekbones weren't as pronounced as usual.

She slammed the brush onto the vanity, furious with herself for caring what she looked like. A far bigger concern was someone in this house had tried to gain access to her service weapon.

WHEN KELLY ENTERED the bar, a tall, slim, gray-headed man in his late seventies turned and pierced her with an appraising look that she suspected was meant to intimidate her. Older than expected, but no question here was Trey's father. Alexander Wentworth had likely once been as handsome as his son.

Trey stood behind the bar. The tense set of his chin and the rigid way he held his body told her he wasn't happy. In fact, she'd never seen him look so miserable.

Their gazes locked and he mouthed, "I'm sorry."

"Mommy's here." Sitting at the bar, his little legs dangling from a tall stool, Jason held up his arms, a signal that he wanted a hug.

"I presume this is the famous Officer Jenkins," Senior said as she gave Jason a quick tight squeeze.

"Yes," Trey said. "Kelly, this is my father, Alexander Wentworth. Dad, this is Kelly Jenkins."

Kelly held out her hand. "Pleased to meet you, sir," she said.

Wentworth grasped her fingers in a tight grip. "Are you really?" he demanded bluntly.

"Dad," Trey said, a warning in his voice.

"Am I really what?" Kelly asked, glancing from Trey to his father.

Senior didn't release his grip. "Are you pleased to meet me?" He said his words as if he knew she was hiding something, but, oh, man, *he* was onto her.

Kelly jerked her hand away. "Why wouldn't I be?"

Still gazing at her intently, Senior said, "She does indeed resemble your ex-wife, Trey."

Kelly shot a glance to Jason. Lower lip stuck out, the child glowered at his grandfather. He looked troubled. Hadn't Trey explained the situation to his father? Didn't Senior realize this conversation had to be confusing for the little dude? Like the boy wasn't mixed-up enough.

Trey handed Kelly a glass of red wine across the bar. "My father has made an unexpected visit to check on Jason."

"And thank God I did before it's too late," Senior said.

"Exactly what does that mean, Father?"

Senior dropped his hand to Jason's shoulder. The child flinched.

"You know what it means, son."

"And I'm telling you you're way off base," Trey said.

"Time will tell."

Kelly took a sip of the wine. Were they speaking in code? The hostility in the room made the hairs on her arm stand up. So much so that she wanted to snatch Jason away from his grandfather. Maybe she wasn't missing anything not having a family.

"Let's conclude this conversation after dinner," Senior said. "My grandson needs food and then bed."

When Senior lifted Jason from the stool, the child gazed at her over his shoulder, blue eyes huge. He extended an arm toward her, obviously wanting rescue. She smiled encouragingly at him as they walked into the dining room.

What else could she do? She wasn't really Jason's mother, but Senior *was* his grandfather, and based on their brief encounter so far, no question good old Grandpa resented her presence. She dared not interfere.

But why didn't Trey? Didn't he realize his son was terrified of the old man?

What galled her most wasn't the way Senior treated her, but how he treated the little dude. He never addressed his grandson directly. He treated Jason more like a possession.

She glared at the old man as he seated himself where Trey usually sat at the head of the table. Senior was nothing but a big bully. Grandfather or not, she wasn't going to let him pick on Jason.

CHAPTER SIXTEEN

TREY PUSHED THE food around on his plate. Nothing wrong with the meal. Even though Greta had had little notice of an extra person for dinner, she'd outdone herself with angel hair pasta covered with savory fresh tomato sauce and parmesan cheese. The bread was fragrant, crusty and delicious.

But he had no appetite.

He just wanted this meal over with so he could put Jason to bed and have it out with his father.

Kelly, of course, attacked her food with her usual enthusiasm. Watching her negotiate a noodle's serpentine progress into her luscious mouth, he lifted his wineglass and smiled. At least there was something to feel good about in a tense, silent meal.

She'd tried to initiate conversation with his father, asking about his flight, where he lived. Senior had shut her down with monosyllabic replies that bordered on rudeness.

"What did you do today, Jason?" Kelly asked when she paused for a sip of wine.

"Went swimming," Jason said, not looking up from his plate.

"Did you have fun?" she probed.

"Uh-huh."

"Did you play Marco Polo?"

"Miss Jenkins," his father interrupted. "We do

not engage children in conversation at the dinner table."

"Oh?" she said, shooting his father a look. "Is that the royal 'we'?"

His father's eyes widened. "What did you say?"

Greta entered the room. His father shook his head and didn't pursue a response when she began refilling his water glass.

"Oh, my God, Greta," Kelly said. "This is the most amazing spaghetti I've ever tasted."

"Thank you, Miss Kelly," Greta said with a nervous glance at his father. She filled Kelly's glass next.

"Thanks," Kelly said.

His father lowered his fork and stared at Kelly. Trey took another sip of wine to hide a smile. His father didn't believe in thanking the help for doing their job. He insisted their salary was thanks enough.

Aware of the attention focused on her, Kelly looked up. "What?" she asked.

Trey was almost sorry when his father shook his head and said nothing.

Kelly shrugged. She tore off a hunk of bread, used it to mop up the sauce remaining in her pasta bowl and devoured the bread with obvious relish. His father followed every step of her process with a disbelieving stare.

When finished, she sat back and took a swallow

of water. "God, that was good. I'm going to get fat as a cow if I stay here much longer."

Regarding her with distaste, his father said, "No dessert, Ms. Jenkins?"

She reached for her wineglass. "What's for dessert?"

"I have no idea," his father said.

"Then how do I know if I want any?"

"I want dessert," Jason piped up in a small voice.

Kelly looked at his plate, which was still half full. "Didn't we talk about how you have to eat your supper before you get something sweet?"

Jase nodded and began shoveling in his pasta.

His father's mouth tightened in that familiar way he had when displeased. Dear old Dad didn't trust Kelly, had accused her of being a gold digger just like Darlene. The old man had agreed not to confront her in front of Jason, but fireworks were definitely coming later.

"Did you play tennis with the island pro today?" Kelly asked.

"I did," Trey replied.

"When are you going to stop fooling around with that game?" Senior asked.

"Never," Trey said. "In fact, I'm about to start fooling around with it in a new way."

"What do you mean?" Kelly asked.

Trey poured more wine into his glass. He hadn't intended to inform his father about his plans, but whatever. He'd find out sooner or later.

"I'm starting a free clinic to teach tennis to kids who want to learn but can't afford lessons or equipment."

Kelly stared at him. "Seriously?"

"You were my inspiration," Trey told her, lifting his glass in a toast.

She paused lifting her own wine for a drink and grinned, which always made him feel good. She smiled so seldom.

"What's this about, Trey?" his father demanded. "A free clinic?"

Trey nodded. "Brian is setting up a foundation to provide rackets and group lessons twice a week over the summer. I've already arranged with the City of Miami to use a public facility when school is out in June."

"That was quick," Kelly said.

"The Wentworth name opens a lot of doors," Senior said. "But it's a ridiculous idea. The hoodlums will destroy the rackets. Or steal them."

"There will likely be some loss," Trey agreed. He had no intention of arguing with his father. Experience had taught him that was a losing game and led to nothing but frustration.

"But it will give a few underprivileged kids something to do over the summer," Kelly said. "Keep them off the streets and out of trouble."

Senior snorted. "Not likely."

"It's a pilot program." Trey shrugged. "We'll see where it goes."

"Surely you won't teach the clinic yourself," Senior said.

"I'm full," Jason said. "Can I go watch television, Daddy?"

"You don't want dessert anymore?" Trey asked.

Jason shook his head with a wary glance at his grandfather.

Trey suspected his son was mainly interested in escaping the tension around this table. Kelly probably thought the same thing because she was no longer smiling.

"Sure, buddy," he said. "Go on."

Jason hopped down from his chair and ran into the media room. Senior frowned at his retreating back but said nothing.

Kelly threw her napkin on the table and stared at Senior. "So tell me about Mean Bull."

"Mean Bull?" Trey asked.

"That's how Jason referred to Grandpa. What's that about?"

"Oh," Trey said. "My father had a small sculpture cast of one of his prize bulls."

"Goliath was a champion," Senior said with his customary pride. He pointed a finger at Trey. "Highest stud fees in the history of Wentworth Farms."

"Jason thought the sculpture was a toy and wanted to play with it," Trey continued. "So Father warned him off by telling him it was a mean bull and would gore him."

"Gore him?" Kelly repeated.

"I meant it as a joke," Senior said.

"But it terrified Jason, and the name Grandpa Mean Bull was born."

"Nothing wrong with a little healthy fear," Senior said.

"How old was he?" Kelly asked.

"Three," Trey said.

Kelly narrowed her eyes on his father. "Man, you are some piece of work, aren't you?"

"I beg your pardon?" Senior said.

"No wonder Jason is so screwed up," Kelly added.

"Now, wait just a minute, missy," Senior thundered. "Who do you think you are speaking to me like that?"

"Lower your voice," Trey said.

"Hey, you don't scare me, Mr. Mean Bully," Kelly said in a quiet but furious tone. "I'm not a frightened child."

"No, you're another hussy trying to take some cash off of my son."

Trey came to his feet. "That's enough, Father."

Kelly also stood, hands curled into fists at her side. "I am so out of here."

Trey blinked at her. Between her blond beauty and the fury flowing off her, she reminded him of an avenging angel.

"And guess what, pal?" she said, glaring at his father. "I don't have to ask permission to leave the table."

HEART POUNDING, KELLY marched out of the dining room. She could hear voices behind her, but didn't look back.

She didn't have to put up with this. The son of a bitch had dared call her a hussy wanting Trey's money. Alexander Asswipe the Third indeed.

She should pack her belongings—at least they were now clean—walk to the ferry dock and catch the next boat. She could take a taxi back to her apartment.

But no. She couldn't leave Jason without saying goodbye. The TV blared as she hurried past the media room, and she hoped it was loud enough that he hadn't heard the angry words. She paused. Should she check on him?

No, she was too upset, and the kid was amazingly perceptive of her moods. She needed to calm down with a swim first. And that could have the added benefit of irritating Senior since he obviously didn't want her in Wentworth Castle.

As she stomped up the staircase, Kelly spotted Maria hurrying down the hall and froze. *What was Maria doing in my room?* She couldn't have been anywhere else.

Maria's hands were empty, but she might have been straightening up. Maybe turning down the bed.

Or was she trying to get inside the gun case again?

Kelly almost called out, but decided not to. She

needed to pay more attention to Maria. Maybe her visit was work related, but maybe not. Maria had already been inside that room at least once today.

Kelly entered her room—which, yeah, was spotlessly neat—and immediately checked the drawer for her gun locker. She glared at the box, convinced it had been moved, but the lock remained engaged. She slid the digits into the opening combination and breathed a sigh of relief that her Glock lay safely inside.

Kelly closed the safe, rearranged the digits into a specific sequence and stuck the box inside a different drawer, memorizing the exact way she placed it. Next time there'd be no question. When she was certain, she'd tell Trey about her suspicions.

But why would Maria want her service weapon?

As she changed into her bathing suit, her thoughts returned to Trey's father. She wouldn't put it past the guy to perform a nightly inspection of the villa to ensure everything was shipshape. Maybe Maria had been tidying up for that.

After a workout where she sprinted more than swam easy laps, Kelly clung to the edge of the pool and rested her head on her arms, breathing hard.

Now that her initial burst of outrage was over, she could think about what had happened at dinner with Senior. She was partly to blame. She'd baited Senior because of how he treated Jason.

But what was the deal with the old man? It was obvious he hadn't liked her even before he met her. What had Trey told him? Was it simply because she resembled the hated ex?

Had Trey showed him the background check? Did Senior know about her mother? No, Trey wouldn't do that. Or would he?

Whatever. Senior obviously didn't think she belonged in his son's home.

And of course the old goat was right about that. She wasn't Jason's mother.

Still holding on to the edge of the pool, she began kicking her legs. She still had some angst to burn off.

How long was Senior staying? They couldn't occupy the same room without spontaneous combustion.

At least Trey had defended her. That was something, right? She suddenly wanted to know what was said after she'd left the room. Maybe they hadn't talked about her at all. Maybe they'd discussed his plans for the free tennis clinic. She loved his idea, if for no other reason than Senior hated it.

The thought that she had been the inspiration for anything proposed by Trey Wentworth sent a rush of warmth into her belly.

Man, was she in trouble. She had to go—before

she got any more entangled with this screwed-up family.

Funny how now she wasn't so eager to leave. The good life must be addictive.

"Hey."

She dropped her feet to the bottom of the pool and looked up at Trey. "Hey, yourself."

"Feel better?"

"Yeah, but I don't like your father."

Trey squatted so they were almost eye level. "Not many people do."

She laughed at his matter-of-fact tone, her mood definitely improved.

"I'm sorry for what he said," Trey said. "He knows you've refused any money."

"Thanks. I love your plans for the tennis clinic."

"I'm glad." Trey rose and grabbed her robe from a lounge.

"Will you come with me to put Jason down?"

Kelly nodded. Maybe she should refuse, but he'd asked nicely.

Keenly aware of Trey watching her every move, she exited the pool via the steps. He held out the robe. When she stepped into it, Trey wrapped his arms around her and pulled her against him.

"You'll get soaked," she said, more breathless than she should be.

"I don't care." He nuzzled her neck, his breath warm against her cool skin.

Kelly closed her eyes. What was she doing? What was *he* doing? This was crazy.

"Where's your father?" she asked.

"In bed." Trey's voice rumbled close to her ear. "He retires early."

"He wakes up at four a.m. every day. One reason he was so pissy tonight was because his dinner was late."

"Because of me."

"Because of Jason."

She closed her eyes. "Did you show your father my background report?"

Trey turned her to face him. "No."

She searched his eyes, wanting to believe him. As far as she knew, Trey had never lied to her.

"Did you think I would?" he asked, his fingers caressing her upper arms.

She couldn't look away from the intensity of his gaze. "I wasn't sure."

"There are private matters in that report," he said.

She exhaled. "Yes."

He lifted his hand, lowered the front of her bathing suit and touched the brand Roy had left with his lit cigarette the night he'd tried to rape her. She sucked in a harsh breath at the memory. And at the touch of Trey's hand.

"Things I'd like you to tell me about," he said softly. He raised his gaze to hers. "Someday."

She swallowed hard. *I don't talk about it. Not ever. With anyone.*

But she surprised herself by saying, "Maybe someday."

CHAPTER SEVENTEEN

THE NEXT MORNING, after a run and a shower, Kelly dressed in her uniform and holstered her weapon. What would she encounter downstairs?

Jason usually waited for her somewhere. She hoped she didn't see Trey today. Or did she want to see him? Maybe share a delightful good-morning kiss?

She smoothed a finger over her lower lip, remembering last night in Jason's room. Their kiss had been soft and sweet. Trey had treated her as if she were precious, something she definitely was not used to. She was no shrinking violet.

So why did his tenderness make her go all tingly and gooey inside? Why had last night been different?

The only thing that had changed was the presence of Grandpa Mean Bull in the house. She hoped he was leaving today. If he didn't, then she'd have to go.

She'd intended to make that clear to Trey last night, but she'd been so breathless after their kiss all she could do was stumble into her room, wishing he would come with her.

What would she have done if he had?

She sucked in a huge gulp of air at the image of him naked and rolling around in bed with her.

Shaking her head, she hurried down the stairs. The mean streets of Miami awaited her patrol. She didn't have time to moon over billionaires or their hateful fathers.

Kelly stepped into the dining room—where she came to an abrupt stop.

Senior sat at the head of the table, eyeglasses perched on the end of his pointy nose, reading the *Wall Street Journal*. Great. Trey had said he was an early riser. Jason wasn't in sight, no doubt hiding from Grandpa Mean Bull.

She'd have to walk by him if she wanted anything to eat.

He took a sip of coffee and gave her a quick nod. "Officer Jenkins."

"Mr. Wentworth," Kelly said, equally formal. Maybe she could just feed her face and go to work.

She stepped past him and heaped eggs and bacon onto her plate. Remembering the tight fit of her jeans last night, she ignored the frosted pastries, but poured herself a mug of coffee. When she took a seat, Senior had returned his focus to reading.

A copy of several other newspapers lay scattered across the table. Kelly slid the front page of the *Miami Herald* toward her, her attention captured by another headline about corruption in the Miami-Dade County Police Department. Not again. In disbelief, she read the story. This was *her* department.

"Just so you know," Senior said, breaking her concentration, "I don't approve of this charade you and my grandson are carrying on. I intend to put a stop to it."

She so didn't want to have this conversation. Maybe she could just ignore him.

"How long are you going to pretend you are Jason's dead mother? It's ridiculous."

She took a deep breath and said, "You need to have this discussion with your son."

"I already have. Now I'm having it with you."

And apparently there was no way out of it. Kelly sat back in her chair. She should just walk away. She could ask Hans to drive through any fast-food place for breakfast. If Trey hadn't set his old man to rights, how could she?

"This charade, as you call it, wasn't my idea."

"But you went along with it. Why?"

"Jason is a sweet kid, but he's confused right now."

"Jason is a four-year-old child. Four-year-olds are always confused."

She glared at Senior. "You don't like kids much, do you?"

"I love my grandchild," Senior said, a defensive edge to his voice.

Maybe Trey had accused him of the same thing.

"You could sure fool me," Kelly said. "Listen, Jason's shrink asked me to hang around until she gets his head screwed on straight. That's the only reason I'm here."

"Interesting," Senior said.

"Surely Trey told you that."

"Oh, he told me. He also dismissed Dr. Carico yesterday."

"He what?"

"Fired her."

Kelly blinked. Trey had fired Carico? Why? Because Jason hadn't regained his memory? Why hadn't Trey informed her?

"I didn't know," she said.

Senior laughed softly. "I'm certain there is quite a lot about my son that you don't know."

Senior's tone was so fricking insulting, Kelly tamped down an urge to toss her hot coffee at him. She took a quick swallow and burned her tongue.

"Will he find Jason another doctor?" she asked.

"We're interviewing them today."

She nodded. So the old goat wasn't leaving. She could still give Trey that ultimatum—*He goes or I go*. Despite Senior's arrogant behavior, something told her she'd be the one staying.

But only as long as Jason wanted her here.

God, what a sticky mess. The poor little dude might be a rich prince, but he was totally screwed by his dysfunctional family. And so was she.

Because she refused to be responsible for a further breach between Trey and his obnoxious father. She'd just have to stay out of the old man's way.

"I think," Senior said, "that the reason you're here isn't so much to help my grandson, but rather you realized you've fallen into a great opportunity."

"Opportunity for what? To be dissed by a hateful rich old man?"

Senior's jaw tightened. "You've got quite a mouth, don't you?"

Kelly shrugged. "Your son thinks so, too."

"And my son is a great 'catch,' isn't he?" the old man asked, making quote signs in the air around the word. "The world's most eligible bachelor and all that media nonsense?"

"You can't be serious."

"You may resemble his dead wife, but you are not anything like her."

Kelly looked down at her plate. She'd been starved fifteen minutes ago. Now she felt nauseated. She pushed back her chair and came to her feet.

"Well, good luck with the interviews," she said, striving for disinterested. "I don't want to keep Hans waiting."

"That is his job."

Shaking her head, she moved toward the door.

"Let me give you a piece of advice, Officer Jenkins."

She kept walking. She didn't want to hear anything more that this bitter old man had to say.

"Don't fall in love with my son."

Kelly closed her eyes, wishing she could block out the condescending voice.

"I'll admit he appears to have an affinity for

women with a little dirt under their fingernails, but you will never get your hooks in him."

LATE THAT AFTERNOON, Trey rose from his desk and stretched his arms high overhead. After an early morning game with Mac, he'd spent most of the day on the phone either talking to child psychiatrists or lining up coaches for his tennis camp. God, it felt good to actually have a project again. He missed that feeling of accomplishment.

It was time to revisit the agreement he'd made with his father and take an active role in Wentworth Industries. Although he hadn't attended a board meeting in years, he followed the various companies from a distance, and it was apparent Senior was slipping.

Trey thought back to the day at the stud farm when he and his father had argued so violently and then struck their deal. He'd agreed to bow out of Wentworth Industries to protect his mother, so Senior would leave her alone in the private sanitarium. His visits agitated her to the point of hysteria. She didn't recognize anyone for months afterward.

As long as Trey generated positive press as the PR face of the companies, Senior left his fragile wife alone. Trey had told himself he didn't mind. He couldn't stomach working with his father anyway.

One reason he'd holed up in his office all day was to avoid the man. That wouldn't be possible when he became more involved with WI.

His pleasant mood trashed, Trey walked to the window. Changes needed to be made. He wanted to move the companies in a different direction. He wanted the Wentworth name to stand for something more than just pure profit. He wanted to do some actual good in the world.

At least he'd had some success today. The pros he'd contacted had jumped at the opportunity to participate in the project, wanting the positive publicity certain to be generated by teaching kids from the inner city.

Trey shook his head. Less than twenty-four hours with his father, and he was becoming as cynical as the old man. No question some of the pros he'd spoken to had gotten on board because they liked the idea of helping disadvantaged children.

On another front, one Dr. Edward Barth, highly recommended by Carico and several other physicians, had agreed to come to the island and meet with Jason tomorrow. What would Dr. Barth think about Jason's condition? Would he recommend that Kelly leave, as Carico had?

Jason liked Carico. Had he missed his session with her?

Trey had eaten lunch with his son by the pool— mainly because he knew his father would refuse to join them there. Jason had spent most of the day with Maria and the new bodyguard. Jase had seemed happy, accepting of the fact that his "mother" had to work every day.

But she would be home soon. Trey looked in the direction of the ferry landing, noting the pleasure generated at the thought of Kelly's return. He'd tried to put on the brakes on his attachment to her, but Kelly Jenkins was like a breath of fresh air in his life. She'd shaken him out of a lethargy he hadn't even known he'd been mired in.

Trey turned when the door burst open without a knock. The only person with the gall to do that was his father.

"We have guests," Senior announced. "You might want to change."

"Guests?"

"I invited the Gallaghers for dinner. They were on the last ferry."

"You arranged a dinner party without bothering to inform me?"

"The Gallaghers are some of my oldest friends," Senior said. "I was certain you'd realize I would reach out to them during this visit. I handled everything with your cook."

Trey stared at his father. "This is *my* home."

"I am well aware of that."

"What if I had plans for the evening?"

"I thought you were staying in to be with Jason."

Trey shook his head. His father deliberately kept him in the dark about his plans so he couldn't interfere until too late. This was the way it always went.

He heard voices at the front door. The Gallaghers weren't bad people, just as boring as a long baseline rally with no net shots. Even worse was their daughter, a gorgeous but vapid redhead he'd once escorted to a benefit at his father's request. Their first and last date. God, he hoped she wouldn't accompany her parents.

Forget a pleasant evening with Kelly. Damn.

Kelly.

What would she think when she returned home and found the Gallaghers? They'd be soused beyond logic by dinnertime, apt to say anything. Outrage ignited in his gut as he understood this dinner party was a calculated move by his father to keep Kelly on the outside. To put her in her place.

"When are you leaving?" Trey demanded.

Senior raised his eyebrows. "I haven't decided."

"Tomorrow," Trey said. "You're leaving tomorrow."

CHAPTER EIGHTEEN

KELLY WAVED GOODBYE to Hans and trudged up the marble stairs of Wentworth Villa, dreading the thought of running into Wentworth Senior. She'd already had one hell of a day—including one particularly nasty domestic call—and was too drained to fend off the old man's energy suck. Plus, the entire precinct remained abuzz over the allegations of fraud in their department. It was all anyone could talk about, even brass, and she was sick of the whole subject.

She just wanted some downtime. Maybe she could read to Jason after dinner and get lost in a silly story.

Over the gentle splash of the fountain in the loggia, she detected voices drifting from the direction of the dining room. She inhaled a delicious aroma that smelled a lot like sirloin and moved toward it. She could eat a good steak.

She slowed her steps as she got closer, hearing the clink of silverware on plates, boisterous laughter. She could make out two distinct women and two men that weren't Trey. One was likely Senior, but who were the others? Trey hadn't held dinner for her tonight, no doubt because he had guests.

She paused, not wanting to make her presence known. Deciding to go into the kitchen and fix herself something to take up to her room, she turned and almost bumped into Maria.

"There you are, Miss Kelly," Maria said. "Thank goodness."

"What's going on?" Kelly asked.

"Mr. Wentworth's father invited friends for dinner. You should go on in."

"No," Kelly said, registering how jittery Maria appeared. Again. Her hands actually trembled as she smoothed her skirt.

"I don't want to interrupt the party. I'll just fix myself a plate and go to my room."

Maria frowned. "But *Jasonito* is refusing to eat until you do."

Kelly closed her eyes. Just when she thought she could escape more drama. "I'll bet Senior loved that."

Maria nodded. "I feared he would strike the child, but they placed him in his booster chair and went on with the meal."

Trey had allowed that? Although ignoring the kid was probably the best thing to do. Jason truly did need a mother to teach him how to behave. Kidnapping or not, he couldn't continue to be treated like a little prince.

"Let me change out of my uniform first." *Get rid of my weapon.*

"No, Miss Kelly." Maria shook her head. "The longer it goes on, the more upset *Jasonito* becomes."

Kelly looked toward the door. "I really don't want to go in there."

"Please," Maria said. "For *Jasonito*?"

"Do these people know about Jason's amnesia?" Maria shrugged. "I don't know."

"Great." Kelly repositioned the heavy gun belt on her hips and walked into the dining room. This could be awkward.

"Ah, here is Officer Jenkins now," Senior proclaimed in a booming voice.

"Mommy!" Jason raised his arms toward her.

She gave Jason a hug and took the open seat next to him.

"Kelly," Trey began, "I'd like you to meet Carol and Jack Gallagher, and their daughter, Courtney."

Kelly forced a smile and nodded at the Gallaghers, all three of them, including a stunningly gorgeous woman of about her age with thick, shining red hair.

"Pleased to meet you," Kelly said.

"And this of course is Kelly Jenkins," Trey continued.

"Jason's savior, I understand," Jack said.

"She's my mommy," Jason stated.

Kelly caught Jason's eye and placed a finger over her lips to quiet him. He giggled and began to eat the food on his plate.

Greta bustled into the room and served Kelly while Courtney narrowed her eyes on Jason. Was this one of Trey's girlfriends? According to Patrice, the number of old flames was staggering.

"The Gallaghers are some of our oldest friends," Senior said.

"And my father invited them to dinner," Trey said. "He wanted to catch up."

Kelly met Trey's gaze. So he hadn't extended the invitation? Maybe he hadn't even known about it.

"It had to be tonight," he continued, "since Father is leaving tomorrow."

The tightness in Kelly's gut released a little.

"Tomorrow? Oh, no," Carol Gallagher wailed. "Can't you stay a few more days, Alex?"

Suppressing a smile, Kelly cut into the grilled steak Greta had placed on her plate. Medium rare. Perfect, just like the fact Senior was leaving.

"I was hoping for a round of golf on this fabled course," Jack said. "I need revenge."

"Better not, Daddy," Courtney drawled. "You know Mr. Wentworth always beats you."

"What do you say we take it up to a thousand dollars a hole?" Jack asked.

Senior shrugged and took a swallow of an amber liquid in a crystal glass.

"How long have you been a cop?" Courtney asked just as Kelly had started to chew.

Kelly swallowed and took a sip of wine. "I'm a rookie."

"What department?" Jack asked.

"Miami-Dade County."

"Oh, my," Carol said, eyes wide. "Weren't they in the paper today, Jack?"

"Yes," Courtney said. "Something about secret payoffs?"

Jack nodded at his wife and daughter. "That was a disturbing report."

"Nothing but allegations at this point," Trey said. "Don't believe everything you read."

Courtney's huge green eyes swept Kelly's uniform. Wearing a superior smirk, she lowered her gaze, and Kelly suspected she was searching for her service weapon. Courtney wore a lovely emerald silk blouse that matched her eyes, and Kelly again wished she'd changed.

"Have you ever seen a cop take a bribe?" Courtney asked.

"Absolutely not," Kelly stated. "Every officer I know is honest."

"Still," Carol said, "where there's smoke, there's usually fire."

"How about you?" Courtney asked with a laugh. "Have you ever taken a bribe?"

Kelly put down her fork. "Did you really ask me that?"

"Just making conversation," Courtney said, looking away.

"Why don't we let Kelly eat?" Trey said.

"Well, yes," Carol said. "The poor thing had to work all day. She must be exhausted."

Kelly took a sip of wine. Too bad the "poor

thing" had just lost her appetite again. She doubted either of these women had ever worked a day in their lives. And Jack had probably inherited his fortune. She didn't know that, of course, but from the looks of all three of them, they had all the cash they wanted.

Pushing away useless resentment, she glanced at Jason to check on his progress. He grinned at her, mouth full. She smiled back and indicated he should chew with his mouth closed.

"Eat your dinner, Jason," Senior barked.

Jason looked at his plate and put down his fork.

Silence fell over the table for several long minutes.

Jack cleared his throat. "Anything exciting happen at work today, Kelly?"

"Well, let's see," Kelly said, deliberately making her tone as light as his had been. "I arrested a man."

Carol leaned forward. "What did he do?"

"Punched his wife in the face. Broke her nose."

Carol gasped, and Kelly regretted her inexplicable need to shock these people out of their white bread lives.

"He hit her?" Jason asked in a thrilled voice. "In the face?"

Oops. How could she have forgotten about Jason? Kelly shot a glance at a stunned Trey. Well, at least she hadn't mentioned all the blood.

"Yep," Kelly told Jason. "And that's illegal."

"What's illegal mean?" he asked.

"Wrong," Kelly explained. "The man did something wrong, so he's going to jail."

"Jail?" Jason's eyes widened. He knew what jail was. "For how long?"

"That's up to a judge."

"When you do something wrong, son, you're punished," Trey said.

Jason screwed up his face as he thought about that, then nodded and began eating again.

Kelly worked on her own food. Did Jason even know what punishment was?

"Are you planning to attend the Parkinson's benefit at Vizcaya next month?" Courtney asked Trey.

"No," Trey said.

"You should fly back down," Carol said to Senior. "That's always such a fun event. They're bringing in an acrobat troupe this year."

"Fabulous," Jack continued. "And we're taking the *Bertram* to Cat Cay for a week afterward. Why don't you and Trey join us for a few days at least?"

"Please do," Courtney said. "Jason would adore the big boat."

"I doubt if I can find the time," Senior said with a frown. "But Trey should go."

"Sorry," Trey said. "I've got a lot going on right now."

Kelly tuned out the voices as the Gallaghers tried to convince the Wentworths to join them on their upcoming cruise to the Bahamas. She forced herself to eat, but the food lodged in her belly.

When dinner was finally, blessedly at an end, Kelly pushed back from the table with everyone else and rose.

"Let's move out to the patio for after-dinner drinks," Senior suggested.

Kelly suspected the location was chosen so she couldn't enjoy her nightly swim.

"Please excuse me," she said. "I have to get up early."

"Oh, that's too bad," Courtney said in a saccharine-sweet voice.

She felt eyes on her back as she marched toward her room. She squared her shoulders and lifted her chin high.

Sixty-foot yachts, fancy-schmancy parties at the most beautiful house in Miami, thousand-dollar-a-hole golf games. If she needed more proof that she didn't belong on Collins Island, the evidence had just been deliberately flung in her face.

There'd be no good-night kiss tonight. Trey could tell his kid whatever he wanted.

This charade had gone on long enough.

THE NEXT EVENING, nursing a glass of aged whiskey, listening for Kelly's return, Trey waited in the bar. He checked the time again. After midnight. Where the hell was she?

He hadn't seen her since dinner last night. The

meal had been brutal, deliberately choreographed by his pretentious father to demonstrate what he considered the difference between her and his friends, and she'd clearly been aware of what he was up to. Trey took a healthy swallow of whiskey.

At least the son of a bitch had gone back to New York.

He'd put his son to bed alone, explaining that his mommy didn't feel good. Jason had fussed only a little. The child had always sensed the tension when Senior was around.

Trey had expected Kelly to emerge for her nightly swim, but she'd remained in her room. He'd wanted to knock on her door, but instinct told him to leave her alone. So, reluctantly, he had, fully intending to speak with her first thing this morning.

But according to Hans, she'd caught the 6:00 a.m. ferry. He'd called her numerous times, but she hadn't picked up and hadn't answered his messages. She'd sent a text at 4:00 p.m.: I'll be late. Don't wait for me.

But *this* late? And why hadn't she returned his calls?

Had she been injured? He couldn't even imagine Jason's reaction if Kelly were killed or hurt on her dangerous job. His fragile son couldn't handle more loss. She'd made an arrest yesterday of a man who had punched out his wife, for God's sake.

Her department had made a media-worthy arrest today in a series of robberies at local electronics stores. He'd searched for her in the footage from the scene, but didn't see her. According to the live report, shots had been fired during the confrontation, but nothing about an officer down.

If she were involved with that case, maybe she'd been bogged down with paperwork.

Or maybe she was with a lover. She wasn't married, but maybe the background report hadn't picked up a casual boyfriend. A boyfriend who might be jealous of time spent with him. Or maybe she'd hooked up with someone new tonight. He had no hold on her.

Jason, already agitated by his session with a new doctor, had cried himself to sleep tonight. He hadn't wanted to go to bed a second night without seeing his mommy.

Damn her. Yeah, she had a right to be angry because of his father's arrogant behavior, but Jason was the one paying the price.

At the sound of quick steps across the marble foyer, Trey closed his eyes, relief flooding him. She was back. She'd never summoned Hans for transportation, but she'd made it home.

By the time he got to the foyer, she was halfway up the staircase, moving fast. She wore tight black jeans, a bright red blouse and carried a duffel bag, likely containing her uniform and gun belt.

So she'd changed. Where had she done that? And why?

Trey followed her up the steps. He intended to

talk to her before she disappeared inside her room. There was a lot left unsaid between them, and he intended to get it out there right now.

CHAPTER NINETEEN

KELLY EASED OPEN the door to Jason's bedroom and peeked inside. Focusing through the dark on the little dude's bed, she saw Jason breathing regularly, and the knot in her belly eased.

Of course the kid was fine. He was surrounded by an army. What had she been so worried about?

She closed the door, turned and bumped into the solid chest of Trey Wentworth, the collision knocking her off balance. He grabbed her upper arms so she wouldn't tumble.

"Trey," she blurted. She glared at him, her heart banging like a drum.

"Keep your voice down," he said. He picked up her duffel and pulled her down the hallway, away from Jason's room. Toward his.

"You'll wake up Jase."

Why wasn't Trey in bed? She'd deliberately stayed out late enough to make sure he'd be asleep. She blinked at his five o'clock shadow. God, but that dark stubble made him even hotter. And a little dangerous. She swallowed. His shirt was open, and she could see a dusting of dark hair on his chest. With a jolt she realized he wore a bathing suit, the type competitive swimmers wore that left nothing to the imagination. She swallowed hard.

At Moe's and Joe's tonight, she'd tried to convince herself and her squad that everyone exaggerated Trey's sultry good looks. Trice and Lana had laughed at her lame attempts to bring him down to ungod-like status.

Trey folded his arms. "Where have you been?"

Well, my goodness. The billionaire sounded unhappy. Too damn bad. She was a big girl. She could do what she wanted, and she'd definitely wanted to avoid him and his obnoxious father tonight.

"My squad was celebrating," Kelly explained. "We took down some bad guys today."

"You didn't call Hans. How did you get here from the ferry landing?"

"One of the guards brought me in his golf cart." She shrugged. "Professional courtesy, I guess."

His lips tightened. "Jason missed you at bedtime."

"I'm sorry about that." She raised her gaze to his. "Did *you* miss me?"

A flash of something sharpened the intensity of his gaze. Some emotion she didn't want to think about. She looked away. Why had she asked that?

"You've been drinking," he said.

"It was a celebration," she said, meeting his gaze again. She'd had only one drink and didn't need to explain herself. "How many have you had tonight?"

He raked a hand through his thick dark hair. Kelly followed the movement with interest. She'd like to run her fingers through that glorious mess of hair. It looked soft, unlike the stubble on his chin.

"God, listen to me," he said, sounding disgusted. "I sound like your father."

She giggled at the thought. "My father?"

He stepped closer. "What's so funny?"

"I never knew my father."

"Lucky you," he said softly.

"Maybe." Unsure exactly what they were talking about, she allowed her gaze to travel the length of his body to that thin strip of nylon that passed for a bathing suit.

Trey stood so close she could detect the spicy scent of his now familiar cologne, one she'd forever associate with him. She bit her bottom lip. What would his skin taste like if she leaned forward and licked his bare chest?

She touched a button on his open shirt. "Why are you almost naked?"

"I waited for you."

"In your bathing suit?"

"I thought I'd join you in the pool tonight."

"Oh," she murmured, liking the idea of swimming with Trey, both of them all slippery and wet. She placed her palm over his heart and felt his heat. "Too late."

"Yes," Trey said, his voice husky. "It is."

And then his mouth was on hers, taking what he wanted. All night long, while telling her friends how much she needed to get away from this man, all she could think about was this: his lips plundering hers and her willingly giving him everything she had without Jason watching.

Trey pulled away. She opened her eyes and found him staring at her. They were both breathing hard, as if they'd just sprinted fifty meters, but that was no reason to stop kissing her. She slid her hands up his chest, and he grabbed them, his dark eyes intent on hers. She ignored his attempt to stop her—it was half-hearted, anyway—locked her hands around his neck and stepped into his body, finding the proof that he wanted her as much as she wanted him.

A shiver of something delicious ran up her backbone when Trey placed his hands on her buttocks and pushed her groin into his. Finally. No more frustrating kisses in front of a little boy.

Suddenly in a hurry, Trey half carried and dragged her into his bedroom, but she resisted and reached for her duffel. She couldn't leave her service weapon in the hall, which meant she knew exactly what she was doing. She was doing what she wanted to do, what she'd fantasized about for days. Ever since that first bogus good-night kiss.

Trey made an impatient noise and grabbed the duffel. Holding her with one hand and the bag in the other, he moved into his bedroom, kicked the door shut and tossed the duffel into a walk-in closet larger than her bedroom.

She only had a second to absorb the fact that she was in Trey's bedroom, that the bed was turned down and that the room was super neat—but of course Maria would keep it that way—before he was back to kissing her and unbuttoning her blouse at the same time. A delicious tug in her belly made her long to feel her bare flesh pressed against his. She stepped away, unzipped her jeans and wiggled out of them.

Wearing only her bra and panties, she faced him, for the first time unafraid that a man would see the brand left on her by Roy. Trey had already seen her scar of shame.

He released her bra, and she sucked in a deep breath, the air cool on her skin. He cupped her right breast with a warm and gentle palm. She closed her eyes to savor the sensation as he ran a finger around her nipple, urging it to a peak.

"You're so beautiful," he said softly.

Kelly opened her eyes. She *felt* beautiful right now. Trey made her feel like a princess, a strange sensation for her. He stared at her with open admiration, the way every woman wanted a man to look at her.

She reached up and slid the shirt off his shoulders, skimming both hands down his arms as the material fell away. His skin was smooth and warm, the muscles hard from years of tennis.

"Kelly—"

"Don't talk," she whispered, interlocking her fingers with his and stepping backward until her calves bumped into his bed. She didn't want to talk. She didn't want to think. She just wanted to feel. She'd chicken out with too much conversation.

She was going to do this, and nothing was going to stop her.

She lay down on the bed—God, the sheets were so smooth they had to be silk—and extended her arms overhead glorying in the sensation. She probably looked wanton, like some hooker from the streets, but didn't care.

Trey placed a knee on the bed, looked down at her, his expression impossible to read. But she didn't know this man. How was she supposed to understand what he was thinking? Maybe he wanted to tell her something, something she didn't want to hear. Not right now, anyway.

She lowered her right arm and used her index finger to circle her nipple, her gaze locked on his.

"No talking," she said in a stranger's breathless voice.

His mouth lifted into a crooked smile. "Whatever you say, Officer."

LOOKING DOWN AT Kelly stretched out like a goddess on his bed, Trey was hard to the point of pain. Maybe this was a mistake, but there'd be no turning back now, no matter what the consequences.

He removed his bathing suit in one quick movement, joined her on the bed and smoothed off her panties. She rolled toward him with a soft moan, pressing her perfect body against his, reaching for his hardness, her touch making him crazy with need.

He slid his hand between her thighs and found her wet and ready for him. Responsive to his seeking fingers.

"I want to feel you inside me," she whispered.

He wanted to ask her what the hurry was, but she didn't want dialogue. And neither did he anymore. He understood her urgency, was glad for it.

He wanted her, wanted her now.

He'd fantasized about making slow, sweet love to Kelly, but that would have to wait for another time. He hoped there'd be another time.

He found a condom in the nightstand, sheathed himself and entered her, watching her face as she closed her eyes in what he knew was pleasure. Bliss was all over her face.

For him, though, this act of love had become more than satisfying a desire for sexual release. His need for her had become something elemental, the feel of being inside her, part of her. The mounting pressure was something essential to his being, his happiness.

She matched his rhythm, making sexy sounds of encouragement that drove all thought out of his mind until he emptied himself into this one very special woman, Officer Kelly Jenkins.

KELLY CAME ALERT with a start, feeling luxuriously soft sheets beneath her. She was stark naked.

She looked for the digital clock on the bedside table and instead found the equally naked body of Trey Wentworth stretched out in the bed beside her. Sound asleep.

Before she could react to this unbelievable development, the door burst open. Wearing his pj's, Jason ran across the room and leaped into the bed. She yanked sheets over her body.

When the little dude came up for air and spotted her, he looked as surprised as she felt to find her in his father's bed.

"Mommy," he squealed in a too loud voice, and snuggled up next to her.

"What?" Trey bolted up in bed, his gorgeous hair mussed out of its normal perfection. "What's going on?"

Maria appeared hesitantly in the doorway, and Trey covered himself.

"I'm sorry, sir, but—" The wide-eyed, open-mouthed shock on the housekeeper's face made Kelly shut her eyes. Unwanted, the memories came flooding back. That couldn't have been her. But, yes, it was, because she'd never forget the exquisite pleasure of her body entwined with Trey's while they rolled around in this bed last night.

Maria shifted her gaze from Kelly back to her boss and finally found her voice again. "I'm sorry, sir. He couldn't find his mother and thought you would know where—" Maria swallowed. "Where she was."

"I found her," Jason piped up in his little boy voice, placing his warm hands on her cheeks. "She was with Daddy."

The expression on Trey's face made Kelly want to laugh. Was that what she looked like? So he was experiencing the same confused panic as her. Jason was the only one of them who appeared to be delighted by last night's sleeping arrangements.

"That will be all, Maria. Thank you." Trey uttered these words with so much formal dignity—considering the circumstances—that a laugh erupted from Kelly.

Trey shot her a look.

Maria fled into the hallway.

"What's so funny, Mommy?"

"Never mind, buddy," Trey said. He met Kelly's gaze and a slow smile curved his mouth.

Kelly took a deep breath. How would this new state of affairs affect the little dude? Would it make things better or worse? Well, the deed was done and there was no going back now. If Trey could act dignified, so could she. And she needed to get moving. She was on duty today.

"What time is it?" she asked. Faint light streamed in around the window, but she couldn't tell how high the sun was. God, her gut was tied into a thousand tight little knots. What had she done?

Trey scratched his head, appearing befuddled. "I don't know."

"It's time for breakfast," Jason said. "I'm hungry."

"I need to go to work," Kelly told Trey.

"I know," Trey said. "How do you feel?"

She narrowed her eyes at him. What was he asking? *How was I? Was it good for you?*

"Other than the fact that I don't have on any clothes under these sheets, I'm fine." She motioned with her eyes toward Jason.

Trey swept a hand through his tousled hair, obviously plotting a way out of this sticky situation. She bit her lip, watching him think.

She'd had sex with Trey Wentworth last night. Unbelievable, but definitely true.

Maybe it was because they'd been intimate, or maybe because no one looked their best in the early morning, but for the first time Trey Wentworth appeared vulnerable.

Well, well. She'd finally succeeded in demoting him from that godlike status Patrice had teased her about.

And then a horrible thought crashed into her brain, making her want to pull the covers over her face. Senior was an early riser. What if Mean Bully heard the commotion and came to investigate? She raised her chin. Well, the hell with him. She had nothing to be ashamed of.

"Do you think your father is up yet?" Kelly asked.

"He's gone."

"Gone?"

"I sent him packing back to New York."

"Did you now?" A wave of pleasure washed through her, making the knots in her belly resolve. Trey had said he was leaving, but she hadn't truly believed it.

Trey wrapped the bedspread around his lower half and scooped up Jason. He looked sexy with his kid perched on one hip. His beard was even longer this morning and that added to his allure.

"Go take a shower," he said, striding toward the door with his giggling son. "I'll take care of Jason."

"Wait," she said, a new kind of worry creeping into her thoughts.

Trey turned back.

"Where's my duffel? My service weapon is in it."

"In the closet," he said, motioning with his chin. "It's safe. Jason can't reach the handle."

Kelly blew out a breath. "Okay. Good."

Trey's gaze pierced hers. "We need to talk."

"Yeah," she agreed. "We do."

"When you get home tonight?"

"This isn't my home, Trey," she said softly. *And I need to remember that.*

His face tightened. "When is your next day off?"

"Tomorrow."

He nodded. "Good."

When father and son had disappeared, Kelly gathered the deliciously sensual sheet around her body and tucked an edge to hold it in place. Man, she'd love to sleep on this material every night. She hurried to the walk-in closet to retrieve her duffel and gaped at the rows and rows of shirts and jackets and slacks and belts all suspended from some sort of machine that moved so their owner didn't have to reach. Everything was perfectly arranged, neat and tidy, photo op ready.

Well, yeah. Hadn't Patrice told her this closet had once been featured in some architectural monthly magazine?

Her uniform would be a wrinkled mess inside the duffel. She'd been in too big a hurry to get Trey naked to bother to hang it up.

She hefted the bag over her shoulder. She'd had her fun. A nice little break from reality. But Jason might never regain his memory. Trey needed to face that fact, and so did she. She was sorry for the little dude, but he wasn't her problem.

He wasn't her son.

A nasty pang shot through her gut at that reminder. She needed to get out of fantasyville before her life spiraled so completely out of control that she'd never get back on track.

But how could she walk away from Jason? The little boy still needed her.

Or maybe she needed Jason. Or was it she didn't want to leave Trey?

When had she become such a damn fool?

She'd tell him about Maria and then she was out of here.

CHAPTER TWENTY

"But you can't go home," Trey told Kelly, placing a glass of wine in front of her on the bar. Why was she talking about leaving?

They'd had a pleasant dinner—one far more enjoyable without his father's glowering presence—and Jason was now watching his allowed thirty minutes of television before Kelly read him a bedtime story. She was off tomorrow, and he had plans for his strange family.

But now she was talking about leaving. Why couldn't he ever figure out what she was thinking?

Trey took a sip of the wine, watching her, trying to read her thoughts. He'd been looking forward to their good-night kiss ritual, which promised to be the highlight of an already satisfying day spent working on his tennis clinic. He wanted her to spend the night in his bed again.

This was certainly a new dilemma for him. A woman wanting to leave wasn't something he'd dealt with before. Usually he couldn't get rid of them.

She'd enjoyed their lovemaking. No question she had. Why was she running away when things were just getting started between them? Good things, in his opinion. Feelings that had been missing from his life for a long time.

"Have you forgotten about the car bomb?" he asked, trying not to sound angry. He had no right to be angry.

"I haven't forgotten," she said, not meeting his gaze.

"You won't be safe at your apartment."

"I'm a cop, Trey. I'll be fine."

"If this is about last night—"

"It's not," she interrupted. She gulped wine, and then finally raised her brilliant blue eyes to meet his gaze. "Yeah, of course it is. Partly."

He leaned across the bar and smoothed his index finger down her arm. She closed those beautiful eyes and shivered.

"I enjoyed last night," he said. "And so did you. Admit it."

She sighed. "Obviously."

He smiled, relieved she could admit the truth. "So you're running away."

"Maybe. But it's time."

"Time for what?"

"For someone to face reality."

Trey straightened up. "What reality are you talking about?"

"Stop glaring at me."

"Sorry. But you're making no sense, Kelly. I want you to stay. Yeah, the reasons are complicated, but we need time to figure it out."

Her eyes widened, but she didn't say anything.

"Obviously Jason wants you to stay, too," Trey added.

"He's a confused kid who doesn't know what's good for him."

"Do you know what's good for you?"

"This isn't about me."

"It's about all three of us."

She shook her head. "You told me Carico thought I should go home."

"And Dr. Carico had an agenda separate from my son's mental health. That's why I fired her."

"But maybe she was right. Think about it, Trey. It can't be healthy for Jason to pretend I'm his mother forever. And now he's seen us in bed together." Kelly threw up her arms in obvious disgust. "I can't even imagine what the shrinks would say about that."

"We'll lock the door from now on."

A faint flush crept into her cheeks. Kelly didn't blush often, but when she did, the effect was stunning.

"We can't," she whispered.

"Why not?"

"The longer I stay here, the harder—"

"The harder what?"

She looked away again, biting her bottom lip, and now Trey *could* read her. She'd grown to care deeply about Jason, yes. That much was obvious. But his father's gambit had worked. She wasn't ready to admit it, maybe not even to herself, but

Kelly was worried about her feelings for him, about getting hurt.

The last thing in this world he wanted was to hurt this courageous woman who had been through so much, but he couldn't give up. Not when she was starting to care about him.

"It's only been a week," Trey said softly. "Give it some time."

"How is Jason supposed to get better? He isn't even seeing a head doctor right now."

Trey nodded. She'd given him the perfect opening for his last good argument. "He's got a new therapist, Dr. Edward Barth."

"Yeah? When did that happen?"

"Yesterday, and that's another reason you need to stay."

"Why?"

"Dr. Barth wants to observe the interaction between you and Jason before arriving at an opinion about his future treatment."

Trey watched Kelly nibble on her bottom lip as she processed that information.

"I'll give you tomorrow," she said. "I'll say goodnight to Jason tomorrow night and won't come back here from work the next day."

"But Dr. Barth had to go out of town. He can't come tomorrow."

Kelly's gaze shifted toward the door just as a voice behind Trey said, "Mr. Wentworth."

He whirled, furious at the interruption.

Jason's on-duty bodyguard stood at the door, shifting from foot to foot, wearing a grave expression.

"I need a moment, sir."

"What is it?" Trey demanded.

"There's been an unauthorized docking at the marina. You and your family need to move into the panic room immediately."

"AND THEY ALL lived happily ever after. The end."

Kelly closed the book she'd just read to Jason and glanced down to the kid. Eyes closed, breathing regularly, he leaned against her shoulder where they sat on a sofa in a claustrophobic twelve-by-twelve room. She peered more closely at him trying to determine if he was asleep.

Trey stood at a bank of four monitors that showed different angles of his property watching people enter and exit the view. Tension flowed off him as if he were a wire strung too tightly.

Kelly itched to be out there with the security team on the hunt. She was a cop, for God's sake. But oh, no. She was stuck with Trey and Jason, stashed in this vault-like room until his team gave the all-clear.

For her own protection? What a bunch of BS. This was not how it was supposed to go.

Jason made a noise and yawned huge. Not asleep, but close.

"Come on, Jase," she whispered, and carried him

to the crib in the corner. This room had been created when Jason was much younger, but he still fit in the old bed just fine.

Trey turned from the monitors.

"This is a baby bed," Jason fussed as she placed him down.

"It's just for fun tonight," Kelly said.

Jason's lower lip stuck out. "How long do we have to stay here?"

Trey moved next to her and said, "Just until the game ends, buddy."

"Okay, Daddy," he said on a deep sigh.

And then, just like that, he was out. He hadn't even demanded the kiss ritual. Was it the change in routine or was he just too tired?

"I wish I could fall asleep that easily," Kelly whispered, unsure if she was sorry or relieved about missing her good-night kiss. She'd been dreading her reaction to Trey's lips on hers again.

Or was it anticipation?

When Trey didn't reply, Kelly shot him a glance. He gazed down at this sleeping son with such obvious love that her heart lurched. Trey might not be a perfect parent, but he would do anything for Jason.

She moved quietly back to the sofa. Hell, and what was a perfect parent? She'd never had one, that was for sure. Her mother hadn't protected her from Roy. She hadn't encountered an ideal mom or dad since she'd been on the job, either, although she had to admit her police work might not provide a fair sampling. She was only called to situations where trouble already existed.

Trey sat beside her. "How are you holding up?"

"I'm antsy," she said.

"You want to be out searching for the intruders, don't you?"

"You got that right."

He smiled. "It'd be a waste of your time. I'm certain this is a false alarm."

"How can you be so sure?"

"Visitors tie up at the marina and forget to ask for clearance all the time. Or, according to my security team, more often than it should. They're usually guests of a resident, apologetic and embarrassed afterward. We don't hustle into the safe room every time."

"But because of Jason's abduction, your team is taking no chances."

Trey nodded, looking toward Jason's crib. "And I agreed with them."

Kelly surveyed the windowless room. Everything they would need for the short term was here, a small refrigerator stocked with water, sodas and frozen meals, a microwave. The sofa made into a bed, and there was even a toilet, although no shower. Thick walls and huge stainless steel doors made unauthorized entrance impossible.

"Why didn't you tell me about this room?"

He shrugged and placed his arm behind her on the sofa. "I seldom think of the safe room except during hurricane season, but you're right. I should have. I'm sorry."

"I assume everyone on your staff knows about it."

"Not everyone, but key people."

"Including Maria?"

"Yes. Anyone who lives in knows it's here and its purpose."

Kelly nodded. "That's a problem if they have access codes."

"They don't."

"Good," Kelly said.

"You still think someone on the staff was involved in the kidnapping?"

"I'm sure of it. And that makes this room all but useless. They'll know exactly where you are."

"But not how to get me out."

"Maybe," Kelly said.

"Have you seen anything concrete to make you suspicious?"

"Not concrete," she said slowly. "Certainly nothing that would stand up in court."

"Hans?"

Kelly shook her head. "No. Hans is in the clear, and so is Greta. But Maria hasn't taken her polygraph yet. She keeps making excuses."

Trey gaped at her. "You can't think Maria would be involved in harming Jason. She adores my son."

"Yes," Kelly agreed. "She does. And I like Maria, but something is going on with her."

"Like what?"

Kelly took a deep breath. She couldn't prove her suspicions about Trey's housekeeper, but she was a law enforcement officer. Her gut told her Maria had a secret.

"I've caught her on her phone several times. When she sees me, she immediately terminates the conversation and hurries away."

"Maybe she didn't want you to know who she was talking to."

"Could be, but why? I'm not her boss. Her actions were, you know, secretive. Plus, she's gone through my drawers."

"I instructed her to do your laundry."

"And I appreciate that, but she leaves the clean clothes on the bed and I put everything away in drawers. Believe me, I know when my stuff has been rearranged. I don't have a whole lot here."

"Why would she do that?"

"I think Maria is looking for something."

"What?"

"My gun. I deliberately put the gun locker in a new place twice, and it's been moved. Someone is trying to get at it. If not Maria, who?"

Trey shifted to face her more directly. "Maria has been with me for four years, since Jason was an infant. She's totally loyal."

Kelly chewed on her bottom lip. Maybe she was wrong about Maria. Maybe there was a good explanation for her behavior, but Trey needed to know her suspicions no matter how much he didn't want to hear them.

Kelly looked away from the denial in Trey's eyes, from the allure of his lips. She was trying to behave like a professional, explain her doubts about his most trusted staff member. He needed to know this information.

But he sat too close, which short-circuited her brain. She could feel his body heat, breathe in the subtle fragrance of his aftershave. It was hard for her to concentrate on the results of her investigation when she wondered what he would do if she licked his throat. Whether they could turn this sofa into a bed without waking up Jason.

She suppressed a groan. What was wrong with her? All she could think about was getting Trey naked again.

She needed to focus on something besides another foolish fling—no matter how enjoyable— with Trey Wentworth.

"You have a traitor somewhere, Trey. I'm trying to find out who it is."

He crossed his arms across his chest.

"Maria's been good to me since I've been here." Kelly released a breath and looked away from his troubled face. "But I think she has a secret."

"A secret?"

She raised her gaze to his. "I've seen signs of a substance abuse problem."

CHAPTER TWENTY-ONE

TREY CAME TO his feet, but had nowhere to go. The room was too small to even pace. What else could go wrong?

He glanced back to Kelly. She avoided his gaze, her mouth tight.

"What signs?" he demanded.

Jason rolled over, and she shot a look toward his bed. "Keep your voice down."

"Sorry." He moved back to the sofa and sat beside her again. "Look, I pay Maria quite well, and she survived a background check when I hired her."

"The FBI cleared her, too," Kelly said. "She's never been arrested. At least not under the name she gave you."

"What makes you think she has an alias?"

"I don't know that she does. I'm throwing out theories."

"I don't like your theories."

"You didn't like your son being kidnapped, either." Kelly sat cross-legged on the sofa, facing him. "Collins Island is just your winter home, right?"

"Right. Usually we live the rest of the year in Manhattan."

"Does Maria travel back and forth with you and Jason?"

"No," Trey said. "Jason has another nanny in New York."

"So what does Maria do the rest of the year?"

He stared at Kelly. "I don't know."

"Does she have another job?"

"I don't know."

"Did you ever think to ask?"

"No. It's her business."

"The day we met, you told me that you and Jason stayed in Florida longer than usual so he could continue therapy with Dr. Carico."

"Yes. Carico thought her continued treatment would improve Jason's condition." Remembering his disgust with Carico, Trey ran a hand through his hair. If he'd gone north, Jason wouldn't have been abducted. He'd been blind to Carico's ulterior motives.

Was Kelly onto something? Could he be blind about Maria, too? He *had* noted a change in her behavior lately—she'd somehow seemed more nervous. He'd attributed that to the horror of the kidnapping and being attacked.

"So Maria just miraculously became available when you remained?" Kelly asked.

Trey hesitated, trying to remember how that conversation had gone. "Well, I told her we were staying and asked her if she could continue on."

"Is she married?"

"No."

"Has she ever been married?"

"Not according to the background check."

"Children?"

"How could she have kids and live in here with us?"

"Relatives. What about a boyfriend?"

"I don't know. I've never heard her mention one."

"Do you have a lot of personal conversations with your staff?"

"Are you interrogating me, Kelly?"

"I'm trying to find out how much you really know about Maria. It doesn't seem like it's a whole hell of a lot."

Trey stared at Kelly.

"And yet you trust her with your son."

His throat tightened at her accusation, and he swallowed to release the tension. But Maria harm Jason? No way. Kelly had to be wrong.

"What evidence have you seen of a drug problem?" he demanded "I've never seen her high. Have you?"

"No. Just jittery in the afternoon, but happy in the morning. Once I saw her take a pill."

"Maybe she's on medication."

"For what?"

"How would I know?" But maybe he should.

"Maybe you should," Kelly said, echoing his own thought.

"Damn you, Kelly."

She poked an accusing finger at him. "Don't blame me, Trey. I'm trying to figure this mess out."

He released a breath. Why was he lashing out at Kelly? She didn't want anything from him, had refused all his offers of payment, had even turned down the watch. She was perhaps the only person in his life who didn't tell him what she believed he wanted to hear.

The FBI took her concerns seriously. So should he.

"Sometimes I forget you're a cop," he said.

She nodded. "Don't do that."

"But I'm convinced Maria loves Jason," Trey said.

"And I don't disagree. The thing is, if she has an addiction, she can't help herself. The capsule she took was out of an orange container, like from a pharmacy, but being hooked on prescription meds is a huge problem in this country."

"I know all about that," Trey said. "Darlene was treated by a quack who gave her whatever she wanted whenever she wanted it."

"I'd like to use the FBI's resources to dig a little deeper into Maria."

"God, I hate this," Trey said.

"I know. Okay. Before we get Agent Ballard involved, let me try to find some real proof."

"How?"

"I want to search Maria's room."

"What do you think you'll find?"

"I'll know it when I see it."

Trey nodded. The idea that Maria had facilitated Jason's abduction didn't ring true to him. He couldn't be wrong about the genuine affection she had for his son. Kelly wouldn't find anything in a search, but he dare not take that chance.

He'd been wrong about people before.

"I'll need you to keep her occupied at some pre-arranged time tomorrow so I can get in there," Kelly said. "I don't want her to know we're suspicious or she'll start being more careful. Or disappear."

"I made plans to take you and Jason out on the *Drop Shot* tomorrow. My boat."

A smile tugged at her mouth. "Of course you have a boat."

"I wanted you to enjoy your day off."

Once again he couldn't read her reaction, but at least she was smiling.

"Since you won't let me do anything else for you," he said.

She threw up her arms. "At least you aren't trying to *give* me a boat."

"Do you want one?"

Her eyes went so wide he had to laugh.

"No!" she said. "Stop it."

"Never." He liked seeing this playful side of Kelly. He longed to see it more often. In fact, he wanted to know everything about her. What was her favorite movie, book? What type of music did she like? He picked up her hand and linked their fingers. She didn't pull away.

"So you're up for a little cruise tomorrow?" he asked.

"Sure. Why not. So give Maria some task to do in the morning, and I'll sneak in her room while she's occupied."

Trey shook his head. Kelly was unlike any woman he'd known. Instead of looking forward to a relaxing day on the water, her thoughts remained focused on her investigation of his staff. She was more excited about searching Maria's room than any pleasure he'd planned for her. Did Kelly even know how to have fun? Had she ever enjoyed a day without worrying about what needed to be done?

"Your quest will have to take place later in the day," Trey said. "We're leaving the dock early, and it makes more sense for me to ask Maria to help clean *Drop Shot* after we get back."

A buzz of static came over the intercom. "Mr. Wentworth," a voice said.

Trey moved to the monitors. "What's your status?" he demanded.

"All clear, sir. The boat belonged to a guest of a resident. You can come out now."

STRETCHED OUT ON a lounge chair on the deck of *Drop Shot*, which was anchored off the coast of Elliott Key, Kelly closed her eyes and relaxed into the warmth of the afternoon sun, wearing the bikini Trey had given her a week ago.

She could so get used to this life.

Get over yourself, Jenkins. You're not some pampered princess, and this is the last day of your little vacay.

She opened her eyes and gazed far across the glistening waters of Biscayne Bay to where another boat had anchored soon after the *Drop Shot*.

Trey's "boat" had turned out to be a sixty-something-foot yacht, one she was certain could easily make a trip across the Atlantic. The yacht came with a captain to keep them out of trouble and a mate to serve her every whim, including a gourmet lunch that was actually healthy, making her think Trey had paid attention to her complaints about the fattening food.

The weather was perfect. Not too hot, not too cool, a pleasant wind, and the *Drop Shot* cruised like a dream. Jason hadn't been bratty. He'd even agreed to wear a life jacket on deck without complaint. Right now Trey was putting him down for a nap. Amazingly, the kid hadn't objected to that, either.

She couldn't remember ever having a nicer day. Even the constant presence of Jason's bodyguards didn't spoil the outing.

Although something was definitely up with the little dude. Not only had he been a perfect gentleman, she'd caught him looking at her in a new way at lunch, a confused expression wrinkling his nose. Was he remembering his real mother?

And of course that would be an excellent development. She took a deep breath and released it slowly. More good news on an already perfect day.

She'd made up her mind to go home. It was time, in fact past time. Leaving was the best decision for her and the Wentworths. Especially Jason. She wasn't his mother, and it was wrong to keep up the pretense that she was. Even more so now if he had remembered the truth.

And why was that thought making her so sad?

"Hey, pretty lady."

Trey appeared beside her, holding two margaritas. "Thanks." She accepted hers and took a taste. Yep. Definitely tequila.

"Is Jason asleep?" she asked.

Trey nodded. "All the excitement wore him out."

"Bodyguards standing by?"

"One by the cabin, one at the bow keeping an eye out."

Kelly smiled at Trey as he sat in a lounge next to hers, but his gaze wasn't on her face. It zeroed in on the burn mark on her shoulder. Without thinking she raised her hand to cover the mark, her fingers icy from the drink.

He shifted his gaze to the same horizon she'd just pondered. Trey was curious about the burn. She knew he wanted her to tell him what had happened. But not now. She didn't want memories from the worst day of her life to interfere with one of the best.

"It's been a lovely day," she said. "Thank you."

"Have you noticed anything different about Jason?" Trey asked.

Surprised, she cut him a look. Of course Trey would have noticed. "Yes. Has he said anything to you?"

"No. But I've caught him studying you."

"Do you think he's regaining his memory of his mother?"

Trey released a breath. "God, I hope so."

"Maybe he's trying to figure out who the hell I am. Should we ask him about it?"

"I don't know. If we say the wrong thing…" Trey took a sip of his drink. "That's something we can discuss with Dr. Barth tomorrow night."

"Dr. Barth," Kelly said. "Tomorrow night?"

"Jason's new therapist, remember?"

"Right, but I told you I had to go home. Do you remember *that*?" The noise from an approaching boat made her raise her voice.

"What's one more night, Kelly?"

"Do you know how many times you've asked me for one more night?"

Before Trey could answer, a sleek black speedboat raced too close along the side of *Drop Shot*, creating a huge wake that rocked the boat. The bodyguards appeared, but these weren't kidnappers, just people out for a joy ride.

Three people on the bow, a man and two young women, held up cell phones to snap photos of them.

Another man stood behind the wheel. All four waved as the boat roared out of sight.

"That should be illegal," Kelly muttered.

"I think it is," Trey said. "But of course there's never a cop around when you need one."

"Very funny. Do you think they recognized your boat?"

Trey nodded. "I'm surprised it didn't happen sooner. We've been lucky today."

They lapsed into silence as the motion of the boat steadied. Kelly stared after the vanishing boat. Trey lived in a fishbowl. God, she'd hate people constantly poking their nose into her business.

"I know I've asked a lot of you, Kelly," Trey said softly, "but has your time with me really been so horrible?"

"Well, I didn't enjoy the visit from your father."

"Neither did I."

"What's the deal with you two?" she asked.

"It's complicated," Trey said.

"Yeah, I get that. Where's your mother? You never talk about her."

"We all have scars, Kelly." Trey shifted his gaze to the boat off in the distance, a muscle working in his jaw. "Some are less obvious than others."

Kelly swallowed. She shouldn't be surprised Trey had wounds. Everyone did. Life was crazy hard most of the time.

"Is your mom still alive?"

He shot her a look, then nodded.

Kelly bit her lip, wildly curious now. He hadn't shut her questions down yet. "Are your parents divorced?"

"No, but they haven't lived together for twenty years. She's in a private treatment center. The Wentworth machine chewed her up and spit her out. She can barely function."

"Are you saying she had some sort of a breakdown?"

"She was—is fragile. Life with my father destroyed her." Trey ran a hand through his thick hair. "Part of the problem was he's twenty-five years her senior. I think she got to a point where she couldn't take his bullying anymore and went somewhere deep inside herself. I make certain she has everything she wants or needs."

Kelly wanted—no, needed—to know more about Trey's mom, but wasn't sure if she should keep pressing.

"Do you visit her?"

"Not often. Seeing me can agitate her. As long as my father stays away from her, she remains calm. That's the deal I made with him, one that unfortunately now has to be altered."

"Deal?"

Trey turned toward her. "Did you ever wonder why I don't go to work, why I don't participate in Wentworth Industries?"

Kelly shrugged. Of course she'd wondered about that strange fact.

"We struck a deal that if Senior left my mother alone, I'd let him run things. I'd be a hands-off face of the company."

Kelly laughed. "You were a face?" *Well, he did have a gorgeous face.*

"You know. I go to parties, benefits, charity events to promote Wentworth Industries. The idea is to keep the name out there. My father is obsessed with good PR."

Kelly nodded, remembering Trey had left wearing black tie her first night at the villa. And how disgusted she'd been that he'd abandoned Jason mere hours after the kid had returned home.

"I had been groomed to take over, but Father refused any loosening of the reins."

"I get that," Kelly muttered.

"So to protect my mother, I agreed to wait. At first I was fine with the arrangement because of my new marriage," Trey continued. "And soon I had my hands full with an unraveling wife and an injured son."

"What is going to change?"

"My father doesn't know it yet, but the board wants me to step in. He's made some costly mistakes lately."

"So you'll begin working full time?"

Trey glanced toward the closed bedroom door. "As soon as Jason is stable."

Kelly wondered if Jason's delusions weren't just from physical and emotional trauma. Maybe he had some kind of genetic predisposition for mental illness.

"Has your mother met Jason?" she asked.

Trey shook his head. "She doesn't even know my son exists."

That meant Jason didn't know his grandmother. Trey's mother sounded like a sweet gentle soul who couldn't stand up to the steamroller also known as Grandpa Mean Bull. Kelly flashed to a sudden and delightful image of giving the hateful old man a good kick in the butt.

"I'm so sorry," Kelly murmured.

"Yeah, me, too."

A warm glow spread through her center. Trey had trusted her with personal information she intuitively knew he didn't share with many people.

But she'd already allowed herself to care too much about both Trey Wentworth and his son. They weren't a real family, although it was easy to play along with that lie on a day as dreamlike as this one. And as appealing as that dream might be, it would never work between her and Trey. Their worlds were too different.

She tried to picture him at Moe's and Joe's tossing back the cheap beer with Dale or Lana, listening to sick cop humor. Yeah, right.

What a joke to even fantasize about a relationship with him. He only wanted her around because of Jason, and proximity had turned her into a convenient bed partner.

Her own foolishness was about to set her up for a whole bucketful of life's harshest pain. She needed to go home.

Why couldn't she manage to do that?

"For Jason's sake, will you stay and meet Dr. Barth?" Trey asked.

"Yes," she answered, hating herself for her weakness. "One more day, Trey. That's all."

"Thanks," Trey said and came to his feet. "We need to get back. I'll have the captain pull up anchor."

Kelly closed her eyes as an unexpected wave of melancholy washed over her. Time to return to reality.

CHAPTER TWENTY-TWO

KELLY PUSHED OPEN the door to Maria's room, hurried inside and took a quick look around. The room was neat, as expected. Interestingly, no photographs on the chest of drawers or nightstand. Did Maria have a life outside of Wentworth Villa?

The view out the window was to a driveway. Ocean views were reserved for the rooms of guests, not staff.

Kelly took a deep breath and moved into the bathroom, the most likely place to find meds. She had plenty of time for a thorough search. Maria was with Trey on the *Drop Shot*, and he would call her cell to warn her when they were done there.

Would the prescription bottles be hidden? Trey claimed to have never visited Maria's quarters, but there were other staff members and all kinds of security personnel roaming the villa, including Hans, so the housekeeper might be cautious. Secretive about a nasty habit.

Kelly opened the medicine cabinet and her gaze immediately zeroed in on a package of birth control pills halfway through a cycle. The prescription, dated two weeks ago, was for Maria Navarre. Interesting. So Maria was sexually active. According to Trey, she got one day a week off and usually took a late ferry to Miami after dinner the night before, returning the following evening about the same time. She hadn't taken a day off since the abduction, but under normal conditions did she meet a lover once a week?

No other meds, either marked or unmarked, were in the cabinet. Plenty of skin creams, though, hairbrush, comb, mouthwash, toothpaste and brush. Kelly shut the door and squatted to look underneath the vanity where she found clean towels and a large plastic container of multivitamins, the type you get at a warehouse club. She opened the cap and sniffed. Definitely that familiar vitamin smell, but she pocketed a tablet for possible testing.

Finding nothing else of interest or suspicious in the bathroom, Kelly moved back into the bedroom. A search of the closet, including the pockets of clothing, revealed nothing. The drawer in the nightstand contained magazines and books printed in Spanish.

She began a search of the six-drawer dresser. In the bottom drawer on the right, beneath a neatly folded stack of T-shirts, she discovered a plastic shopping bag from a well-known department store stuffed with orange prescription bottles. She removed one of the containers to read the label, and the pills rattled inside.

Oxycodone. One hell of a lot of oxycodone. Trey paid Maria a good wage, but perhaps not enough to keep up with her habit. Sorry that her suspicions had proved correct, Kelly shook her head and set an empty container aside.

So much for her perfect peaceful day.

Continuing to search beneath the clothing, she found a frame face down and flipped it over.

The face of Jason's kidnapper sneered back at her. Adam looked younger, less gaunt, but no question she was staring at the man who had blown up her car.

TREY STARED AT the photograph Kelly placed on his desk. She'd discovered this frame hidden in Maria's room and insisted this was one of the men who had kidnapped Jason.

"You're certain?" he asked. But he knew. Kelly was too smart, too competent to make a mistake on something as important as this.

"Yes."

He picked up a plastic bag she'd also found. "That's a lot of pills."

"The bottles are empty."

Trey met Kelly's gaze. "You were right."

"Where is she?"

"In her room. I told Hans to keep an eye on her."

"That's one good thing about this island," Kelly said. "She can't run, at least not very fast."

"How could she do this?" Trey demanded. A terrible rage ignited in his gut, pulling him out of the shock Kelly's words and their meaning had created. A woman he had trusted to run his home and care for his son, a woman he'd treated like family, had betrayed him. Maria had caused Jason's regression. Would his son ever be right again? He picked up the photograph again and stared at it.

"This man could have killed Jason."

"She's sick, Trey. Addiction is a disease."

"I don't care. I want her out of my home."

She nodded. "Agent Ballard will be here in about two minutes. He's flying in on a Bureau chopper."

"You called the FBI?"

"I had no choice. I actually got worried he'd arrive before you two returned from the boat. I didn't want him to show up without you knowing what was going down."

"Will he arrest her?"

"He'll read Maria her rights and question her first, but, yes. I have no doubt she'll be cuffed and arrested. She's just as guilty as the two men."

Trey collapsed into his chair. "I can't believe this."

"Focus on the fact that with Maria's help, Jason's kidnappers should be off the street soon."

"What if she doesn't help?"

"She will. Especially when she can't get her meds in jail. She'll do anything to help herself."

Trey shook his head. "I never doubted her loyalty for a second. She had a black eye, for God's sake."

"No doubt they slugged her to make it look good," Kelly said. "Jason might be a child, but he could tell what happened."

"Jason." Trey closed his eyes and sat back in his chair. Losing Maria would be another blow to his son. On top of Kelly leaving tomorrow.

"I know," she said softly.

"What can we tell him?"

Kelly bit her bottom lip. "Maybe we can ask the new shrink how to handle it."

"Good idea."

"Do you want to be present for the questioning?" Kelly asked.

"Yes," Trey said, staring at the photo again. "I want to hear her explanation."

He looked up at a knock on the door. Agent Ballard entered the office and went directly to Kelly to shake her hand. "Good work, Officer Jenkins."

"Thank you, sir."

Ballard turned to Trey. "Wentworth."

Trey nodded at the agent.

"Is that the photograph?" Ballard asked, his gaze falling to the frame on the desk.

Trey handed the photograph to the agent who studied it.

"No question that's one of the kidnappers," Kelly told him.

Ballard nodded. "Where is our suspect?"

Trey called Hans's cell. "I need to speak with Ms. Navarre. Escort her to my office."

"Will she come willingly?" Ballard asked in the silence that followed.

"She doesn't know anything is wrong," Trey said.

When Maria entered his office, Trey could hardly stand to look at her. Where he'd once seen a trusted member of his household, he now saw a snake in the grass waiting to lunge with a fatal strike. Even the black eye, supposed proof of her loyalty, had faded.

"Yes, Mr. Wentworth?" she said, casting nervous glances to each of the people in the room.

"Maria, this is Agent Ballard from the FBI. He wants to ask you some questions."

Maria turned to Ballard. When her gaze zeroed in on the frame in the agent's hand, her eyes went wide and she raised a hand to her mouth as if to stifle a scream.

She bolted for the door.

Trey jumped to his feet, but Hans blocked her exit, and Kelly quickly moved to assist.

"No! Please." Wild-eyed, trapped, Maria turned back to the center of the room, tears streaming down a face distorted with the agony of knowing she was caught. Her shoulders heaved with silent sobs.

"I'm sorry," she said. "I'm sorry."

Ballard pulled her arms behind her and snapped plastic restraints around her wrists. "You have the right to remain silent."

Maria closed her eyes as if trying to block out the world. Trey tried to muster sympathy but couldn't. She'd forfeited any right to his pity by endangering an innocent child.

"Do you understand these rights?" Ballard asked when finished.

"Yes," Maria whispered. "I understand."

Head down, shoulders slumped, Maria looked like a stranger to Trey as Ballard led her to a chair before his desk.

When she was seated, Ballard placed Adam's photo on the desk and slid it toward her. "We want to know the location of this man."

She raised her head from the photo and met Trey's gaze with a pleading look.

"Why, Maria?" Trey demanded. "For God's sake, why?"

"I never meant for *Jasonito* to be hurt."

"I trusted you with my son."

She looked away. "I needed money."

"Why didn't you ask me for it?" Trey said.

"I was afraid. Adam told me…" She shook her head as she trailed off.

"What did he tell you?" Ballard demanded.

"He told me a lot of lies," she whispered.

"Where is he, Maria?" Ballard demanded again, tapping the photograph.

Maria took a deep breath and nodded. "I will tell you everything."

WHEN KELLY ENTERED her station house the next morning—thankfully on time—she had so much to think about she couldn't concentrate on one issue. She was itching to know what was going on with

Maria, but hadn't heard from Ballard since the arrest. He'd promised to keep her in the loop, but of course he hadn't. Jerk.

But she had other problems, worse problems. Trey had been devastated by Maria's betrayal, and she'd ached for him last night after Ballard took the housekeeper away, and had lain awake in bed for hours tempted to go to him, make love to him to make him feel better. To make them both feel better.

And what did that say about her? She was in way too deep. Tonight would be her last night at Wentworth Villa, although Trey would no doubt use Maria's absence as leverage to get her to stay and comfort his son. She had to resist any persuasion he might use.

She needed to return to reality. Until a week ago, being a cop had been all she cared about.

"Hey, Kelly."

Kelly refocused and smiled at Sean O'Malley, a friend and fellow rookie from her class.

"How's it going, Sean?" He'd been part of the study group created by her, Patrice, Lana and Dale Baldwin, another trainee.

"Can't complain," Sean said. "Although nothing like *your* life these days."

Kelly paused. She'd always liked Sean, but why was he grinning at her so strangely? In fact, as she became aware of her surroundings, everyone was staring at her, looking away quickly when she made eye contact. That many people acting squirrelly couldn't be her imagination. What was going on?

Lana appeared and grabbed her elbow. "I need to talk to you."

"Okay," Kelly said, pushing open the locker room door. "What's up?"

"Wait," Lana said, her voice low and urgent. "Before you…"

Kelly heard laughter as her gaze zeroed in on a large photograph stuck to her locker. A photograph of her on the deck of Trey's yacht. Holding a margarita. Wearing her bikini.

Beneath a three-inch headline that screamed Wentworth Heir Picks New Mother, on the front page of *The National Intruder*.

"They wouldn't let me take it down until you saw it," Lana said.

Kelly marched into the locker room, ripped the newsprint off her locker and stared at it.

"Is this real?" she demanded.

Lana followed her inside. "There's one in the men's locker room, too."

"But is this really the front page of this stupid tabloid or did someone Photoshop it to haze a rookie?"

"It's real," Lana said. "Today's edition. Someone bought a stack of *Intruders* and placed them in the break room."

"Oh, my God," Kelly breathed.

Patrice appeared at her side. "At least you look

good, girl. I gotta say I understand why Wentworth wants to keep you around."

"Jenkins."

Kelly looked up at the barked command. Sergeant McFadden lurked at the door of the locker room.

"A moment of your time, please, Officer."

Kelly crumpled the paper into a tight ball and slammed it into a trash can as she moved to the door, her heart pounding. But McFadden passed his own desk and marched her straight into Lieutenant Marshall's office.

A copy of *The National Intruder* lay on Marshall's desk.

She stood at attention before her lieutenant, her gaze straight ahead. How bad was this going to be?

"That will be all, Sergeant," Marshall said.

When the door closed, Marshall said, "As you were, Officer. In fact, why don't you sit." Marshall motioned to a chair.

Kelly gratefully collapsed into the padded seat, but kept her spine as erect as she could manage.

Marshall held up the front page. "I take it you've seen this?"

"Just now, sir. I haven't read the text."

"They have your name and the fact that you are a Miami-Dade County police officer. The story suggests you're involved in the payoff scandal being reported by the *Miami Herald*."

"What? That's impossible. I never even patrolled

the district involved." She gaped at her lieutenant. Surely he didn't believe such a ridiculous fabrication.

"Understood, but you're living on the most expensive piece of real estate in the county."

Kelly swallowed, tasting something bitter.

"Paparazzi are also surrounding police headquarters downtown," Marshall continued. "Brass isn't happy."

"I don't know what to say, sir."

"Can you explain this photograph?"

"Yesterday was my day off. Wentworth took his son out on his boat and asked me to go with them." She shrugged. "Another boat went by and its occupants snapped photos with their phones. I had no idea one would end up on the front page of a tabloid."

"This photo is from an expensive long range lens," Marshall said. "Not a cell phone."

She'd assumed the photo was courtesy of the idiots who had zoomed too close to *Drop Shot*, but remembered the boat anchored in the distance. Had they been paparazzi?

"Of course, your private life is your own business, Officer Jenkins. You can date whoever you want."

"Sir, I'm not dating Wentworth. Yes, I've been pretending to be his son's mother, but that ends tonight."

Marshall's brows went up. "You're leaving his residence?"

"Yes, sir."

"The son has regained his memory?"

"No, sir. Not yet."

"You're sick of being the guest of a billionaire?"

"I just want my life back." *But is it already too late?*

Marshall nodded and stared at her as if he knew precisely why she was leaving. The fact that she'd wear a skimpy bikini in front of Trey obviously left the wrong impression. She could have worn her competition swimsuit.

"That's probably a wise choice," Marshall said.

"Yes, sir."

"Because of the corruption allegations, the department has no choice but to take this report seriously. Internal Affairs has opened an investigation."

"Oh, my God," Kelly breathed. Internal Affairs? This couldn't be happening.

"As of today, you're off patrol, Officer Jenkins," he said in a firm voice, one that told her there would be no discussion.

"Off patrol, sir?"

"You'll have to ride a desk until IA completes their investigation."

CHAPTER TWENTY-THREE

IN HIS OFFICE digging through the disaster that was the latest quarterly statement from Wentworth Industries—even analyzing his father's mistakes was better than thinking about Maria's betrayal—Trey heard his cell buzz. He checked the readout and relaxed. Joe Schwartz. Despite the fact that the man was his father's PR genius, Trey had always liked Joe.

"Yeah, Joe?"

"I just sent you an email," Joe said. "There's a photograph attached. You need to open it."

With a sense of foreboding, Trey opened his email account and found Joe's message. He clicked on the attachment, and a grainy photo of Kelly on the deck of *Drop Shot* materialized.

"What is this?" he asked. "Does someone want money?"

"It's the cover of today's *National Intruder*."

"You mean it's already out there?"

"Yes."

Trey enlarged the attachment and stared at the huge headline: Wentworth Heir Picks New Mother.

He cursed. How did the *Intruder* get that part of the story? Hell, the media always found a way.

He hated this. Kelly was going to hate this.

Did she know about the story yet?

"You know Wentworth Industries shies away from any tawdry publicity," Joe said.

"You mean my father does."

"He wants to do damage control."

Trey sighed. Of course he did.

"I wanted you to know what was happening on this end," Joe said.

"I appreciate that, Joe, but wouldn't it be better to just ignore the story?"

"Your father doesn't think so."

"And what do you think?"

"I think it's time you took your rightful place on the board of directors."

Trey laughed softly. "Not yet, Joe."

"When?"

"Has my father announced his retirement?"

"If that's what you're waiting for, there could be a hostile takeover before you make your move."

Trey glanced at the financials. "It's not that bad."

"His time has passed, Trey. You need to step up."

"Soon, Joe. Sooner than I originally planned."

"Don't wait much longer," Joe said. "Listen, I'll be issuing a statement later today with our usual denial of any relationship with this woman."

"I'm not certain that's accurate."

"Obviously. She's living in your home."

Trey nodded. Of course the tabloids had figured that out. And the *Intruder* cover wouldn't help his case to convince Kelly to stay. Or would it? If she moved back to her apartment, photographers would be all over her. The paparazzi couldn't get to her while on Collins Island.

But should he publicly deny any relationship with her? A sexy photo on the cover of the most sensational tabloid in the country wouldn't be good for her career. Could she be disciplined for something that wasn't her fault? A quick denial might cool things off for her, placate her bosses.

"All right," Trey said. "Issue your usual denial."

AFTER HER SHIFT, where she sat at a desk answering the phone the whole day and didn't hear one fricking word from Ballard, Kelly exited the station and came to a stunned halt.

"Kelly, over here! How is Jason?"

"Do you take kickbacks?"

"Are you and Trey Wentworth involved?"

In the middle of the mob of shouting photographers, she spotted Hans holding open the door to the limo. She ducked her head, dashed toward him and jumped inside.

A horde of loud motorcycles followed the limo. At the first stoplight, she pulled the curtains so no one could snap her photo.

"You all right back there?" Hans asked over the intercom. The privacy shield was up.

"Just peachy," she said and folded her arms waiting for the limo to move again. She couldn't block out the world in her patrol car. Marshall had been right to bench her.

How had she descended into this madness? This was not her life. And now IA had opened an investigation on her. They'd find nothing, but would it always be a blemish on her record?

Her cell phone buzzed. Ballard at last.

"Jenkins," she answered.

"Maria lawyered up," Ballard said without preamble. "We got her a public defender. It took a while, but we struck a deal and she gave up Adam."

"Is he in custody?"

"Not yet. He's holed up in Homestead, and we're taking him down at first light. Do you want in?"

Yes! Kelly made a fist and thrust it into the air. "You bet I do."

"Yeah, well, this is partly your collar. I'll clear it with your lieutenant."

"Thank you." No way would Marshall say no to the FBI considering the circumstances. Between the corruption allegations and the *Intruder* cover, a little positive press would be welcome. And a good outcome could help her problems with IA.

"This operation won't be a cakewalk," Ballard continued. "Maria claims his home is like an armory. From her description, there may be an assault rifle. Wear your vest."

"Understood. What's the story with Adam and Maria?"

"They're both junkies. Her habit started with prescription meds after a car accident two years ago. They met at rehab."

"Nice," Kelly said. So Maria's addiction began subsequent to her employment with Trey, which explained why the background check didn't reveal her problem. And Trey wouldn't know what to look for once it started.

"When her new boyfriend found out where she worked, he cooked up the kidnapping plan," Ballard continued.

"Hard to believe she'd go along with it, though."

"He's abusive. She's afraid of him. He even instructed her to get at your service weapon."

By the end of her conversation with Ballard, the limo was safely on the ferry. Kelly stashed the tactical information about when and where to meet Ballard's team in a pocket, and gave it a quick pat. She lifted her feet into the air and pumped her legs, wishing she could break into a run.

Finally some good news. The FBI had invited her along on Adam's takedown. She could function like a real cop again. She just had to get to the meet location without being followed.

When the limo arrived at Wentworth Villa, Kelly went straight to her room, locked up her weapon and tossed belongings into her suitcase. She only had to get through one more night. One more night, and then she would have her life back.

Or would she?

She collapsed on the bed, hugging a pair of shorts to her chest.

So many things had changed. For one thing, she

didn't have a car, and the insurance company hadn't yet issued a check. Trey would loan her a vehicle, but for how long? She couldn't keep a loaner forever. How was she supposed to get back and forth to work? Would the media continue to hound her? If so, would Marshall suspend her? Terminate her?

"You're going away, too, aren't you?"

Kelly looked up at the sound of a small voice. Wearing a solemn expression, Jason stood at the threshold of her room, his gaze glued to her suitcase.

She sucked in a deep breath. She had to have this conversation with him sooner or later. But how could she explain why she had to go?

"Hi, Jason," she said brightly as he moved toward her. "Did you have a nice day?"

He shook his head. "I miss Maria."

"I know you do, and I'm sorry," Kelly said. God, but the timing of her departure couldn't be worse. Feeling like a jerk, she hugged him close. As she breathed in his sweet fragrance, she closed her eyes against an unexpected rush of tears. She'd miss seeing him every day. Obviously, she'd allowed herself to care about Jason too much. Yeah, maybe he was a little spoiled, but that wasn't his fault. He'd been through so much, and now she was adding to his losses.

He wiggled away and sat on the bed beside her. "I know a secret," he told her.

"You do?" she asked.

He nodded. "Yes."

"Do you want to tell me?"

"I don't know." He focused on her suitcase behind her on the bed.

"Is it about Maria?" she asked.

"No." He picked at the hem of his T-shirt. "It's about you."

"Is it a good secret or a bad secret?"

He shrugged. "I know you're not my real mommy. You're Kelly."

She blinked. So she and Trey had been right. "That's right, Jase," she said carefully. "I'm Kelly."

He gazed at her with incredibly sad blue eyes. "My mommy is dead," he said in a tiny voice. "The angels took her."

"I'm so sorry, sweetie," Kelly said.

"Me, too," he whispered, looking away. "I got mixed up."

"How long have you not been mixed up?"

He shrugged again. "A while."

"Why didn't you say anything? Why keep it a secret?"

"Because I knew you'd go away. Are you?"

"Yes," she said.

"But I want you to stay. Can't you stay?" His voice was pleading.

"This isn't my home, Jason. It's your daddy's home."

"He won't mind. I'll ask him if it's okay."

"But I have a different home somewhere else."

His eyes widened. "You do?"

"Yes, a little apartment."

"Where is it?"

"Not on this island, but not too far."

"Could I come visit you there?"

"I hope you do."

He smiled for the first time. "I have a new doctor."

"I heard that. Do you like him?"

"He's okay. Will I get a new nanny, too?"

"Probably. Yeah, I think so."

He entwined his fingers with her. "I wish you could be my new mommy."

So do I. The thought came out of nowhere. Was that what she wanted? To be Jason's replacement mother?

Or did she want to be Trey's replacement wife?

Wishing for the moon never did anyone any good. She'd learned that a long time ago. The cold reality was now there was no longer any reason for her to remain. Trey wouldn't even try to persuade her.

Jason had accepted the truth. He was sad, naturally, but otherwise okay with the fact that his mother was gone. Certainly no more hysterics. He had a new doctor and would soon get a new nanny.

And maybe he'd even get a new mommy someday.

She closed her eyes. She suddenly knew she'd

follow Trey in the tabloids like some obsessed fan girl. She'd have to know what he was doing, where he was, if his tennis clinic ever came to fruition. How Jason was.

"Come on, Jason." Still holding his hand, she stood. "Let's go talk to your daddy. He needs to know you're not mixed up anymore."

CHAPTER TWENTY-FOUR

TREY TUCKED THE sheets around his son and kissed his forehead. "Sweet dreams, buddy."

Jason's eyes were wide open, however, and boring into his. "Do you miss Mommy?"

After a moment's hesitation, Trey said, "Of course," and sat on the edge of the bed. Did Jason want to talk about Darlene? Maybe the fact that he'd remembered his mom was gone lessened the impact of Maria's absence, which he'd explained by saying she had to help out her own family for a while.

He was beyond relieved that Jason had realized the truth on his own. Of course that meant there was no longer any need for the ritual good-night kiss. With Barth's approval, Kelly wasn't even in the room. She was packing.

He hadn't quite processed the fact that she was really moving out. This house was going to feel like a museum without her.

"I like Kelly," Jason said.

Startled at the change of subject to his own thoughts, Trey said, "Me, too."

"Can we go visit her at her real home?"

"I'm sure she'd love to see you."

"You can come, too."

Trey laughed. "Thanks, buddy. Is there anything you want to talk about? Do you have any more questions?" He and Kelly, along with Dr. Barth, had spent a lot of time after dinner explaining about Maria, why she wasn't here, why Kelly had to leave. Jason was sad, but had accepted the changes.

"No," Jason said. "I love you, Daddy."

Trey swallowed hard, wanting to remember this moment forever, the first time his son had expressed any love for him since Darlene's death.

"I love you, too, Jase," he said in a hoarse whisper. He blew his son a kiss, and Jason blew one back.

At the door, Trey took a last look at his son, thankful that the long nightmare was finally coming to an end. They'd have to remain in Florida awhile longer so Jason could begin treatment with Dr. Barth, but that wasn't exactly a hardship. He already had feelers out for a new nanny. He looked forward to working on the tennis clinic. He'd soon take his position on the Wentworth Industries Board of Directors. It was time.

Plus, thanks to Kelly's detective skills, Jason's kidnappers should soon be in jail.

Yeah, and there was the only rub. Kelly. Everything in his life was under control except for his feelings about Officer Kelly Jenkins. The fact that she was moving out overshadowed all the other good news.

She was good for him, had somehow dragged him out of the funk he'd been in since the disintegration of his marriage, making him want to rejoin the productive world instead of hiding behind a life of parties. She'd given him the motivation to defy his father.

She was also good for his son. She'd taught Jason more about sharing and good manners in a week than Darlene had in all their time together. Darlene had loved Jason, but didn't have the faintest idea about parenting and had had no interest in learning.

Trey quietly closed the door to Jason's room and went to find Kelly. This would be the last night she spent under his roof, and he wanted to make the most of it. Yeah, he wanted her in his bed, but that wasn't all he wanted. He wanted her respect.

For the first time in his life, he wasn't sure how a woman felt about him. Understandable, of course. He hadn't exactly been at his finest when they'd met.

He didn't want to lose contact with Kelly, but could they have any kind of relationship? They came from such different worlds. Was it possible to even try?

He stepped outside into a clear, cool night and found her hanging onto the edge of the pool, lazily kicking her legs. He kept the water at the exact temperature she preferred. She'd finished her workout and was waiting for him.

When she noticed his presence, she smiled and exited the pool. As far as he was concerned her body was perfect. He held out the robe for her, encircling her with his arms as she stepped into the terrycloth. She leaned against him and sighed.

"I'm going to miss this pool," she said.

Will you miss me? "You don't have to go."

She stepped away. "You know I do. For Jason's mental health if for no other reason. Dr. Barth agrees." Gesturing toward the lounge chairs she said, "Can we stay out here a few minutes? It's such a perfect evening. I think I want to soak it up."

Trey followed and sat on a lounge next to her.

"How is Jason?" she asked. She pulled a large comb from a pocket in the robe and used it to untangle her wet hair. "Any problems putting him down?"

"Out of nowhere, he told me he loved me," Trey said. "On a day filled with loss, he decided to forgive me."

"Kids are amazingly resilient," she said. "They can recover from all kinds of trauma."

"Like you did?" Trey asked.

She paused combing and looked out over the pool. "My childhood was way different than Jason's."

"Your mom had a drug problem, didn't she? That's how you recognized it in Maria."

"Yes, a bad one. She couldn't keep a job because of her addiction, so often resorted to the world's oldest profession."

"Where was your dad?"

She shrugged. "Who knows?"

"Did your mom give you that burn mark on your shoulder?"

"No." Kelly swung her gaze back to his. "She never harmed me, but couldn't stand up to a man who wanted to. Mr. Roy Brown." She spat out the name.

"Did he rape you?" Trey asked, holding his breath for the answer.

"Oh, he tried, but it didn't go that far." She shook her head.

Trey reached for her hand and intertwined their fingers. He wanted to know everything about Kelly. But did she trust him enough to confide in him?

She didn't say anything for a moment as she stared at the lit pool, its water now calm. "My mom was working as a maid in a no-tell motel, and I was in a room doing my homework when Roy came in high on something really nasty. Whatever it was made him super strong. I couldn't get away from him, but screamed my fool head off and got lucky. A police officer intervened, Officer Ricardo Morales, who became my savior in more ways than one."

"How so?"

"Ricardo was a dinosaur, a few years from retirement, and took an interest in me and my mom. He couldn't stop Roy from killing her a few months later," Kelly said bitterly, "but he watched over me in the system, made sure my foster homes weren't abusive."

"You said he moved to Daytona Beach?"

"He's in an assisted living facility near where his own kids live. He's got dementia. I used to visit him every now and then, but he no longer remembers me."

"I'm sorry." He gave her hand a gentle squeeze.

"Thanks. Ricardo is one reason I became a cop."

"You love being a police officer, don't you?"

"I really do. I'm totally jazzed that Ballard invited me along on the takedown of Adam." She stared at her comb. "My lieutenant cleared it even though I'm riding a desk these days."

"You're on desk duty?" he demanded. "Why?" Kelly would hate desk duty.

She sighed and looked out over the pool. "Because one of the tabloids suggested I'm a dirty cop."

Trey went still. "Based on what?"

"Because I'm living here."

He stared at her. "Surely your superior officer doesn't buy into that nonsense."

"Maybe not, but Internal Affairs opened an investigation."

"Why didn't you tell me?"

She shrugged. "We've got a lot going on."

Stunned, Trey dropped her hand. Kelly was under investigation because she'd agreed to remain in his home, and that was on him. "Is there anything I can—"

"No!" She pointed the comb at him. "Stay out

of my career, Trey. If you try to pull strings, you'll only make it worse."

"Okay, okay." He held up his hands in surrender. She must not have heard about Joe Schwartz's press release where Wentworth Industries denied any romance between himself and one Officer Kelly Jenkins. Would she consider that interfering?

"Anyway, this op in Homestead in a few hours will be the real deal," she said. "Maria claims Adam's house is like an armory, loaded with guns, even an assault rifle."

An assault rifle? And Kelly was looking forward to this operation with the FBI?

"But you'll stay back as an observer, right?" he asked. "You won't be rushing into the structure with the federal agents?"

"Hell, yes, I'm going in with them. I'm not hanging back anywhere."

"Don't go," Trey said before he could stop himself. "You could be hurt."

"Don't worry," she said. "I'll be wearing my vest."

He'd noticed how bulky her upper body was under her uniform. Jason called it lumpy. That meant she wore a Kevlar vest, but the reality of that fact, what it actually meant, hadn't truly registered.

Kelly was a law enforcement officer doing a job she loved, maybe a job she was meant to do—and he understood why, now that he knew her history.

But this beautiful new light in his life could be extinguished in a matter of hours. What would that loss do to Jason?

CHAPTER TWENTY-FIVE

KELLY PEERED CLOSELY at Trey. He looked like he'd just seen a ghost. Or maybe that he'd just learned Santa Claus was a big fat myth.

"What's wrong?" she asked.

He shook his head. "Nothing. Not really. It just hit me how dangerous your job is."

"I'll be fine, Trey."

He nodded and ran a hand through his hair, something she'd recognized as a tell that meant he was anxious.

Was he worried about her? She ducked her head to hide a smile. She shouldn't want anyone to worry about her, but the thought that this sexy and powerful man might care about her safety on the job created a warm glow in her chest.

Pathetic. Really pathetic. The sooner she got off this island the better.

"Have you finished packing?" he asked in a tone that told her he'd accepted the fact she was leaving.

"Yes," she replied. "Listen, can I borrow a car for a few days until I can make other arrangements?"

"Of course," Trey said. "Keep it as long as you like. How about an Italian sports car, maybe a convertible?"

"Maybe not. Do you have anything a little less showy?"

"An SUV?"

"That'll work. Thanks." She'd need to disguise herself, put her hair under a cap and wear sunglasses when she drove off the ferry. She'd be in an unfamiliar vehicle, and the paparazzi—if they were even waiting—would ignore her.

A silence fell between them, and Kelly followed his gaze to look out over the stunning elegance of his lit pool deck. She breathed in the sweet fragrance of Trey's night-blooming jasmine, a scent she'd always associate with these amazing nighttime swims. She really would miss this place.

And its owner.

Feeling a chill now that she'd stopped moving, Kelly tightened the robe around herself. She'd fallen into the luxury of Trey Wentworth's life far more easily than she could have imagined. Would she ever see him again? Yeah, in a tabloid or maybe on an entertainment television show.

She switched her gaze to his profile. What was he thinking? With a sinking feeling she understood he wasn't going to say anything about them hooking up after she'd moved out. Or even about her spending tonight in his bed.

Of course she'd planned to refuse that offer, if it came—it would only make her leaving harder—but damn if she hadn't wanted the invitation.

God, she was such a loser. She'd actually been holding out the ridiculous hope that Trey Wentworth would want to see her again. Would want to make love to her again. He might not want her standing in front of a bullet, but that was just common decency. It didn't mean anything more.

"Well, I'd better turn in," she said. "I've got an early morning."

"I'll make sure there's something for you in the breakfast room," he said.

"That's not necessary."

Trey shot her a look, which only confused her. Why was it so hard to say goodbye to this man?

"About that car?" she prompted.

"I'll instruct Hans to leave the SUV in the driveway for you. The keys will be in the ignition."

"Perfect," she said, coming to her feet. Should she stick out her arm and shake his hand? No, she'd just pretend this was like any other night, even though it was likely the last time she'd speak to him.

She took a deep breath, hoping to get away without him noticing she was fighting tears. He'd read too much into that, want to know why. If she did, she could always tell him she'd miss Jason. That was the truth.

"Good night, Trey." She couldn't bring herself to say *goodbye*.

Trey reached out and gently pulled her into a hug. "Promise me you'll be careful tomorrow," he said, his voice sounding muffled and far away.

"I promise." She held herself stiffly, afraid to release into his warmth, afraid she'd never want to exit his embrace, terrified she'd raise her chin and beg for her good-night kiss. She closed her eyes telling herself she could get through this. She'd certainly gotten through worse.

He released her and ran a gentle hand down her cheek, staring into her face with eyes that spoke of loneliness and regrets.

"Thank you, Kelly."

"For what?" she whispered.

"For being you." He kissed her then, his lips meeting hers with a brief feather light touch. But his face remained close, his breath hot on her chin. She had the distinct impression he wanted to say something. And then his mouth was on hers again, kissing her as if he didn't want to let her go, pressing his body into hers. She couldn't help but lean into him and slide her arms around his waist. Yes, this was what she wanted, what she needed.

But when she heard moans of pleasure rumbling in her throat, she pulled back, a hand to her lips, knowing those little noises gave her away as surely as a signed confession. Their gazes locked and understanding passed between them. Yes, he did want to make love to her.

But it would be the last time. There'd never be anything else but one more night of mind-blowing passion, and that wouldn't be enough. Not for her anyway. Still, she hesitated for a moment, tempted, wanting to open his shirt and place her cheek against his bare chest and feel his heart race, even if it would be the dumbest thing she'd ever done.

No way. This parting was already too hard.

Without saying a word, she turned and fled to the safety of her room. Trey didn't follow her.

"ADAM CHANDLER, THIS is the FBI." Ballard's voice boomed into the quiet dawn. "You are surrounded. Come out with your hands up."

Crouched behind an FBI vehicle, gun drawn, her heart racing, Kelly waited with dozens of FBI agents for a response to Ballard's demand. Everyone focused on a one-story concrete block home with peeling paint and a blue tarp suspended over one section of the roof. A rusted truck sat in the front yard full of weeds growing higher than the truck's bumper.

Ballard raised the microphone to his mouth and repeated his instructions, his amplified voice sounding loud, yet thin and grainy, through the speakers.

Still no response. Kelly shifted her weight. What was Chandler doing inside that house? Not taking her focus from the front door, she raised a shoulder and brushed sweat from her cheek. The early morning was cool, but she was beyond excited.

Ballard raised his microphone again.

A barrage of gunshots exploded out a front window before he could speak. Definitely an automatic weapon. Ballard cursed.

"Anybody hit?" he yelled.

Kelly held her breath, but everyone was okay.

Now what? If this were her department's op, they'd use a negotiator and try to talk Chandler down.

"Make the call," Ballard ordered a woman at his side.

So the FBI followed the same protocol. Kelly exhaled roughly and lowered her weapon, as did the other agents. Likely they were in for a long morning.

Two hours later, Ballard summoned Kelly and introduced her to Agent Alexa Nardi, a striking woman who looked to be of Indian descent, maybe forty years of age, the FBI negotiator.

"Agent Nardi has initiated communication with a gentleman inside that structure who claims to be Caleb Chandler, Adam's cousin," Ballard said. "The morning you rescued the Wentworth kid, did you learn the name of Chandler's associate?"

"Yes," Kelly said. "Caleb."

"Caleb insists Adam isn't in the house, that he left in the middle of the night," Ballard said.

"Could they have gotten a warning?" Kelly asked.

"Good question," Ballard said.

"If so, why didn't Caleb flee, as well?" Nardi asked.

"I'm surprised Caleb doesn't surrender," Kelly said. "He was definitely not on board with violence that morning. He fled the scene, which really pissed off Adam."

"He's high on something," Nardi said. "Not thinking clearly."

Kelly nodded. "My initial impression was that they were both users."

"And I think he's getting higher," Nardi added. "He's not coming down anytime soon."

"Great." Eyes narrowed, Ballard glanced toward the house, obviously considering his options.

So what would he do now? Stage an assault on the residence? That could result in people injured or dead, including law enforcement. The FBI needed Caleb alive so they could pump him for information about Adam's possible locations. So would they wait Caleb out? Wait until he crashed? He could possibly OD and they'd never get any intel.

She was an observer, nothing more, a rookie cop without the experience to offer any tactical solutions. But, man, was she ever enjoying herself.

The phone in Nardi's hand buzzed, the one dedicated to communication with Caleb. Kelly stared at Nardi as she answered.

"Yeah, Caleb. Okay. I'm glad to hear that. Yeah, keep your hands in the air. No sudden moves."

She disconnected. "He's coming out."

"Heads up," someone shouted. "The door is opening."

Kelly and everyone else looked toward the residence. Caleb, now sporting a ragged beard, looking even more emaciated than he had in the park, exited the front door. She tensed. His arms were over his head, but a rifle of some sort was suspended in his hands.

Did this fool have a death wish?

She went for her weapon and bent her knees to make herself a smaller target.

"Take cover," Ballard shouted.

Caleb lowered the rifle and began firing.

TREY SLAMMED HIS most recent letter from Wentworth Industries' comptroller onto his desk, pushed back in his chair and scrubbed his palms over his face. He glanced at the time on his computer monitor again. After 11:00 a.m., and he hadn't heard word one from the FBI.

Or from Kelly.

An hour ago his anger at the lack of communication had grown to fury. Now he was ready to explode.

He'd intended to spend the morning plotting his return to WI. But it had been hours since the FBI's operation to take down Adam Chandler had begun, so instead he left his desk every twenty minutes to wander around his home, check on Jason, trying not to give in to his worry.

Until he knew what occurred this morning in Homestead, he couldn't concentrate on anything, much less the questionable decisions his father had been making.

He moved to a window and glanced outside at his pool deck where Jason played, watched over by two bodyguards. Trey smiled at the sight of his son's antics, grateful his son was happy, safe and secure.

He understood the Bureau's negligence, but Kelly knew how anxious he was to learn if Jason's kidnappers had been apprehended. She definitely should have phoned him by now. Or at least sent an impersonal text. She *knew* he was worried about her.

True, he hadn't asked her to keep him informed, but he didn't think he needed to. This silence wasn't like her.

Something was wrong.

He grabbed his phone. No voice mail. No text. He'd already left half a dozen messages on her voice mail. No point in leaving another.

What if something *had* gone wrong, dangerously, life-threateningly wrong?

He had to know. But once again he was powerless. As he'd been when Jason was abducted. As he was to help his mother.

If an FBI sting had turned violently sour, there might be something on the noon news. He looked at the pool where Jason still played. He'd probably stay there awhile.

Trey picked up the remote and activated a door concealing a huge flat-screen inside a bookcase. After the door slid open, he turned on the television, found a local channel that featured noon news and sat on the edge of his desk to watch.

He stared at the screen not listening or seeing

anything until loud, familiar music filled the room and a voice blared, "Stay tuned for Action News."

After the station's graphics ran, an image appeared of an active police scene, obviously shot from a helicopter. Dozens of marked police cars, unmarked cars, uniformed and plain-clothed officers swarmed the area.

Trey rose and moved closer to the screen, confirming the uniform was the same one Kelly wore. Where was she?

"Breaking news," the female voiceover announced. "Shots fired during a violent FBI operation. One shooter and two law enforcement officers are down."

His gut clenched. Trey swore harshly, searching for her in the confused video, which the station claimed was live. Would he even recognize her? It was impossible to make out facial features.

Or was Kelly one of the injured officers? No ambulance appeared on the screen, so whoever had been wounded had already been rushed to a hospital. Could he call and get a name? No way. Only family.

He wasn't family. Not even close.

As the live feed continued to play, the voiceover reported the shooting was in connection with the kidnapping of the heir to the fortune of Wentworth Industries. The station's sources maintained a suspect exited the structure approximately two hours ago and opened fire on law enforcement with no provocation. There was no further information because the scene was still active.

He paced the room. What could he do? Storm the hospital and make demands? Embarrass the hell out of Kelly? Tough. If she were alive, he'd deal with...

The ring tone he'd programmed for Kelly sounded. He grabbed his phone. "Kelly?"

"Yeah, it's me."

He closed his eyes in relief and collapsed into his chair, sending a prayer heavenward. She was alive. Thank God she was alive. He took a deep breath and released it slowly, wondering at the force of his reaction.

And realized he was in love with her.

"Are you all right?" he demanded, muting the TV. "I'm watching the television coverage live."

"I'm fine. My phone was off. This is the first second I've had to call you."

"But you're all right?"

"I'm good. Just so you know, Adam wasn't here. Caleb is critical."

"What do you mean Adam wasn't there?"

"He either got advance warning of the op or lucky. We've searched the residence. This is definitely where he'd holed up, but he fled."

"So he's still out there?"

"Yeah, but likely no longer in the area. Ballard thinks he's on the run. The FBI will apprehend him eventually."

"But you weren't shot? You're okay?"

"I said I'm fine," she said, sounding annoyed. "Listen, I've got to go. I just wanted to fill you in."

"Kelly, I—"

But the phone went dead. She was gone, to a place where he didn't belong, where he couldn't reach her.

By some sick twist of fate he'd fallen in love with Kelly Jenkins, a woman totally unlike any other woman he'd known, a woman who worked with a bull's-eye on her back. Even if the FBI caught Adam Chandler, there were plenty of other sickos in this world gunning for cops these days.

His son had already lost one mother. It wouldn't be fair to let him get attached to another woman and lose her, too. Jase had been through too much in his short life. He might never recover from that loss.

Better to make this break with Kelly complete and permanent.

Jason was young. He'd forget her in time.

Trey turned away from the television, a sense of cold emptiness creeping into his limbs.

His son might forget Kelly Jenkins, but he never would.

CHAPTER TWENTY-SIX

THE MORNING AFTER the shoot-out in Homestead, Kelly stood at attention before the desk of Detective Monroe DiSilva for her interview with Internal Affairs. She wasn't worried. She'd never patrolled the district where the alleged payoffs took place. They had no evidence against her.

This interview was just a formality, something to satisfy the brass. Or the media.

Although, interestingly, the paparazzi hadn't followed her today.

DiSilva, a dark-haired man of maybe thirty-five, shuffled through papers on his desk. He glanced up at her with a steely glare.

"As you were, Officer Jenkins," DiSilva barked.

Kelly stood at ease, eyes focused on the wall over his head.

"Is it true you were with the FBI in Homestead yesterday?" he demanded.

She cut him a quick glance. Uh-oh. DiSilva didn't sound happy. "Yes, sir."

"Why? You were placed on restricted duty."

"The Bureau cleared it with my lieutenant," Kelly protested.

"No one cleared it with Internal Affairs."

She raised her chin. "I'm sorry, sir."

"Brass wanted you out of the field."

"Yes, sir."

DiSilva shook his head. "I've been ordered to suspend you, Officer Jenkins."

No way. Kelly stared at the grim-faced IA detective. He wasn't kidding.

She swallowed hard. "I'm suspended?"

"Please surrender your weapon and badge."

THAT AFTERNOON, KELLY moved restlessly around her apartment.

DiSilva had suspended her. He'd taken her weapon and badge.

Nothing she said could dissuade the IA detective. Not the fact that she had permission from her lieutenant, not even the fact that there was zero proof that she'd taken kickbacks. At least the suspension was with pay.

She'd already completed a long run and a brutal strength workout, one she'd pay for later with sore muscles. Out of desperation, she'd even attended a yoga class, which Lana claimed would quiet her thoughts. She was willing to try anything to help her stop thinking about what a disaster her life had become.

Suspended. Unbelievable.

She hadn't heard from Trey since she'd called him from the scene in Homestead. She hadn't tried to contact him, either, but why should she? She still needed his car, and what else was left for them to say to each other?

Apparently nothing.

She'd thought he'd want to know about the investigation, if the FBI had managed to interview Caleb, if they'd developed any leads on the whereabouts of Adam. But maybe Ballard had kept Trey informed. There was nothing new to report anyway.

Caleb was still breathing, but barely. The doctors had him sedated and wouldn't let the FBI near him. Without good intel from Caleb to aid in the search, Adam remained a ghost. The Bureau had checked every location Maria had given them, but so far the kidnapper remained in the wind. Convinced he'd fled the area, they'd suspended surveillance on her apartment.

Her stomached grumbled, so she took that as a clue and walked into the kitchen, jerked open the refrigerator and wrinkled her nose at the odor. Any produce or dairy had gone bad in the two weeks she'd been gone. Now, there was a fun project—she'd dispose of all the rotten food.

She looked under the sink for plastic gloves, but before she could finish snapping them on, her phone sounded. Caller ID revealed Patrice was checking on her again. News of her suspension had spread through the ranks like wildfire.

"Hey, Trice," Kelly said. "Are you on break?"

"At the Coral Bagel with Sean."

"Anything going on? God, I miss patrol."

"It's pretty quiet today. How long will you be suspended?"

"No way to know."

"At least the paparazzi should leave you alone. You're old news since Wentworth issued the denial."

"What denial?" Kelly asked.

"The Wentworth PR machine issued a release denying any truth to the rumors of a relationship between you and Trey Wentworth. You didn't know about that?"

"No, I did not." Kelly slid her back down a lower kitchen cabinet and plopped her butt onto the floor.

"Yeah. Sorry, kiddo."

"Where did you hear that?"

"It was on all the television entertainment shows last night. They even dredged up old photos of him with his ex and reported he was still in mourning, not yet ready to date."

"Well, the release is absolutely factual. There *is* no relationship whatsoever. There never was."

"If you say so."

"I do."

"Okay, then."

Kelly disconnected and, still on the floor, stared across the kitchen without seeing anything. She lowered her head and wondered why it felt like her heart was collapsing in on itself. Why was she so disappointed by the press release? There'd never been any chance of a continued connection between her and Trey once Jason regained his memory. She'd known that all along.

Still, a little heads-up from Trey would have been nice.

He obviously didn't think a warning was necessary, that they'd said all they needed to say to each other.

So the thing—whatever it had been—between her and the billionaire was over. Really and truly over.

They came from different worlds, worlds that had nothing to do with each other. He was one of the beautiful people, while she'd had a big fat *L* for *loser* tattooed on her forehead most of her life.

But not anymore.

Get over yourself, rookie. Get your ass off the floor.

Kelly pulled herself to her feet. She might be suspended, but she was still a cop.

And she had an idea.

Ballard had already sent agents to the rehab facility where Adam and Maria had met in their support group. Of course the feds got nothing useful. Federal agents always wore suits, and in certain situations, that tended to put people on edge. She, however, was her mother's daughter. She could rock a pair of ragged jeans and a faded T-shirt. She could walk the walk, and talk the talk.

And nothing slammed the difference between her and Trey into her face more clearly.

KELLY PARKED TREY'S SUV across the street from a rambling concrete block structure. Signage featuring a huge yellow sunburst read: Sunshine Center.

She checked her surroundings. Adam was still out there somewhere. She wouldn't drop her guard until he was in custody.

Trice had been right about the paparazzi losing interest in her. No one had followed her when she drove away from her apartment. She was now last week's news.

Telling herself she was relieved by this development, Kelly released a breath and exited the SUV. But she still couldn't return to patrol. Not until IA was done with her. God, was it really possible she could lose the only career she'd ever wanted?

She heard shouts indicating a soccer game in progress and headed toward an athletic field on one side of the two-story building. No bleachers or scoreboard, but maybe fifty people of all ages stood on the sidelines encouraging the young teenagers on the field, both boys and girls.

Not exactly the depressing scene of downtrodden addicts she'd expected to encounter, but the relaxed atmosphere of an amateur athletic competition might be a great place to pump onlookers for information.

Or not. When she arrived, spectators were so

intent on the game that no one took notice of her. She waited for a time-out and turned to the dark-haired woman beside her who had been a vocal critic of the goalie.

"Who's winning?" Kelly asked casually, keeping her gaze on the field.

Still focused on the field, the woman cursed and in a Hispanic accent said, "Sunshine can't do squat today."

Kelly nodded. These players looked too young and healthy to be recovering addicts.

"I thought this was a rehab center," Kelly said. "What's with all these kids?"

"And halfway house," the woman said. "And shelter for abused women. Father Hernandez does what he can for those in need."

Something in the woman's voice made Kelly glance her way.

"Are you in need of aid?" the woman asked softly.

"Maybe," Kelly said. That was the impression she'd wanted to create, that she was a druggie in search of a safe spot to crash.

"A friend of mine says he got clean here," Kelly said. "Did I get that wrong?"

"Who is your friend?"

"Adam Chandler."

"I don't know him, but go inside and talk to Sister Aleta," the woman said.

"Yeah, maybe," Kelly muttered, not wanting to

seem too eager. Sister Aleta? Father Hernandez. Was this facility run by a church?

"Tell her that Nancy sent you."

"Thanks."

Kelly moved off, scanning the crowd one more time for any sign of Adam. She didn't see him anywhere, or even anyone that looked like him, so retraced her earlier path and entered the doorway beneath the large sunburst design, which made her think of a benevolent all-seeing eye.

A plump fortyish woman wearing jeans and a T-shirt with the same logo of the sun greeted her with a smile. "May I help you?"

"I'm looking for Sister Aleta," Kelly said, deciding to go with Nancy's advice.

"She's in the gym." The woman pointed. "Down that hallway, two doors on your right. Just follow the noise. You can't miss it."

Kelly moved in the direction indicated. Was this place a rehab facility or the YMCA? Maria and Adam had met in group therapy, but no one here looked like they were in recovery.

She passed an open door and peered inside to find rows of chairs before what appeared to be a chapel. Responding to shouts further down the hallway, she pushed into the gym where a basketball game was in progress with players from six to ten years old, all boys.

An ebony-haired woman in her twenties raced up and down the court with the contestants trying to officiate what appeared to be bedlam. Kelly watched a bit of the action. When two of the players fought over the ball and one of them went tumbling to the ground, the official raised a whistle hanging around her neck and blew shrilly, bringing the dispute to a halt.

"That's it," she shouted, hands on her hips. "Game over. I warned you guys." The boys wandered off amid much grumbling and pushing and light punches on each other's shoulders.

Kelly walked across the now deserted court where the official stuffed equipment into a duffel bag.

"Sister Aleta?"

The woman turned, pushed sweaty hair that had escaped a ponytail away from her face and smiled at Kelly. "Can I help you?"

"Are you Sister Aleta?"

"That's what they call me."

"Are you a nun?" Her mom claimed to be Catholic, but Kelly could count on one hand the times they'd attended mass. Kelly didn't know much about the church, but was surprised a nun would wear shorts.

"No," Aleta said. "But the kids all call me sister anyway."

"Nancy sent me," Kelly said.

"Ah," Aleta said, her smile fading. "What are you on?"

"Oxy."

Aleta nodded. "Do you want help?"

Before Kelly could answer, cries of "Sister Aweta, Sister Aweta" bounced off the high gymnasium ceiling.

A little boy close to the size of Jason Wentworth ran up to Sister Aleta and tugged on the hem of her khaki shorts. "Aweta," he wailed in a childish voice, again reminding Kelly of the little dude.

Kelly gazed down at the child and her heart squeezed. He had a bruise on his right cheek where someone had slapped him so hard she could make out the outline of a palm. Suddenly she longed to see Jason, missing him with a physical ache in her core. Was he okay? Did he miss her?

She shook her head. Of course the little prince was okay, at least physically. He was safe, unlike this child. Trey would never strike his son.

And the Wentworth men had already forgotten she existed.

Aleta knelt so she was eye level with the child. "What's wrong, Julio?"

"It's my mommy. She won't stop crying. Can you talk to her again?"

"Of course, sweetie." Taking his hand, Aleta stood. "Will you wait for me?" she asked Kelly.

Kelly shrugged, playing the druggie unsure if she wanted to get clean.

"Go to your mom," Aleta told Julio. "I'll be right there."

Julio bit his bottom lip, but trudged out of the gymnasium, glaring at Kelly over his shoulder.

Guilt made her release a sigh. The people here may not all be addicts, but they were definitely in bad situations.

"What's the deal with all the kids in this facility?" Kelly asked. "I was told it was a place to get clean."

"Sunshine Center provides a multitude of services."

"How can you have druggies hanging out in the same location with children at risk?" Kelly used her chin to motion the way Julio had exited.

Aleta's gaze sharpened on Kelly. "Who sent you?"

"A friend told me she got help here," Kelly said.

"Who is your friend?"

"Maria Navarre."

"Is that so? I'm surprised Maria recommended us."

"Why is that?"

"We were unable to do much for her."

"She met a guy here," Kelly said. "Adam Chandler. Have you seen him around?"

"Do you know Chandler?" Aleta's tone turned sharp, so likely she knew Adam was a fugitive. Or maybe the FBI had already questioned her.

Kelly rubbed her cheek, as if she'd been slugged there. "He used to be my supplier. The thing is, he's a bad dude. I owe him money and don't want to see him, don't want him to know where I am."

"I can promise you he won't come here."

"Because?"

"Because he knows we'd call the police on him."

Kelly nodded, as if she totally knew the score. Even if the counselors here didn't know Adam was hunted by law enforcement, most likely they knew he'd abused Maria, and could do nothing to stop it.

Kelly looked toward the door, as if nervous. "Are any of his friends still around?"

Aleta issued a harsh laugh. "Adam doesn't have any friends."

"That sounds right," Kelly muttered.

"Listen—what's your name?"

"Kelly."

"Kelly. I'm sorry, but I need to go. If you want help, I promise this is a safe place. Adam won't be able to get to you here. Please wait for me to come back."

Kelly nodded, but didn't commit to waiting. No point in it. She believed Aleta that Adam didn't have any friends here, so no one would have information on where he was holed up.

She watched Aleta hurry from the gymnasium, presumably to assist Julio and his weeping mother.

Kelly returned to Trey's SUV and drove away, her gaze on the rearview mirror making sure she wasn't followed.

Back in her apartment, Kelly again found herself with time on her hands. Her trip to Sunshine had been a bust, so she no longer had that bit of undercover police work to look forward to. Where else could she look for Adam?

It hadn't even been twenty-four hours and suspension totally sucked.

She glared at the refrigerator, knew there was no help for it and shoved her hands into yellow latex gloves. Her garbage can was almost full when the phone rang.

"Jenkins."

"Kelly, it's Trey."

She closed her eyes, willed her heart to slow down and managed to say, "Hi."

"Are you at home?"

"Yes."

"Would it be convenient if I brought Jason over to see you?"

Trey wanted to come here? "Sure. When?"

"Now."

"Now?" She swallowed. Surely she'd heard him wrong. "Are you serious?"

"Yes. I know I should have given you more warning, but we're in the area, and he's been begging me to arrange a visit."

"Since when are you in my area?"

"Dr. Barth believes Jason needs to get off Collins Island more often."

"Trey, Adam is still out there somewhere."

"I have adequate security in place. Hold on. Someone wants to talk to you."

Oh, no. Kelly clutched her phone tighter.

"Hi, Kelly," Jason said in his sweet little voice.

"Hi, Jase. How are you?"

"I want to come see where you live. Daddy says it's okay."

Kelly shook her head, doubting that was exactly how the discussion with his father had gone down, and examined her apartment with a critical eye. Not so bad. Then she looked down at herself and groaned. She likely stunk from rotten tomatoes. Did she even have time to take a shower?

But she couldn't say no. She wanted to see Jason. She wanted to see Trey.

Did he want to see her?

CHAPTER TWENTY-SEVEN

TREY PUNCHED THE intercom when Hans braked the limo to a stop in front of Kelly's brick apartment building.

"Wait here until we hear from Scott," he told his driver.

"Yes, sir."

Trey gazed at the building, noting the lack of media frenzy. Joe's press release had worked.

He'd tried to stay away, knew that he should for Jason. He'd convinced himself a clean break was best, and not only because of his son's mental health.

They needed to stay away from each other for her sake, too.

Maybe she'd made *him* better, but thanks to the Wentworth name her existence had become a living hell. She was well rid of his disruptive presence in her life and career.

But God forgive him, he couldn't ignore Jason's pleas. Or his own emptiness.

He wanted to see her. One last time. Was there anything left unsaid between them? A lot, in his opinion, but maybe it was better to leave it that way.

Ballard had informed him that the Bureau had ceased surveillance of Kelly's home, but the Protection Alliance had thoroughly vetted the premises and surrounding area. Scott was clearing Kelly's floor before he and Jason went up.

Kelly thought it was risky to bring Jason here, but Adam Chandler didn't want to harm his son. Why would he? He'd only wanted money. It was Kelly, the woman who could identify him, who remained in danger.

Once again because of him.

"Is this where Kelly lives, Daddy?"

Trey nodded. "Inside that building on the third floor."

"Why don't we go see her?"

"Scott will call me when Kelly is ready."

"Okay." Jason got up on his knees and peered out the window.

Trey tried to make sense of his thoughts as he waited for the all-clear. They shouldn't be here, and it wasn't because of any danger. He'd brought a small army with him. No one would get to Kelly or Jason this afternoon.

But what was this stunning sense of urgency he had to see her? She hadn't sounded pleased to hear from him. So why was he here?

Because he couldn't stay away.

His cell buzzed, making Jason turn from the window. Trey smiled at his son, and then read a text from Scott giving the go-ahead.

"You ready to go see Kelly?" he asked Jason, reaching for his hand.

Jason nodded and grasped his fingers.

The limo door opened, and four armed PA operatives surrounded them as Trey lifted his son and hurried to the entrance. They rode up the elevator in silence, Jason's foot softly kicking his thigh during the ride.

Scott waited in the hall when the doors opened. He motioned with his head to the right. Trey glanced that direction and found Kelly standing in a doorway. Looking even more beautiful than he remembered.

Her gaze locked onto his, and he moved toward her.

"Kelly," Jason shrieked.

She shook her head, but a smile softened her lips.

"I see you brought your own military force," she said as he approached.

Her skin was damp, and she smelled of citrus. Trey wanted to pull her into his arms and breathe in her fragrance.

"Hi!" Jason reached out his arms.

"The building is surrounded by my private security," Trey told her as she took Jason from his arms and stepped into her apartment. "You and Jason will be safe."

She hugged Jason, closing her eyes. "Hey, Jase. I missed you, sweetie."

Jason wrapped his arms around her neck and said, "Me, too."

"I swear you've grown an inch," she said.

"No, I didn't."

Kelly pulled back and poked a finger into Jason's belly, making him squirm. "And I think you gained ten pounds since I saw you."

Jason giggled and clutched at Kelly's finger.

"Have you turned into a fish yet?" she asked.

"I swim every day, Kelly," Jason said, still holding on to her finger.

Trey turned to Scott who waited in the hallway. "Stay by the door."

"Yes, sir," Scott said.

"Stay in touch with everyone in the field and keep me informed of anything suspicious."

"Of course, sir."

Trey shut the door, flipped the deadbolt and turned to face Kelly, noticing she wore faded jeans and a tank top, looking casual and nothing like a woman who policed the dangerous streets of Miami.

She smiled at him and lowered Jason to the floor. His son immediately looked around as if assessing the room. Her home was small, a one-bedroom apartment. The rooms were neat, efficiently furnished, the furniture appearing new. He saw no homey touches, indications that the woman he'd come to admire lived here. But exactly what would those signs be? Framed guns hung on the wall? FBI wanted posters?

A photograph of her late mother?

He knew next to nothing about Kelly's private life.

"This is where you live?" Jason asked.

"Yes, it is."

"You don't have a pool?"

"Actually, yes, I do. Down on the first floor. Everyone who lives here can use it, but it's much smaller than yours."

"Oh," Jase said, and scampered into the kitchen, obviously intent on a thorough exploration.

She focused on Trey and said, "So small it's hard to do laps."

"How are you?" he asked.

She hesitated, but said, "I'm fine. How are you?"

"Lonely. The house is empty without you."

He watched her chest rise as she sucked in a breath. He'd surprised her with that answer. Hell, he'd surprised himself.

"How is Jason?" she asked.

"He's doing well."

Was this how it was going to go? Polite conversation? Would they discuss the weather next?

She shook her head, as if having similar thoughts, and rubbed her palms on her jeans. Was she nervous to have him here? He'd never considered that idea.

"Can I get you something to drink?" she asked. "I wasn't really prepared for guests, but I can make some iced tea."

"I'm fine," Trey said. "If you like, I can have Scott bring up some wine from the limo."

Jason reappeared. "Do you have any potato chips, Kelly?"

"Jason," Trey said warningly. "What did we talk about?"

His son stuck out his lower lip. "Kelly doesn't mind."

"How do you know?"

Jason gave Kelly his most winning smile and said, "Daddy says I have to be good or we can't visit you anymore."

Kelly shot him a questioning look.

"That's not what I said, Jason."

His son merely shrugged.

"I'm trying to set boundaries," Trey told her. "Someone told me he might be spoiled."

She laughed, a full-on belly laugh, which somehow broke the tension in his gut. Had he ever heard her really laugh before?

"I don't have any chips," she told Jason. "How about a cracker?"

"That's okay," Jase said. "Where is your bed?"

She colored, shot Trey another look, but pointed toward a doorway. "In my bedroom."

Jason hurried into the room, and Trey followed. Of course he wanted to see where she slept every night.

Trey waited at the doorway while Jason leaped onto the yellow comforter and placed his head on her pillow, giggling again. This was all a big game to him.

When Kelly moved to Trey's side, he wanted to reach out and touch her.

"He seems happy," she said.

Trey glanced at her, but she remained focused on Jase. He'd found a remote control device and punched buttons in an attempt to turn on the small television that sat on a dresser.

"He's getting better," Trey said.

"Does he like the new therapist?"

"He seems to."

"So he doesn't miss me."

Was that a touch of sadness in her tone? Longing even?

"He misses you," Trey said. "So do I."

She lifted her gaze to his. "Do you?"

"More than you can imagine."

Her eyes widened as she stared at him. What was she thinking?

"I'm surprised you came here."

"It's safe. No one will breach my security. The Protection Alliance even cleared rooftops for snipers before we got out of the limo."

She shook her head. "That's not what I meant."

"What did you mean?"

The television blared to life, and Kelly broke their connection, glancing back to Jason.

"Turn it down, son," Trey said.

"Do you have any cartoons, Kelly?" Jason asked.

"I don't know," she said. "Maybe."

"Are you sure you want to watch TV?" Trey asked. "I thought you wanted to talk to Kelly."

"But this is *Kelly's* TV," Jason said in an aggrieved tone indicating such ownership made a huge difference.

Kelly stepped into the room, away from Trey's pull. She needed to escape the emotions that welled up when he looked at her. When he said he *missed* her, for God's sake.

How could he miss her? Trey had denied to the world there was anything between them. He'd only come for a visit because Jason wanted to see her. And she'd been glad to see the little dude. Too glad. She'd had to hide unexpected tears when Jason had reached for her, but now apparently even the kid preferred to watch TV.

She took the remote from Jason and surfed until she found a channel with children's programming.

"How's that?" she asked.

"Okay," Jason said. He clutched her hand and pulled her down close to his mouth. "Go talk to Daddy," he whispered.

CHAPTER TWENTY-EIGHT

KELLY STARED AT JASON. "What did you say?"

"Talk to Daddy," Jason insisted again.

She jerked up. What was the little prince up to? She glanced at Trey. He raised his eyebrows, probably wondering what they were whispering about.

Had Jason insisted Trey bring him for a visit so his pretend mother could talk to his real father? But why? Was this child so spoiled that he thought he could play matchmaker? She'd often noted how intuitive the kid was about the feelings of grown-ups. Especially when his grandfather was around.

No way. Jason was barely four years old. He didn't know anything about the convoluted emotions of adults. As if she did.

Kelly shrugged and moved toward Trey, who definitely appeared confused.

"Sorry," he told her. "Jason was so thrilled to come see you, I didn't expect him to park himself in front of the tube."

Kelly nodded, immediately suspicious. Had father and son cooked up a scheme so she and Trey could be alone? But why would they? If Trey wanted to be alone with her, the man would have no problem making that happen.

"Maybe he's exhausted from all the excitement," she said.

"Maybe," Trey said.

"Did he get a nap today?"

"No. Now that he's down, he'll likely conk out in few minutes."

Kelly nodded and shut the door, muffling the sound of the manic cartoon characters. "Are you sure you don't want something to drink?" she asked on the way to the sofa.

"I'm fine," Trey said. He waited for her to sit first. She did, and he sat beside her. Too close.

"How long have you lived here?" he asked.

"Not quite a year."

"I didn't see any sort of alarm system on your front door."

"Because there isn't one."

"The Protection Alliance informed me there are problems with the security on this building."

"It could definitely be better," she agreed. "Ballard was furious because the cameras on the parking lot weren't working the day my car was bombed, which meant he got no video of Adam."

"Are there any new leads on my son's kidnapper?"

"I wish," Kelly said.

Trey placed his arm on the sofa behind her. "That's all the more reason for you to have an alarm."

"The feds think he's left the area."

"What do you think?"

"I'm not so sure. I visited the rehab center where

he and Maria met to try and stir something up, but no luck."

Trey's mouth curled into one of his sexy grins. "Congratulations. So you're back on patrol?"

"No. In fact, I've been suspended," Kelly said. "The visit was made on my own time."

"Suspended?" Trey's smile faded. "What happened?"

"Politics. The IA detective disagreed with my lieutenant's decision to let me go on the FBI op."

"I'm sorry." Trey shook his head. "I hoped the press release would help."

Kelly looked away when he mentioned the press release. So he did know about it. She'd been harboring the faint hope that his father had engineered the statement and had kept Trey in the dark.

But no.

She'd found a copy online and had memorized the important section: "The family is grateful to Officer Kelly Jenkins for her aid in rescuing Jason Wentworth, but rumors of a relationship between the officer and Trey Wentworth are completely unfounded and harmful to the child's recovery."

Harmful to the child's recovery. Did Trey now believe she was hurting his son? If so, why did they come?

"Hey," Trey said softly. "What's wrong?"

She sighed. As if her suspension wasn't enough. "I guess I'm wondering how the press release was supposed to help me."

"It got rid of the paparazzi, didn't it?"

She nodded, but doubted the original intention behind the statement had been to help *her*. It had all been for the benefit of the Wentworth image, denying any connection between Trey and a rookie cop from the seedy side of town. He apparently had no clue how foolish the blunt denial had made her feel.

Because it had never occurred to him that she'd developed feelings for him. She ought to be grateful for that.

"How long will you be suspended?" he asked.

"I don't know. These things take time."

"None of this would have happened if you hadn't helped Jason," Trey said in a tight voice.

"It's not your fault," she said. Time to change the subject. "How are the plans for your tennis clinic coming?"

He hesitated, but said, "Everything is falling into place nicely. You should come to the opening day. It was your idea, after all."

She shrugged. "Hardly my idea, but send me an invite."

"If I did, would you come?"

She lifted her gaze to his and found him staring at her intently. She hesitated. "Probably not."

"Why not?"

"We—we're different people, Trey. I'm not part of your world."

After a long moment he said, "What if I wanted you in my world?"

Her heart began to pound. Yes, this was what she wanted him to say, even if it was all wrong for them both.

"You know I don't fit."

He picked up her hand and laced their fingers together. "Maybe we could make it work."

"Could we?"

"I think Jason wants us to."

"And whatever the little prince wants, the little prince gets?"

Trey's eyes widened. "The little prince? I haven't heard that one in a while."

"Sorry. It's one of my pet names for Jason."

Now wearing a sad smile, Trey squeezed her hand. "Funny thing. I was once a little prince."

"You?"

Trey nodded, seemingly fascinated by the connection of their fingers.

"I've met your father," Kelly said. "I find it hard to believe the man spoiled you when you were Jason's age,"

"Not my father." Trey shook his head, obviously thinking back. "My mother. I was her little prince."

Kelly held her breath as Trey continued to speak. He seldom mentioned his mother.

"I've often wondered if that's one reason Darlene turned to drugs," he said. "Two different women, two different ways of reacting to the pressure of being a Wentworth. Hell, I was happy to back away from that life myself."

"And you're about to be sucked back in."

"I knew my absence was temporary, but things will be different when I take over. I'm nothing like my father."

"No," Kelly said. "You're not."

"Thank you for that," Trey said.

He fell silent, and so did she. Canned laughter from the television was the only sound as she remembered what he'd said on *Drop Shot* about some scars being less visible.

Her family history might be sad, but so was his. No matter how much money anyone had, everyone had to do the best they could with the hand they were dealt. Sometimes the cards sucked.

Jason was getting better. That was the important thing. He didn't need her anymore. Perhaps she was even a reminder of a confusing and scary period in his young life. With a sharp stab of regret, she wondered if she needed to step away. She should cut off all ties with the little dude, which meant any connection with his father would also be lost.

A connection that didn't really exist anyway. Or only in her imagination.

"Kelly—" Trey broke off, shaking his head.

"What?"

"I'm sorry if the press release hurt your feelings," he said. "That wasn't my intention, but I should have warned you."

"I understand," she said.

"Do you really?"

"You explained the reasoning," she said. "And after all, the statement was the truth." She raised her gaze to Trey's and got caught by the raw emotion glittering in his dark eyes. She swallowed.

"Wasn't it, Trey?"

CHAPTER TWENTY-NINE

TREY RAISED A hand and caressed Kelly's soft cheek. She was so lovely, so good for him in so many ways, and he was desperately in love with her. And this time his feelings were the real deal. Not the crazed infatuation he'd had for Darlene. He knew the difference now.

Jason loved Kelly, too. No doubt she was the perfect woman to nurture his son. Her influence would turn him into a fine man.

He wanted to make Kelly his wife and build a life with her, have another child, if she was willing.

Yes, it was possible the dangerous job she loved could end her life too soon, but he'd become willing to take that chance. He better than anyone knew there were no guarantees.

Except one.

Marriage into the Wentworth family destroyed women. Ground them down until there was nothing left but a shell of their original vibrant spirit. His grandmother had died too young and under mysterious circumstances that his father refused to discuss. His mother was rotting in a sanitarium. His wife had drunk herself into a horrifying and violent death, nearly killing her own child.

He couldn't—wouldn't allow that tragic story to shape Kelly's life. To prevent it, all he had to do was walk away from her. If he let her go, she would at least have a chance to live a normal life, a happy existence.

But could he do it? Could he say goodbye to this woman who had become so important to him? To Jason?

He'd lived a life of privilege and had always taken whatever he wanted. Who was going to stop him? He was self-aware enough to know the arrangement with his father had been as much for him as for his mother.

Confusion clouded Kelly's clear blue eyes as he remained silent, stroking her cheek with his thumb. She'd asked him if the press release was the truth. He owed her an answer.

"You're safer if it is the truth," he said softly.

She blinked. "I'm safer? What does that mean?"

He dropped his hand and stood, interrupting her questions. If he stayed here any longer he'd give in to his own need and tell her how he felt. He suspected she was half in love with him already. And with *him*, surprisingly, not his money, which was perhaps the quality he admired the most about her.

Or was it his own raging arrogance that made him think he could make Kelly his? He'd never met a woman like her, a woman with an unwavering internal compass about right and wrong. She'd made him a better person, given him the courage to take Wentworth Industries in a new direction.

If she fell in love with him—and maybe it *was* arrogance, but he knew he could make that happen—life with him would devastate her. That was a tragedy he had to prevent because the world was a better place with a healthy and happy Kelly Jenkins living in it. She'd already saved one little boy. Maybe others would need her help someday. She'd chosen the right career to help people, a job that she loved.

And her contact with him had put that career in jeopardy.

He shouldn't have come.

"Trey?" she asked in a quiet voice. "What's wrong?"

He turned back to her. "I need to focus on Jason's recovery," he said.

"Of course you do." She closed her eyes.

"He's been so confused about you, his mother, losing Maria, the change in therapists. Jase doesn't need any more turmoil in his life right now."

She opened eyes glittering with unshed tears. He longed to move to her, comfort her, tell her everything would be all right. That he loved her. But he couldn't do that to her.

"And being around me is harmful to his recovery," she said, her voice catching. "Just like the press release said."

No, he wanted to scream. But Trey nodded, unsure what he'd say if he tried to speak. It was better this way. Easier.

At least easier for him. This way he didn't have to pretend he didn't care about her.

"I understand," she said. Moving slowly, she used her arms to push herself to her feet.

"I'm sorry," he managed, knowing his apology meant little to Kelly, that he'd hurt her. Worse, he could see the pain it had caused her to think she was damaging his son.

He moved to the front door and opened it. Scott focused on him immediately, alert and attentive. Trey informed him they were leaving.

"I'll wake up Jason," Trey said, stepping toward the bedroom.

Arms folded across her chest, Kelly offered him a brave smile. He wondered how much that had cost her.

He shouldn't have come. No matter how much Jason begged, he couldn't bring his son to see her again. They should fly back to New York tonight. He needed to put distance between himself and Kelly so he wouldn't be tempted to give in to his own selfish desires.

But no. He couldn't escape Miami. Jase had just started with a new therapist, one he liked even better than Carico. His four-year-old was adjusting to the change. He was the adult and needed to find a way to do the same thing.

As predicted, Jason was sound asleep on Kelly's bed. When Trey gathered his son in his arms, he fussed a little but didn't fully wake up. Trey exhaled a sigh of relief that they were all three spared a tearful scene, and turned toward the door.

Jason had had enough goodbyes in his short life.

Kelly stood in the doorway watching. Their gazes locked as he moved toward her. At least he couldn't touch her. Not when he was holding a child who had thankfully gained weight since returning home.

When he drew near, she focused on Jason, then reached out and gently stroked his hair.

"Tell him goodbye for me," she whispered.

"Of course," Trey said, his voice hoarse.

Kelly cleared her throat. "As soon as the insurance money comes through, I'll get your SUV back to the island."

"Please keep it," Trey said. "I can transfer the title."

Another half smile curved her lips. "Still trying to buy me off, Mr. Billionaire?"

Trey wanted to hug her close, but shrugged instead. "Can't blame a guy for trying."

"You know I can't accept it," she said.

"Yeah," he said. "I know."

He stared into her lovely but unhappy face, trying to memorize it. Did he even have any photos of her? He hated that his visit, this final goodbye, had made her sad, and his resolve wavered.

She rose on her toes and lightly kissed his cheek. He turned her head to capture her mouth with his, but she was gone too fast.

"Stay well, Trey," she whispered.

"You, too," he said, and walked out her door.

"Papa is on the move," Scott barked into the mike at his mouth as he moved ahead of Trey down the hallway.

Before entering the waiting elevator, Trey looked back.

In her doorway, Kelly raised a hand and waved. She didn't smile. Trey nodded and stepped into the car, wishing again that he could leave this city. Instead, he'd be trapped in his walled estate longing for a woman who was so close and yet totally out of his reach.

A WEEK LATER, in full uniform except for her cap, Kelly stood at attention before Lieutenant Marshall's desk.

"As you were, Officer Jenkins."

Kelly moved her feet apart, clasped her hands behind her back, gaze straight ahead. Marshall had summoned her into his office. Why?

Was he finally going to fire her?

"Internal Affairs has cleared you," he said. "Congratulations."

She released a breath and closed her eyes. Thank God.

"Plus it appears you are no longer of interest to the media," Marshall continued.

Kelly cut her gaze to his. Eyes narrowed, Marshall scrutinized her, waiting for her reaction.

"Are you ready to go back on patrol?"

"Yes, sir."

Marshall opened a drawer, withdrew her badge and service weapon and placed them on his desk. "Report to your sergeant for roll call. He's expecting you."

Kelly grabbed her badge and holstered her gun. "Thank you, sir."

Marshall leaned back in his chair. "I expected a smile at least."

Kelly swallowed. "Sorry, sir,"

"I know the suspension seemed harsh, but you needed to stay off the streets for your own protection."

"I understand, sir." But she didn't. Why was everyone, Trey Wentworth included, trying to protect her? She raised her chin. She didn't need anyone to take care of her.

"You did a good thing rescuing that Wentworth kid," Marshall continued. "You did the department proud at a time when we needed a little positive press." He sighed. "Make that a lot of positive press."

Kelly nodded. He was talking about the corruption allegations. She'd seen the headlines, read the stories. Hell, she'd even been part of the story for a while. Fortunately, things had died down on that front. Just as with her brief flirtation with celebrity, hungry journalists had moved on to newer, more sensational stories.

"I'm proud of you, Officer Jenkins. You should be proud of yourself."

Kelly forced a smile. Proud of herself? She wished she'd skipped her run that fateful morning. If she had, she would have never met Trey Wentworth.

"Thank you, sir."

"You're dismissed," Marshall barked, as if uncomfortable about his uncharacteristic praise. "Be safe out there."

Kelly saluted and marched out of the lieutenant's office. She was pleased, of course she was. Resuming patrol was what she'd wanted, had prayed for, but lately she couldn't muster much enthusiasm for anything. Not even eating. She'd lost the weight she'd gained from Greta's gourmet meals, and maybe a couple pounds more.

She ought to be elated about her career, on that proverbial cloud nine. Instead she felt as if she trudged around inside a dark rain cloud.

What she needed to shake her out of her slump was a good callout on patrol today. She needed an incident that summoned her entire squad, sirens wailing. Something exciting—no, something worthwhile. She needed to do something that made her proud to be a cop.

Kelly gave herself a swift mental kick in the butt as she pushed into the women's locker room. Was she fantasizing about rescuing another little boy? *If I'm going to daydream, why not reach for the stars? Why not save the mayor of Dade County? Or the governor. The Dalai Lama.*

The whole thing with Trey was just as much of a fantasy.

Lana, standing by her locker, looked up and grinned at Kelly, eyebrows raised.

"Kelly?"

Kelly raised her arm for a high five. "I'm baaack."

"All right." Lana slapped Kelly's palm. "Welcome home, girl."

Kelly slammed open her locker. Welcome home. That sounded right. This police station *was* her home, the only home she had ever wanted. Truly the only home she'd ever known.

She smashed her cap onto her head. What did she know about a family? She'd never actually been part of one. The make-believe with the Wentworths didn't count.

The locker room door swung open. Grinning, Trice entered and said, "I heard a rumor."

"Please," Kelly said, holding up her hand. "I've had enough celebrity gossip to last a lifetime."

"Rudy says you're off suspension."

"Damn straight," Kelly said.

"Make it count," Trice said.

"Make it count," Lana repeated.

Kelly nodded. "Make it count," she said again, the mantra the three of them had cooked up during training.

Make it count. She *had* saved a little boy. She pictured Jason in the park when he crashed into her that morning, and the tightness in her belly loosened just a little.

Okay, yeah, maybe he was spoiled and rich and would have eventually been rescued when the ransom payoff got straightened out. But what if he wasn't? Her lieutenant was right. She should be proud of herself.

So why did she feel so empty inside?

AT HIS DESK, Trey looked up at a knock on his office door. He was expecting Brian, and that was who stood in the doorway looking as intense as ever, toting his massive brown leather briefcase.

"You're late," Trey said, smiling to soften his accusation.

"Sorry. The two o'clock ferry was full, and I had to wait," Brian said. "Has the meeting started?"

Trey glanced at his computer screen, which showed a long empty conference table. A woman carrying a tray with a pitcher of water and glasses moved in front of the camera and disappeared. The sound was muted, but Trey knew she'd placed the water on a sideboard for use by directors during the upcoming emergency board meeting.

"Any minute now," Trey said.

He sat back, rubbing his eyes. It had been a long day. A long week. Between plans for the tennis clinic and preparing himself for the CEO position at Wentworth Industries, he'd tried to keep too busy to think about Kelly. She'd texted that she was off suspension, which was of course excellent news. But he couldn't help wonder if she blamed him for almost destroying her career.

And he couldn't help wondering if she missed him.

"You need a secretary," Brian said, glancing at the various stacks of paper on the desk. "And a file cabinet."

Trey followed Brian's gaze and winced. "I've got a temp coming tomorrow morning."

"I think you'll need more than a temp." Brian settled himself so he could see the screen. "Are you certain this is the way you want to go with your father?"

Trey cut him a look. "You said there were no problems legally with the board's decision."

"Absolutely not," Brian said, withdrawing a thick packet from his briefcase. "A majority vote is all that's needed to make a change. But—" He hesitated. "The man *is* your father."

"And I would have preferred to wait a few more months, give him a little more time to get used to the idea of stepping down. But the board is adamant. Senior's recent decisions have been too costly." Trey paused, then said, "I thought you agreed."

"I do," Brian said. "As your new corporate counsel. It's your old friend who is worried about the consequences to your family."

Trey shook his head, refusing to dwell on the meaning behind the word *family*. He pushed away an image of Kelly reading Jason a bedtime story, his son gazing adoringly at the woman he'd chosen for his new mother.

"Father refused to resign," Trey said. "It's either me as CEO, or they bring in someone new. I'm certain Senior would rather have me than an outsider he'd have less influence over."

"Will he show to protest the vote?"

"Unknown," Trey said with another glance at the monitor. Two men and a woman were now seated around the table. The board had acquiesced to a teleconference due to Jason's situation. Trey wasn't ready to leave his son yet since one kidnapper was still at large.

"Alexander could file suit," Brian said. "He doesn't have a case, but the litigation would be expensive and cause a stock dive."

"I hope he doesn't go that route." Trey sighed. "My father is slipping, and he doesn't want to admit it."

"How bad is it?" Brian asked. "Could you have him declared incompetent?"

Trey shook his head and didn't reply.

"I take it you don't want to go there."

"Not if I can help it," Trey said.

The phone rang. Trey checked caller ID, wholeheartedly agreeing with Brian that he needed a permanent assistant, if for nothing else than to screen calls. His life was definitely about to make a radical change. He'd be attending fewer fund-raisers and answering more phone calls. He couldn't help but think that had to be a good thing. He'd have less time to obsess about what was missing in his life.

One Officer Kelly Jenkins.

And this call was from the company that managed the apartment building where she lived. He'd been expecting to hear from them. He heard a chime from the computer and glanced at the monitor. The table was now full, so this conversation had to be quick.

The meeting to depose his father as CEO of Wentworth Industries was set to commence.

CHAPTER THIRTY

ALREADY SEATED WITH Sean at their usual table at the Coral Bagel, Kelly waved Trice over when she entered.

"Man, what a slow day," Patrice said as she slid into the booth.

"That's the way we like it, ladies," Sean said.

"Speak for yourself," Kelly muttered.

"I know you like to rock and roll, Kel," Sean said. "But we can't be heroes every day."

"And you know where you can shove it, Sean," Kelly said.

Sean laughed. Trice opened her mouth to say something, but shook her head and looked down at her menu. As if she didn't already know what she'd order.

"What?" Kelly demanded.

Trice waved her hand. "You don't want to know."

Their server appeared, interrupting the conversation. Kelly scrutinized her friend as she requested her usual lunch. Trice knew something. Something big, no doubt juicy gossip about Trey. Kelly had been careful to avoid even hearing his name, but now she had to know.

When the server moved away, Kelly leaned forward. "What don't I want to know?"

Patrice smiled knowingly. "That your lover is now in charge of Wentworth Industries."

"What?"

"Trey staged a coup d'état and threw his dad out," Trice said, picking up her water.

"Close your mouth, Kelly," Sean said. "Even I couldn't miss hearing that news."

"What do you mean?" Kelly asked, unsure who to glare at now.

"It's all over the news," Sean said. "Don't you watch TV?"

"He's apparently some big financial wizard," Trice said. "Who knew your party animal was a business genius?"

"Wentworth Industries stock went through the roof," Sean said.

"That's good, right?" Kelly asked.

Sean shrugged. "For the stockholders. The whole stock market is happy. Even my little 401K has gone up. I'll bet yours has, too. Do you ever check?"

"When did this happen?" Kelly asked.

"The market started reacting to rumors three or four days ago, but the official announcement was made yesterday morning," Sean said.

"Why the delay?" Kelly asked.

Trice met Kelly's gaze. "No one knows."

Kelly nodded and fell silent. So Trey did it. He booted Senior and took over the family business. Good for him. Would he become so immersed in

Wentworth Industries he'd ignore Jason? No, Trey wouldn't do that. He loved his son too much.

She needed to return his SUV. She'd received her insurance check yesterday and planned to rent a car while she searched for a vehicle she could afford. She should drive to the ferry tonight, but knew she wouldn't. She wasn't ready to sever that last connection.

What did another day or two matter? Trey had more vehicles than anyone needed. She could wait until her next day off.

"Have you heard from him?" Trice asked quietly.

"Only indirectly," Kelly said.

"What does that mean?"

"My entire apartment complex has been wired with a new state-of-the-art security system courtesy of Wentworth Industries." She shook her head. "I can't believe how quickly it happened."

"Money talks," Sean said.

"There are new video cameras at every entrance or exit, and get this. I have four monitors in my apartment so I can view every one of them."

"No way," Sean said.

"Yep. I came home from work one night and there they were, along with detailed instructions on how to scroll through each access point."

"Surely he didn't put monitors in every unit."

"No," Kelly said. "Just mine and the manager's office. Apparently Trey wanted them to hire guards 24/7 to monitor the cameras, but when management said that would mean raising everyone's rent, he had the screens placed in my unit."

"And he paid for the whole deal?" Sean asked.

"Well, I sure as hell didn't," Kelly said. "There's also an alarm on my front door. So far I've set the damn thing off twice when I couldn't disable it quickly enough with my password."

"He wants to make sure nothing happens to you," Trice said. "I think that's sweet."

"The man is in love," Sean said with a grin.

"He's grateful because I rescued his son," Kelly said, relieved by the arrival of their food.

"Oh, yeah," Trice said. "I'm sure that's it."

Sorry she'd even mentioned Trey's ridiculous security system, Kelly picked up a fork to signal she was done with the discussion. Too bad her traitorous stomach roiled at the thought of food.

The fact that Trey had been so high-handed rankled, although her fellow residents had been delighted with the extra level of security. She'd actually made a couple of new friends. Turned out most of the building knew who she was and that she'd rescued Jason Wentworth.

Kelly stabbed a French fry. Yeah, but her neighbors didn't have to enter a security code into a blinking box within sixty seconds every time they came home. She'd been tempted to refuse to set the alarm, but that just made her feel stupid.

She'd like to call Trey and give him a good piece of her mind. But she didn't dare do that. Hearing his voice would only make her loneliness worse. And she'd want to talk to Jason. Better that she stay away.

Funny how lately every small child she saw reminded her of the little dude, made her wonder how he and his dad were doing. Made her want a child of her own.

She forced herself to take a bite of her tuna sandwich. She was trying to forget Trey, move on. So how was she supposed to do that when his security system was in her face every single day?

KELLY ENTERED HER APARTMENT, hurried straight to the alarm pad and entered the password. When the blinking light changed from red to green, she released a sigh. At least tonight she wouldn't have to place an embarrassing call to the alarm company to call them off.

After locking her front door, she went to her bedroom, unbuckled her duty belt and looped it over the chair where she always kept it. No need to lock away her service weapon. No small children in the house to worry about.

She changed into workout clothing and stretched her arms toward the ceiling, feeling lighter now that she was free of her belt and the Kevlar vest she always wore on duty. But she never minded the additional weight. The vest and the belt protected her on the job. They were the only security system she needed.

In the kitchen she grabbed a bottle of cold water from the fridge and stepped to the four new monitors that took up too much space in her tiny living room.

The first monitor showed a view of her hallway leading from the camera over her door to the elevator and the fire escape stairwell beyond. Every five seconds the view flipped to show the hallway to the second fire escape. She could see anyone who exited the elevator or the stairs on her floor.

She unscrewed the cap on her water. Right now the hallway was empty.

The second monitor revealed the main entrance of the building. Even before the new system, every door was always supposed to remain locked and residents used a fob to enter and exit any egress point. Management provided a phone so guests could notify residents of their arrival, but the phone and camera to view guests seldom worked, so someone had disabled the locks.

Trey's new electronic door couldn't be tampered with, and the camera functioned perfectly. Taking a long drink, Kelly watched people enter and exit the doorway on her monitor. It was 8:00 p.m., so the view was fairly active.

She waited while the third monitor rotated between two separate views of the parking lot, the two fire escape exits on the ground floor and the various stair landings on all six floors.

No monsters anywhere. At least not in real time.

The system kept the video for forty-eight hours, and then recorded over the loop. She switched on the fourth monitor and scanned the recordings in triple time, looking for anyone that resembled Adam Chandler. She'd done this for three nights and had come up empty. She pulled up a chair and wondered how long she'd continue this routine. She was already bored. That was the problem with these passive types of security systems.

She yawned, her mind wandering to the workout she'd do later. When Kelly refocused on the screen, she bolted forward to freeze the recording on a figure trying to open the east fire exit door. Hadn't she seen the same person trying to access the west door at some point? She made note of the time signature, backed up the video and slowed the recording to normal time to watch the man again.

Yeah, maybe this guy was Adam Chandler, but maybe not. Body type was the same, but the face was in shadows. Definitely similar hair. Long sleeves, so no way to make ID through his tats.

Well, whoever he was, he definitely wanted in her building but didn't have a fob to open the door.

She checked the instructions from the security company, located the time signature for the west door and sure enough the same guy was trying to gain access. He even kicked the door in frustration, and that was likely why she'd remembered him.

He'd made a mistake.

She repeated the process for the main entrance

and found the man again. The lighting was better here. Kelly's heart pounded. He definitely resembled Adam Chandler. The FBI could confirm it with their face recognition program.

The timing, if it was accurate—but then of course it was; Trey paid for it—showed he'd started with the fire escapes and then moved to the front door. Why would a resident do that? Or a guest?

Last night this man had tried to get inside where he didn't belong. It didn't mean the man was Chandler, but Trey's new security was working to keep whoever he was out.

She watched him read the instructions that told guests how to notify residents of their arrival. He picked up the phone and punched in some numbers. He turned his face away from the camera, so she couldn't tell if he spoke to anyone. Maybe no one answered. Whatever occurred, he dropped the receiver and stomped off the visual field.

She waited. When he didn't return, she sped up the recording. According to the time stamp, forty-five minutes later a resident she recognized from the gym approached. Shaking his head, he placed the phone back in its cradle and used his fob to enter. This had all happened yesterday evening at midnight when the front door was fairly quiet. And she'd been at her most vulnerable. Sound asleep.

When finished with her review, Kelly switched off the fourth monitor and sat back, her gaze falling to the current view of the building's main entrance. No one was currently visible, but her gut told her Chandler had been here yesterday.

She took another long drink of her water.

Jason's kidnapper hadn't left the area, and he still wanted to eliminate her as a threat.

The FBI needed to know. Kelly grabbed her phone and punched in Ballard's cell. He answered immediately.

When she told him the reason for the call, he sounded doubtful, but promised to send an agent to retrieve the video for review.

"Wentworth wasted his money," Ballard said.

"I don't think so," Kelly replied.

"If Chandler is still in Miami, he's gone to ground," Ballard said. "Somewhere deep that Maria didn't know about."

"What about his cousin?" Kelly asked, her gaze still on the monitors. She blinked as a familiar figure at the main entrance caught her attention.

"Caleb has regained consciousness, but he's not giving us anything useful."

Only half listening to Ballard, Kelly stared at the monitor. A man had been standing off to the side, out of the visual field. When a female resident she didn't know moved into the frame carrying grocery bags, he stepped forward to speak to her. He held a bouquet of flowers in his right hand.

He also wore a cast on his wrist.

Ballard said, "Caleb insists they didn't know we were coming, but I—"

"Hold on," Kelly interrupted. "Adam Chandler is downstairs right now."

"You're certain?"

"Yes," she said, her heart hammering. The cast confirmed it. He'd been wearing long sleeves last night.

"Oh, no," she moaned.

"What?" Ballard demanded.

Kelly's breath caught as she watched the resident awkwardly juggle her bags so she could raise her key fob and release the lock. Smiling, Chandler pushed open the door for her and slipped in behind her.

Adam Chandler had found his way inside.

CHAPTER THIRTY-ONE

MOVING FAST, KELLY disconnected with Ballard and phoned dispatch on the way to her bedroom. Yeah, Ballard claimed the FBI was en route, but her department could respond much quicker.

And by God they were going to get Adam Chandler tonight.

She donned her Kevlar vest, retrieved her service weapon and moved back to the monitors, barrel pointed down.

Did Chandler know her unit number? She wasn't listed anywhere, but he'd somehow unearthed this address.

She focused on the monitor showing her empty hallway. Would he come up the stairs or use the elevator?

The bigger question was if he was armed. She had to assume so. He'd had a weapon that day in the park. She'd disarmed him with a kick. She'd broken the jerk's wrist.

He wouldn't come here without his Glock.

Her phone clattered as it vibrated on top of the monitor where she'd placed it, startling her, kicking her heart into overdrive. A split second later her ring tone sounded.

After a deep breath, she averted her gaze from the screen and read caller ID.

Dispatch had notified her lieutenant.

She pressed the speaker button and refocused on the monitor. "Jenkins."

"What's your status, Officer Jenkins?" Lieutenant Marshall demanded.

"I'm in my home waiting for Chandler to bang on my front door."

"Good. Do not leave your apartment. That is a direct order. You're far safer inside. Is that understood?"

"Understood, sir."

"Multiple units are minutes out. We're coming in silent to surprise him. We'll cover all exits so Chandler can't escape."

Kelly nodded. "Good."

Nothing yet on the monitor. She rotated her neck to release tension.

"Listen, Jenkins, I know you're a rookie and haven't seen much action, but you're well trained. You were top of your class. You'll do fine."

She swallowed hard. She could actually use a pep talk about now. Waiting for someone to come shoot you pretty much sucked. "Yes, sir. Thank you, sir."

"You'll be ready for him," Marshall said confidently.

"Yes, sir." She tightened the grip on her weapon.

"Don't try to be a hero if he shoots your lock and comes in firing. Take your best shot. I don't want to lose an officer tonight."

"And if he knocks?"

"Don't do anything unless he tries to breach. We'll nab him when he exits. I'm in front of your building now. Stay frosty."

The phone went quiet. Kelly waited, her gaze glued to the monitor showing the hallway, her breath ragged and harsh in the quiet of her apartment. She sent a silent thank-you to Trey for installing his security system. Without it, Chandler could have accessed the building last night and caught her asleep.

It had been ten minutes. Where was Chandler? Maybe he didn't know her unit number. Had her fellow officers already nabbed him or—oh, God. Had he done something to the woman who'd let him inside? Would he have followed her and killed her so she couldn't identify him?

No, that made no sense. But nothing Chandler did had any logic to it.

The elevator doors slid open. Kelly tensed.

Chandler exited still carrying the flowers, a prop to make him appear harmless. Striding toward her door, he reached into the arrangement and extracted a weapon. With a silencer attached. He dropped the bouquet.

Kelly bit her lip. This was it. What would he do? *Where was backup?*

She raised her own weapon, held it steady in a two-handed grip and aimed it at her front door.

She glanced to the monitor. Chandler leaned forward and peered in the safety peephole. He nodded, raised the gun and fired at her lock.

He kicked the door open, making more noise than the gunshot. Chandler entered fast, holding his weapon in one hand.

"Freeze. Police," Kelly shouted.

Chandler swung his gun toward her.

Take your best shot. Kelly squeezed the trigger. She aimed for center mass. Exactly as she'd been taught.

She hit Chandler in the right chest, and he went down.

She heard a crash in the hallway but didn't move her weapon or focus from Chandler. He lay moaning on her carpet.

Uniformed officers in riot gear holding shields appeared in her doorway.

"Stand down, Officer Jenkins," one barked.

Kelly lowered her weapon.

She'd shot a man.

She didn't think the wound was fatal, but still. She released a breath. She had a long night ahead of her.

But she'd done her job. A dangerous man was off the streets.

It was finally over. She couldn't wait to tell Trey.

So maybe it wasn't over after all.

I SHOULDN'T BE doing this. This is a really bad idea. Repeating that thought over and over, Kelly drove Trey's SUV off the Collins Island ferry and into the spray of water that washed away any salt residue from the short ride. She wished she could flush away her nerves as easily.

She should have stuck with her original plan to dump the car on the Miami side and let Hans retrieve it. Trice promised a ride to the car rental agency, or she could call a taxi.

But Trey had asked her to come to the house. She'd heard hesitation in his voice, but the rat had allowed Jason to grab the phone. When Jason had begged her, she couldn't say no.

Kelly used the wipers to clear the windshield as she drove away from the spray. So she now spoiled the little prince just as much as Trey did.

All she had to do was get through a brief recitation of the arrest and thank him profusely. She nodded to herself. She could do that. She'd have to keep the story G-rated, though, because she didn't want to be alone with Trey. She definitely needed the little dude around as a buffer.

Besides, she owed Trey a personal visit. He'd saved her life. If there had been no security system to warn her, who knows what would have happened when Chandler had come to her door. For sure nothing good.

Chandler would live, but would spend the rest of his miserable life in jail.

And Trey deserved to know details about Chandler's takedown. She could just imagine the terse version Ballard had given him. He had been none too happy to arrive on the scene and discover the Miami-Dade PD had gotten the collar. Kelly grinned. Score one for the local guys.

Although Ballard wasn't such a bad sort. He'd actually invited her to apply for the FBI, telling her she had fine instincts and would be an asset to the Bureau. That had made her feel good, but she had found her home with the PD.

She braked to a stop in front of Wentworth Villa and found Jason and Trey waiting for her on the marble steps.

Almost, but not quite.

Jason wore his bathing suit. Trey looked like a Greek statute come to life in shorts and a light blue knit shirt.

When she exited the vehicle, the kid jumped up and ran toward her. She raised her gaze to Trey's and went still at the emotion she read in his eyes.

As JASON LEAPED into Kelly's arms, Trey resisted the urge to move toward the pair and hug them both tight. Sometimes he thought the two of them were all he needed in the world to make him happy.

Unfortunately, life was never that simple. At least not his life. And definitely not today. He shoved away disturbing thoughts. He'd deal with that when the time came. Kelly was here. He'd enjoy her company for whatever time they had.

She lowered Jason to his feet, grabbed his son's

hand and moved up the steps toward him, her blond hair shining in the sun. Why was it that each time he saw her, she appeared more lovely than even his most vivid memories?

"Daddy says you arrested the bad guys," Jason told Kelly.

Kelly flashed Trey a look, eyebrows raised.

"Dr. Barth said to be honest with him," Trey told her.

"Well, thanks to your daddy," Kelly said, "the mean man is in jail now and can never harm anyone ever again."

Jason screwed up his face. "What did Daddy do?"

Kelly knelt in front of Jason and pointed to a video camera over the wrought iron gate. "See that little box?"

Jason nodded.

"That's a camera. Your daddy put lots of boxes like that at my house so the bad guys couldn't get in."

Trey's heart lurched when his son beamed at him with wide-eyed approval.

"Wow," Jason said and ran over to hug his daddy's legs.

With a hand on his son's head, Trey met Kelly's gaze and mouthed, "Thank you."

She shook her head and said, "Thank *you*."

Trey stared at her, committing every feature on her face to memory. He'd expected fury from her over the security system. What a surprise that she was actually grateful. He wanted to tell her so many things—most of all how he felt about her—but knew that he shouldn't. Couldn't.

Jason pulled back. "Do you want to watch me swim, Kelly?"

"Of course I do," Kelly said, as if there were nothing else in the world she would enjoy more.

And he loved her for how good she was to Jason, for Jason. He knew asking her to come in person had been unfair. Unfair to everyone, but when she'd called to tell him the news, he hadn't been able to stop himself. He'd had to see her one last time.

Chatting about how far Jason could swim underwater with one breath, the three of them moved into the house and out onto the patio where Jason immediately jumped into the pool. He and Kelly sat at a table where, in anticipation of Jason's wanting to swim, Trey had arranged for a chilled bottle of champagne in an ice bucket.

She cocked an eyebrow. "It's five o'clock somewhere?"

"Don't you think we deserve a celebration?" Trey asked.

She grinned. "Indeed, I do."

Trey busied himself opening the wine, loving the idea that he'd gotten such a beautiful smile from her. He wished he could be the one to make that happen more often.

Olga, his new housekeeper, appeared asking if

they needed anything. Trey requested a cheese-and-fruit plate.

"Still trying to fatten me up, Mr. Wentworth?"

"You've lost weight," he said tersely.

She shrugged and motioned with her chin toward the bodyguard sitting on the other side of the pool watching Jason.

"Are you going to keep the Protection Alliance around now that Chandler's in custody?"

Trey poured wine into the glasses and said, "I've cut down the operatives to two and will leave it at that for another month. I've decided to keep one on duty at all times."

"Just in case," she said, raising her glass.

He raised his glass to her. "Just in case."

"Kelly, watch this," Jason shouted from the pool.

"I'm watching, sweetie," she yelled back.

"Tell me now while he's in the water," Trey said, leaning forward.

Starting with her review of the video, Kelly detailed for him how they'd nabbed Chandler. When she'd related how he'd been cuffed and wheeled away on a gurney still breathing, Trey sat back and took a long satisfying drink of very delicious champagne. How fitting that Kelly had been the one to take down Jason's kidnapper, although she seemed uncomfortable with the idea that she'd shot a man.

She was a smart woman, a good cop, careful and alert. He shouldn't worry so much about her on the job.

Olga appeared with the cheese, and Kelly eyed the display appreciatively.

"Thank you, Trey," she said, reaching forward for a cracker. "I mean that. Without your cameras in place, I don't know what would have happened."

"Actually, Kelly," he said, "I think you'd have managed to take down Chandler without them."

"Oh, right," she said, grinning again, pointing the cracker at him. "I definitely have some sort of weird Spider-Woman sixth sense while I'm sleeping."

He shrugged, watching her as she topped her cracker with a slice of cheese and took a bite.

"So it's finally over," he said.

A shadow crossed her face, erasing her smile. "Yes. All but the paperwork."

She glanced at Jason, then back to him. "I heard you fired your father from Wentworth Industries. Is that true?"

He'd been tempted to call Kelly and tell her about the changes, but had decided against it. He needed to cut the connection between them. Why couldn't he?

He didn't want to waste this precious time with Kelly discussing his father, but she should know the truth, not the speculation in the tabloids.

"He can remain on the board, if he wants, but he's no longer chief executive officer."

"You are?"

Trey nodded.

"How did Senior take it?" she asked.

Without answering, Trey leaned forward and took her hand, linking their fingers together. He was relieved and more than a little surprised when another lovely smile bloomed across her face.

"I know what that means," she said. "The old man was well and truly pissed." She laughed and raised her glass to his. "Good work, Mr. Wentworth."

After they'd clinked glasses, Trey said, "The truth is my father and I haven't spoken since the vote."

CHAPTER THIRTY-TWO

TRYING TO SORT out the sequence of events, which seemed beyond confusing, Kelly stared at Trey. "Your father wasn't at the meeting?"

"Yes, but he stormed out, shouting we hadn't heard the last from him."

She nodded. That sounded like Senior. "Is there anything he can do?"

"He can try, but the articles of incorporation are clear." Trey raised his glass and took a swallow. "He's out."

Kelly fell silent, twirling the wineglass. She couldn't stand Senior. The man was mean and the worst kind of bully. But he was Trey's father.

She'd never even met her father, and although what she'd heard about him suggested he was far worse than merely a bully, she could now admit to herself she would still love to meet him just once.

She glanced at Trey, who was deep in thought.

"Have you reached out to him?" she asked.

"He won't return my calls. We delayed the announcement so I could ask him how he wanted to spin it. In the interim, the truth leaked to the press."

Kelly nodded. "And now he's hurt."

"Hurt?" Trey made a dismissive sound. "The man doesn't have feelings. He's angry. To punish me, he tried to visit my mother."

Kelly reached over and touched Trey's hand. "Oh, no. Did he upset her?"

Trey enveloped her hand in his and squeezed. "Fortunately, I anticipated that move."

"So he didn't get in to see her?"

"Not this time."

Kelly heaved a sigh. "Good. If he's that vindictive, maybe you should move her."

Trey nodded. Looking down, he focused on where their hands were joined. After a long moment, he raised his gaze to hers. She read a bucketload of pain in his dark eyes.

"What's wrong?"

"Senior's plane landed in Miami an hour ago," Trey said. "I have no doubt he's on his way here right now."

"Why would he come here?"

"I'm not sure." He shook his head. "Please believe me that I wouldn't have asked you over if I'd known. I wouldn't do that to you."

"Yeah, we didn't get along too well last time, did we?"

Trey released her hand and sat back. "You should go. Before he arrives."

Suddenly knowing she shouldn't leave Trey alone with his father, she shook her head. "I just got here."

"My father could be in a rage."

She nodded. "Maybe. He wants to have it out with you."

His jaw set, Trey glanced toward the pool where Jason splashed. "Whatever his purpose, it won't be pleasant."

She leaned forward. "Do you think I can't handle unpleasant, Trey?"

He swung his gaze back to hers.

"Do you know what a cop does on the job most of the time?"

A faint smile softened his expression. "Arrest bad guys?"

"I wish. Mostly we calm people down."

"Senior can be cruel," Trey said, looking away again.

"I am not afraid of your father, Trey."

Trey returned his speculative gaze to hers. "Maybe you should be."

She issued a harsh laugh. "I've seen far worse." When Trey didn't reply, she said, "But I'll go if you want me to. Do you *want* me to go?"

He closed his eyes. When he opened them, he stared across the pool again and said, "Actually, I don't want you to ever leave."

Kelly sucked in a breath, her heart thudding so loudly she could hardly hear herself think. Trey was now talking about more than a confrontation with his father.

Focusing on her again, he raised a hand and stroked her cheek. "Don't you know that, Kelly?"

Their gazes held, and she swallowed, unsure what to say other than, no, she didn't know that.

"And please don't ever think that you are harming Jason," Trey said. "My son adores you."

At a shout behind her, Trey broke their connection and looked toward the house. He narrowed his eyes.

When another yell sounded, closer this time, he leaped to his feet so abruptly the chair almost toppled over.

"Well, isn't this just nice and cozy."

"Father," Trey said.

Kelly whirled to find Senior standing on the patio, legs planted wide, hands on his hips, a sneer on his face.

Damn, but the man had lousy timing.

"I'm sorry, Mr. Wentworth," Olga said, her face flushed, hurrying up behind Senior. "I couldn't stop him."

"That's all right, Olga," Trey said. "You can go."

With a final glare at Senior, Olga moved away muttering to herself.

"What is *she* doing here?" Senior demanded, jabbing an accusing finger at Kelly.

"Didn't anyone ever teach you it's not polite to point?" Kelly came to her feet and faced Trey's father. Had he been drinking?

Senior's lips curled back from his teeth. She almost laughed. Was the man actually snarling at her?

"I think a better question is what are you doing here, Father," Trey said.

Breathing hard, Senior whirled back to Trey. "Son, you and I need to have a conversation."

"The time for that has long passed," Trey said. "You should have taken my advice a year ago. You should have returned my calls this week."

Trey's father raised his chin. "Well, I'm here now."

Aware the splashing in the pool had ceased, Kelly focused on Jason. The child stared at his grandfather with a horrified expression. The bodyguard had come to his feet, alert and watching for the need to intervene. *Good man.*

"Jason shouldn't see or hear this," Kelly told Trey. "Either move inside or let me take Jason."

"Is this slut calling the shots now?" Senior demanded, pointing at her again.

Raising his arm as if to strike his father, Trey lunged forward. But Kelly was closer and moved faster. She batted away Trey's arm. If Trey and his father came to blows, there'd be no going back for them.

"Watch the name-calling, pal," she said with deadly menace, jabbing Senior in the chest. "In case you didn't know it, I'm armed."

The slack-jawed shock on the old man's face almost made Kelly relent. Almost.

"And not only that," she continued. "I've been known to break a man's wrist with one swift kick. Do you want me to prove it?"

She shot a glance to Trey. Her words had had

their desired effect, and he'd backed off his white-hot rage. He stared at her, mouth open, obviously suffering from a bit of his own shock.

Well, that was fun.

Quite the day for the Wentworth billionaires.

She grabbed a towel, moved to the pool and called Jason over to her. He came quickly, and she scooped him in the towel and made her way into the house without looking back at Trey and his father.

She buried her face in the towel to hide her smile. Nothing had ever made her feel so cherished as when Trey had raised his hand against his father to defend her. Of course she couldn't allow that to happen, but still.

Trey and Senior might need to have a conversation.

But so did she and Trey.

TREY WATCHED THE love of his life move away carrying his—no, their—precious son in her arms. She'd remembered Jason before he had. Right now Jase was as much hers as his.

Wrapped in a bright yellow towel, Jason hugged her neck tightly, holding on for dear life. Trey had a crazy notion to go after her, get down on one knee and propose this very minute. In front of his son and his father.

Hell, in front of the whole world.

He glanced to his father, who appeared deflated,

as if Kelly's words had sucked the air out of him.
He looked old and very tired. Confused.

Why had he ever worried that the Wentworth
dynasty would defeat Officer Kelly Jenkins? His
warrior princess could stand up to anyone and was
more likely to cause hiccups in his family's creaky
empire. She'd help him instigate the much-needed
changes.

"Sit down, Dad," Trey said.

Senior nodded and collapsed into Kelly's chair.
"Were you celebrating my betrayal?" he asked, focusing on the champagne bucket.

"We were celebrating the arrest of Jason's kidnapper," Trey said, pouring champagne into a fresh
glass for his father.

"She's a pistol, that one," Senior said, his gaze
fixed on the door where Kelly had taken Jason.

Surprised at the begrudging respect in his father's tone, Trey slid the glass toward him.

"Yes, she is. You need to get used to having her
around if you want to be part of my life."

"Apparently you don't *want* me in your life." His
father focused on him then, his eyes distant. "They
wouldn't let me in to see your mother."

"And you know why." Trey settled back, hoping
for a long, civil conversation. "Let me explain the
way things are going to be now, Dad."

AFTER A WARM BATH, Kelly helped Jason change
into dry clothing and settled him in bed for a nap.

She selected one of his favorite stories and pulled up a chair beside his bed.

"Why is Grandpa Mean Bull here?" Jason asked before she could start reading.

Kelly lowered the book. Jason deserved some sort of an explanation, but what? She suspected Trey and Senior would be in conference for a while.

"He and your daddy need to talk about some stuff."

"Is he going to stay?"

"I don't know, but if he does, it probably won't be for long."

Jason gazed at her with wide innocent eyes. "Why is he so mean?"

Feeling like someone had taken hold of her heart and squeezed hard, Kelly shook her head. Mothering a child was a far more difficult job than she'd realized. She'd had training to be a cop. Where did a woman find instructions to nurture a child into a healthy adult?

"I think," Kelly said slowly, "that maybe he's unhappy and takes it out on other people."

"Why is he unhappy?"

Kelly nodded. This one she could answer. "Today he's mad because he didn't get his way. You know how you get when your daddy or I tell you no?"

Jason nodded.

"It's not very nice to watch Grandpa get mad, is it?"

He grinned at her sheepishly. "No."

"Any more questions?"

He shook his head.

"Okay then." Kelly raised the book and read out loud, not at all surprised when Jase fell asleep after four pages. He must have swum the length of the pool fifty times.

She closed the book and watched his steady breathing, wishing she could read him to sleep every nap. No, every night. She loved this little boy.

She loved his father.

And maybe, just maybe, his father loved her, too.

Now that she had the luxury of being alone with her thoughts, her mind wandered back to what Trey had said, to the raw emotion in his eyes just before Senior had shown up, and her heart began to pound again.

They were different people. They came from different worlds. Was there any possible way love could last between them? Even under ideal circumstances—and hers and Trey's were far from ideal—for a relationship to endure two people had to work at it, compromise, make adjustments.

Love was hard. No question about it.

But life itself was damned hard, too.

And didn't everyone deserve a chance at happiness?

Kelly quietly left Jason and moved into Trey's bedroom. She'd made her decision, and she would wait for him there. They needed to talk. For the first time in her life she'd be totally honest with a man and take that giant leap into the unknown.

TREY DIDN'T KNOW HOW, but he knew he would find Kelly in his bedroom. What he didn't expect was to find her asleep on his bed.

She looked beautiful, of course, with her long blond hair spread out on the pillow, one hand resting on her abdomen, the other flung over her head. Peaceful.

Totally unlike the angry warrior princess who had threatened to shoot his father.

He moved to the bed, slipped off his shoes and lay down beside her. Her eyes flew open. She smiled and reached for him.

"Hey," she said.

"Hey." He gathered her close, feeling the strength of her body, her heat merging with his. She snuggled in closer.

"Where's Senior?" she asked, her voice muffled against his shoulder.

"In his room."

"Everything okay?" she asked.

"It will be."

Trey pulled back, brushed the hair away from her face and kissed her. His warrior woman opened completely to him, held nothing back.

When she pulled away, her startlingly blue eyes appeared unfocused. Trey cupped her cheek. "I'm in love with you, Officer Jenkins."

"And I'm in love with you, Mr. Billionaire."

Trey exhaled his relief. He'd been wanting to hear her say that for so long. "I should never have let you leave."

"I kind of insisted on going."

He propped his head on a bent elbow so he could see her better. "Why?"

She exhaled, rolled onto her back and stared at the ceiling. "I was afraid."

"You? Afraid? Not possible."

"I was afraid of not being good enough, of not fitting in, of losing myself to you." She sighed and swiveled her head toward him again. "In case you don't know it, you're a bit, you know, overwhelming. I didn't think you could ever love me."

He lowered his head and kissed her.

"Mmm," she said, opening her eyes.

"You're pretty special yourself, Kelly," he said, his voice husky.

"Thanks for thinking so."

"How did I get so lucky?"

She hesitated and then said, "So why *did* you let me go?"

He knew that he owed her the truth. It was time to get everything out in the open. "The same reason. Fear."

His answer appeared to confuse her. "Of what?"

"That you would be killed on your job. I worried what it would do to Jason to lose another mother."

Her mouth tightened. "That's a legitimate concern, but I'm careful."

"I know you are," he said. "And I realized I was being very stupid to throw away our chance at happiness, and decided not to let that particular fear rule my life. I intend to cherish you for whatever time we have."

She smiled and closed her eyes. "Oh, I like that," she breathed.

"You've already made me a better person."

She turned on her side then, her eyes glistening. "That's the sweetest thing anyone has ever said to me."

"But I thought a life with me and my horrible family would destroy you, as it destroyed my mother."

"Oh, Trey."

"I know now that you're strong enough to stand up to anyone—kidnappers, overbearing patriarchs, pushy bodyguards."

"Damn right," she muttered.

"I just couldn't stand the idea of spoiling perfection."

"What?" She quirked a brow. "You think I'm *perfect?*"

"Pretty much, yeah," he said. "Although there is the one thing."

She laughed. "Just *one* thing? What is it?"

"Were you really going to break my father's wrist?"

Color crept into her cheeks. "The man is a bigger baby than Jason. He needs to behave."

Trey grinned. "But other than that," he said. "Yeah, perfect."

"Well, you're in for quite the shock."

Trey cupped her cheek. "I'm willing to take that chance."

She smiled, but didn't reply.

"Are *you?*" he asked.

"Am I what?"

"Willing to take a chance. On life with me, on happiness." When she didn't answer, he said, "I'm asking you to marry me, Kelly."

"I know," she whispered.

Trey held his breath, searching her face. Did she really have to think about her answer?

"I just wanted to soak up this moment a little longer so I could always remember what sheer joy felt like," she said.

"Are you done soaking?"

She nodded. "I will marry you, Trey Wentworth. Life with you will make me better, too, because, believe me, I am a long, long way from perfect."

He gathered her close and kissed her, sealing their promise to each other, to the start of their new life. To their new family. He'd reached a truce with his father. Maybe he'd take Kelly's advice and move his mother to Collins Island. Because of Kelly's job, he and Jason would live here full-time. He'd never ask her to leave a career she loved.

Warmth spread through him as he thought about telling Jason, who would be beyond ecstatic at the news Kelly would be his new mother.

"I can see the tabloid headlines now," Trey said, as Kelly laid her head on his chest.

She groaned. "As if Wentworth Heir Picks New Mother wasn't bad enough."

"We'll get through it," he said.

"I know."

"My son certainly has good taste," Trey said. "I must remember to thank him."

"How? Another toy?"

Trey laughed softly. "Jason will have what every child in the world needs."

Kelly remained quiet, still reveling in the joy of this moment, thinking about Trey's words.

"He'll be surrounded by people who love him," she said softly. Maybe it wouldn't be a traditional family, but it was the love that mattered.

"And that's all any of us truly need."

* * * * *